"This novel brought home the point once again that the God we serve will never go back on His word! I read every word with awe and wonder. This novel isn't just something that you read, it's something that you experience! I highly recommend it as it is a spirit lifter!" —Judith

"*His Last Hope* is a perfect combination of love, faith and family. This inspirational novel ministered to my spirit. As I read each chapter, I found myself being pulled deeper into the story because of the author's writing style and the real-life issues involved." — Ann

"It reminds the reader that there is life after heartbreak; there is hope in the Lord, *always*. It is also an awesome study guide for those of us trying to rebuild our relationship with God, as all the scriptures and passages used in the novel can be applied to our everyday trials and tribulations." — Alison

"When reading this book, I felt God's omnipotence. I knew that He guided this phenomenal author to write every single line and that He knew the importance of having this story reach as many readers as possible as lives would be changed by it. What a compelling read." — Jorja

"A heart-filled, Holy Spirit-led reading experience. Although it's a work of fiction, I was able to recognize myself in several characters. Thank God for the movement of the Holy Spirit in clarifying and bringing to the surface certain real-life issues and how they might be dealt with. Our Lord and Savior will surely get the glory from this novel." — Robin

"I have never read a book that had so much spiritual, life changing and fictional balance at the same time. This was a story of love, redemption, salvation and forgiveness.... I would recommend *His Last Hope* to everyone, especially those who desire to be reminded of God's awesome power, love, grace and those who need a breakthrough from any chains that seek to hold them captive or those who would just like to read an inspiring love story." —Sackeisha

HIS LAST

HOPE

A Contemporary Christian Romance

M. A. Malcolm

HIS LAST HOPE
Copyright © 2015 M. A. Malcolm
All rights reserved.
Published by M. A. Malcolm, 2015
Westmoreland, Jamaica.

Books may be purchased by contacting the publisher/author directly. For more information, please visit authormamalcolm.com.

This is a work of fiction. Names, characters, businesses, places, events and incidents are either the products of the author's imagination or used in a fictitious manner. Any resemblance to actual persons, either living or dead, or actual events, is purely coincidental.

All Scripture quotations, unless otherwise noted, are taken from the King James Version.

Author's photo: Kiffa Davis Photography (kiffadavis@outlook.com)
Cover design: Helen Evans (www.fiverr.com/helenevans)
Cover images: Copyright: <a href='http://www.123rf.com/profile_hugofelix'> / 123RF Stock Photo</a>
Copyright: <a href='http://www.123rf.com/profile_stockbroker'> / 123RF Stock Photo</a>
Editing: Amy Vanhorn (amyevanhorn@gmail.com)
Formatting: Nitpicking with a Purpose (nitpickingwithapurpose.com)
Writing consultant: Terri Whitmire (www.funcreativewriting.com)

ISSN 0799-494X (Print)   ISBN 978-976-95815-1-7 (Paperback)
ISSN 0799-4958 (Mobi)   ISBN 978-976-95815-0-0 (Mobi)
ISSN 0799-4965 (ePub)   ISBN 978-976-95815-2-4 (ePub)

This version was updated on February 15, 2017.

Printed in the United States of America by CreateSpace.
First Printing, June, 2015

In memory of:
O. David Gray

I (still) miss you most when I'm happy.

ଓଃ

In honor of:
"Little Praise"
"Little Bit"

The reason this project was possible.
The reason it was necessary.

Therefore, as the elect of God,
holy and beloved, put on tender mercies, kindness, humility,
meekness, longsuffering; bearing with one another,
and forgiving one another....
But above all these things put on love....

Colossians 3:12-14

PROLOGUE

The North Florida weather was flawless on the morning that Victoria Abellard Donahue drove off a bridge. Although her mind had been occupied with a dozen issues vying for her attention, she still noticed that it was bright and sunny. It was funny how the overly made-up weather presenter on the local news that morning had insisted that viewers take their umbrellas. So the woman was wrong. Didn't everyone make mistakes now and then?

Victoria hadn't driven for months—not since her OB/GYN had advised her to go on bed rest for the health of the unborn child growing in the so-called 'hostile environment' that was her womb. As she leaned a little heavier on the accelerator, she absentmindedly noticed that the little boy she was carrying had been uncharacteristically quiet since the argument that had caused her to flee her modest town home. At this time of the afternoon, he was usually doing somersaults inside of her, making it difficult to forget that within a few weeks she would become a mother. She sighed. She didn't think she'd ever be ready.

She passed a car that was older than her twenty-two years and cut in front of it smoothly. Though she was hardly concentrating, she didn't miss a beat. Driving was second nature to her; she had learned early that it was one means of escaping the humdrum life she led at home with her old-fashioned parents.

She thought of them now, and of how pleased they'd been when she had introduced them to Daniel Donahue during her final year in college. Daniel had been in graduate school then, and had great academic potential. He was no doubt going to make it big as an author, and Mommy and Daddy had been thrilled that their once-wayward daughter, who had been expelled from a private high school for her lack of discipline and focus, had chosen a bright young man, a Christian who espoused the allegedly 'old-fashioned' values their only child had always seemed to despise.

When Victoria and Daniel had married only a few months after meeting each other, her parents had been thrilled, even though she was in the final semester of her senior year in college and he was just beginning his Master's degree and working as a graduate assistant. The couple had rented a modest two-bedroom town home in St. Augustine, where they attended school, and she had announced her pregnancy almost immediately. The Abellards were going to be grandparents, and their formerly rebellious daughter was leading what they definitely considered a charmed life. Victoria wondered how her parents would feel if they knew the truth.

The scene she had left behind had been an uncomfortable one in which her past and her future had collided in the present with a resounding crash, and she'd seen fit to remove herself from the situation and face the music later. Much later.

She grinned. She'd forgotten how much she enjoyed driving. As she shifted the manual transmission into a higher gear with a flourish characteristic of everything she did, she wondered what was going on at home at exactly that moment… not that it mattered; she would deal with it all when she got back home. By then, she would have braced herself for Daniel's look of disappointment, for his very *Christian* decision not to condemn her, and for his eventual forgiveness. She would probably force herself to cry a little. Still, there was no doubt that the dramatics would be unnecessary. Daniel was so in love with her, he could forgive her anything. And he would. Of that she was sure. She was convinced that he would keep her and her little secret safe. In a few hours, she would go home and all would be well. She'd figure out what to do with Franklin's car before then.

Ten minutes later, Victoria smiled as she felt the wind whipping through her shoulder-length black hair. She was glad she had taken Franklin's impressive convertible instead of her husband's modest sedan. She knew she was cut out for the finer things in life. These last seven months masquerading as Daniel's devoted wife had been a real challenge. She'd chosen Daniel Donahue because of his ambition, and she expected that one day he would be truly great; she just hoped it would happen soon. She wanted to drive a luxurious coupe of her own, to have a nanny or two at her beck and call, to travel and to live in a lavish home. Her personality was too large to be confined in a home chosen for its low rent and proximity to the university. Daniel, though on scholarship, had continued to work part-time to be able to give her the kind of lifestyle he thought she wanted. He didn't have a clue what she wanted! But at least she didn't have to work.

She had finished her degree in English Literature during her first trimester, but around the four-month mark, she'd been diagnosed with an incompetent cervix and had been placed on bed rest, so she'd never actually found a job. How concerned Daniel had been that she might lose the baby! She hadn't lifted a French-tipped finger since then.

She wiped the lazy smile off her face when she realized the possible repercussions of the situation at hand. It was unfortunate that Daniel had found out the truth, but she knew he was head over heels in love with her. He would soon see reason. After all, she could have chosen just about anyone. So many men were attracted to her, with her olive skin and wavy hair, but she had chosen Daniel. He would never abandon her. He was lucky to have her, whatever the circumstances.

She gritted her teeth. It would take more patience than she possessed to continue to live a life she knew was beneath her. Soon, she would return home to the too-small house and face her too-gullible husband, but for now, she would drive. She smiled and accelerated. This was the life!

Victoria would never know if her husband would have forgiven her as she had expected him to. She picked up speed in the 'borrowed' sports car, failing to notice that the driver of the heavily-laden truck she had been tail-gating was braking to enter a narrow bridge. Pulling herself from her reverie, she saw that she was way too close for comfort. She braked hard and picked up a skid. Trying desperately to maintain control of the spinning vehicle, she had the presence of mind to recite the prayer her parents had said with her every night until she had grown tall enough to lock her bedroom door. She knew Psalm 51:10 by heart, but all she managed to get out was, "Create in me a clean heart and renew a right spirit within me..." before she broke through the guard rail. As the car plunged into the murky water below, Victoria was vaguely aware of a strange darkness engulfing her.

CHAPTER ONE

Eight years later

The cabbie never knew what hit his car. One minute, he was speeding along the Miami highway, which was a bit damp after a late evening shower, and the next minute the car was hurtling towards the roadway below the ramp. All the driver could hear was the screaming of the lone passenger in the back seat. The car landed in a crumpled heap directly in the path of an eighteen-wheeler whose driver was late in making a delivery. The trucker and the passenger survived, but for a long time to come, life would seem very gloomy for the family of the cabbie who had been the sole breadwinner in his family of five.

ଔ

Thirty-six hours later, the passenger who had been in the taxi would finally open her swollen eyes. The young lady's head was pounding and it took quite a bit of effort to open her eyes against the bright artificial light that seemed to surround her. She blinked. There were voices all around her, but she couldn't seem to isolate any of them. As she continued to blink her eyes in an effort to get used to the lighting, someone noticed that she had gained consciousness. There was a bit of scuffling as a group of people she didn't think she knew surrounded her, but everything they said was coming at her as if through a buffer of some kind. She didn't understand a word at first.

Eventually, she was able to isolate an authoritative voice that came from somewhere to her left. "Give the young lady some air. If you all frighten her like that, she'll probably want to go back to wherever she's been for the last day or two. One of you should go call a doctor, don't you think?"

The young lady realized she was probably in a hospital room. She wasn't sure whose voice she had heard, but she was grateful that all the mumbling in her immediate vicinity had stopped. The curious faces that had been peering down at her were gone now. She closed her eyes again, trying to see if she could identify exactly which part of her body hurt the most.

"Well, hello there." Unlike the first one, this voice was male. She slowly opened her eyes against the light to see a pale, graying man with a receding blond hairline bending toward her. "How about I get one of these interns to help you sit up? There you go."

She was vaguely aware of someone adjusting her bed so that she was soon in a sitting position.

"Now, if you don't mind, I'll just check your pupils." The gentleman shone a bright, unwelcome penlight into first one eye and then the other. "Ah, good… your eyes are responding to the light; that's a good sign."

The doctor made what the young lady assumed to be other routine physical checks before asking, "Do you know what day of the week it is?" She tried to think, but she had a hard time getting her thoughts together. Her throat was dry, and with some effort, she was able to move her right hand and point at her throat. Someone close to her held a straw to her parched lips, and she drank thirstily from a cup. Even though all she had to do was raise her head off the pillow, it felt as if every body part was crying out in rebellion.

"Okay," said the doctor with an understanding smile, "let's go with an easier question: what's your name?"

The young lady mustered up a short-lived smile that hurt her cracked lips. She might not know what day it was, but *this* was a question she could answer. "My name is… is…." She tried to shake the cobwebs from her brain, but it hurt too much to move her head.

She tried again, "My name is…." Her eyes opened to what appeared to be twice their normal size. "Oh, my goodness… what's my name?" She wasn't even aware that she was already slipping out of consciousness again.

ᛤ

The next morning, she felt herself swimming back to the surface. Though she did not immediately open her eyes, she was aware of a hushed conversation going on in her immediate vicinity. She wasn't deliberately trying to listen, but every now and then she heard a word or phrase: *retrograde amnesia, traumatic brain injury, total recovery, prognosis, fetus*. She knew they were not talking about her, so she tried to ignore them and focus instead on her own body. It felt strange, almost as if it were not her own. With great effort, she put her hand to her throbbing head. Eventually, the voices moved closer, so she opened her eyes.

The light was still too bright. She heard the same authoritative voice as before saying, "Perhaps you all should turn off some of these lights. They can be pretty bright when you're just waking up. Go on, turn off the lights over her bed. That'll make it easier for her, don't you think?" The woman who was speaking was still somewhere on her left, but it hurt too much when she tried to turn her head to see whose voice it was.

With the lights dimmed, she was able to identify the same doctor who had examined her the day before. He had a pleasant facial expression, and tended to look over his glasses as he smiled at her. "Hello again. I'm Dr. Fields. How are you feeling today?"

"I... I... I ache." It was the absolute truth.

"That's to be expected. Because of your condition, we haven't been giving you too many painkillers. By the way, your baby, miraculously, is doing very well."

"Baby?" She was confused. "What baby? I have a baby named Miraculously?" She was incredulous.

The doctor continued to smile even as he shook his head and turned to look at someone close to him, who seemed to be a nurse. "This is what I was afraid of."

"What are you talking about? I'm afraid I'm confused." Her brows knitted together.

"Your confusion is typical. We haven't been able to fill in all the blanks yet, but this is what we have been able to deduce: you were the passenger in a taxi that went over a guard rail and was hit by an eighteen-wheeler. The driver didn't survive."

She gasped.

The doctor continued, "You suffered a head injury and were unconscious for a day and a half after you were brought to the emergency room. This, by the way, is Hartman Memorial Hospital in Miami, Florida."

"Florida?" She couldn't remember much, but the name of the state didn't spark anything.

"Yes. You've now been here for two days and we have not been able to identify you because all your possessions were lost when the car caught fire. So, young lady, what's your name?"

She tried to say something, but no words came. "I... I'm sorry." Her eyes welled up.

"Don't apologize. It's not at all your fault. We did an MRI and CAT scan while you were unconscious. It seems you have some brain swelling that might be causing some amnesia."

"Amnesia?" She was alarmed. She might not remember her name, but she remembered that amnesia was serious. "How could I be having amnesia? I still remember what amnesia is. If I had amnesia, wouldn't I have forgotten everything I know?"

Dr. Fields smiled. "That's not an unreasonable question. There are different types of amnesia, and we believe you have retrograde amnesia as a result of a traumatic brain injury. Retrograde amnesia is the inability to remember events that happened before a particular episode. It's usually temporary and can last anywhere from a few hours to a few months, depending on the severity of the case."

"A few months!"

"Yes," his voice was calm and controlled as he went on, "but that's not the usual case. A part of your brain is responsible for the memory that's associated with events and particular information, facts and knowledge. It's different from the part that handles habitual actions that become unconscious over time, like reading, writing, walking, riding a bicycle or driving a car. In your case, it seems your non-declarative memory—where habits are retained—is still intact, but your declarative memory before the accident has been impacted."

He could see the patient becoming a bit agitated. "Before you ask, there have been cases where this kind of injury has been permanent, but in the vast majority, the patient makes a full recovery."

The young lady was relieved. "And there's no indication of when this might happen?"

"It depends on the individual case. Every case is different."

"And in my case?"

"Well, that's hard to say. Until the brain swelling recedes, we won't be completely sure what we're dealing with. We have to be careful what kind of medications we give you because of your... condition."

At first she wasn't sure what he was talking about, and then it hit her: she had a baby named Miraculously. She felt as if she might faint again as despair threatened to overtake her.

"Doctor, you mentioned something about a baby... Miraculously? I don't have a baby, do I? And certainly not one named Miraculously!"

"Not yet, but you should be having a perfectly healthy baby in another six months or so. I'm not sure why you think the baby's name is Miraculously. *I* certainly didn't say that it was!" He chuckled, his cheeks turning red with the effort.

She looked toward her abdomen. There wasn't even a slight rounding of her abdomen. "Doctor, even with a brain injury, wouldn't I remember something as significant as a pregnancy?" She automatically looked at her bare left ring finger. "Or a husband?"

"It really depends on the extent of your injury. We are unable to make any definitive statements until the swelling goes down. In the meantime, we'll take the very best care of you and your baby."

He smiled reassuringly, but the young woman wasn't convinced. She felt like her brain had somehow become disconnected from her body. *Who am I? How can this be happening to me?* She wrinkled her brow, and even that tiny movement caused her head to pound even more than before. *A baby? Who's the father? Where is he? Am I even married? Where's my family? Why haven't they come for me? The doctor said I've already been here two days!*

She felt her breath becoming shallow. Dr. Fields, who was still standing by her side, said, "You should try and calm down. I know it's difficult and confusing, but you're going to get through it. With the exception of your brain swelling, you're in excellent condition... at least physically speaking. Your baby is doing well, and you are on the path to mending. As soon as the swelling recedes, we'll bring in a neurologist, who will examine you in an attempt to clear up all our questions. While we're waiting, just take it easy—which I know will be difficult, under the circumstances—and continue to rest."

"I'll try my best," she lied.

"Great. We're going to give you some more medication now, so that you can get some sleep." He gestured to one of the nurses, who moved towards the patient to administer an injection. Soon, the patient was drifting off into a dreamless sleep.

CHAPTER TWO

The next morning, the early morning sunlight streaming through the window onto her bed and warming her face caused the patient to awaken. It took a while for her to remember where she was and why, and although her body continued to ache, she felt more rested than she could remember. Not that she could remember much!

She let out a slight moan as realization forced its way into her consciousness and she became reacquainted with her plight. She couldn't remember who she was. And she was pregnant. With a baby. Miraculously. She immediately began to miss the blissful ignorance of sleep, and wondered if they would give her some more of whatever they had given her the day before that had allowed her to escape the reality that was crowding in on her.

She took a few calming breaths and despite the discomfort, sat up in bed and began to look at her surroundings for the first time. She was startled by a voice that came to her from the other side of the room.

"Good morning!" The greeting had come from an older woman with skin the color of butterscotch and silvery-white hair cropped close to her scalp. She recognized the voice from before, and could see at once that her roommate was a morning person. She was sitting up in a bed that occupied the left side of the double room, her right leg encased in a pristine white cast and lying on top of the hospital-issued sheets. On her lap was an assortment of open books. Before her younger roommate could respond, she continued, "I'm Ruby Crawford, but just about everyone calls me Aunt Ruby."

"Good morning, Miss Crawford—"

"*Aunt Ruby,*" the correction was accompanied by a wide smile.

"Good morning, Aunt Ruby. I'm... I'm...." She was stuck. She opened her mouth to explain, but was stopped by Aunt Ruby's raised palm.

"Don't worry about it, my dear. I know you're having a challenge putting things in their right places in your mind."

The young woman couldn't help but think that she had just heard the understatement of the century, and she rewarded Aunt Ruby with a half-smile, "You can say that again!"

"Well, sweetheart, the good news is that I hear you're in great physical condition, considering the accident. And the even better thing is that even though you may not know who you are, God does," Ruby smiled.

At the mention of God, the young woman's mind wandered off even though Aunt Ruby continued to talk. She couldn't understand how she could remember that there was a God and yet not remember her own name or the fact that she was expecting a child. Noticing that Aunt Ruby was still waxing eloquent, she tried to rein in her thoughts.

"—been praying ever since they wheeled you in here two days ago, not long after I got myself settled." Aunt Ruby removed the reading glasses that were perched on the tip of her nose and tapped the cast that started just above her knee. "I busted this seventy-three-year-old leg up pretty good on Sunday. I was just coming off the cruise liner—I'd been on a week-long seniors' cruise to the Western Caribbean and Mexico—and just as I was congratulating my accident-prone self on not having any accidents for a whole week, I tripped and rolled all the way down that gangway." She chuckled. "I must have been quite a sight, head over heels as I was, but I was in so much pain that I couldn't have cared one iota what those other seniors thought of me. I just knew I'd broken something." She finally came up for air, causing her audience of one to smile.

"When they brought you in, you were so still, so peaceful-looking, that I thought for a second you were... well, you know. But then I said to myself, 'Ruby, you old fool, they wouldn't be bringing a dead woman into your room, now would they?' And they weren't. And I've been waiting to meet you for two whole days since then."

The other woman was exhausted just listening to Aunt Ruby speak, but she was glad she wasn't expected to say much. What could she say? "Well, it's nice to meet you, Aunt Ruby." Her smile was genuine.

"The pleasure is mine, my dear." Aunt Ruby reached for the remote on her nightstand, and for the first time, the young woman noticed the television in one corner of the room. "Now, if you don't mind, I'd like to turn the set on. I don't want to miss my favorite preacher."

Her roommate shrugged, and soon they were both watching a recorded sermon. The woman on the stage was in the midst of saying to the enraptured audience, "You are the Lord's! The Word of God says that you live for the Lord, and you die for Him, so whether you live or die, then, you belong to Him! Isn't that comforting?"

The crowd seemed comforted enough, and Aunt Ruby nodded her head vigorously. Neither woman said a word as they watched the minister walk from one side of the stage to the other.

"I don't know about you, brothers and sisters, but I'm *glad* I'm the Lord's! I'm *relieved* I belong to Him. I'm *secure* in His arms. No matter what you do to me, brothers and sisters; no matter how you mistreat me or how you ridicule me; even if you choose to take my very *life*, I belong to Him! Amen?"

The congregation and Aunt Ruby agreed, "Amen!"

The two continued to watch the program. When it ended, Aunt Ruby asked if it was okay to switch to the news. The other woman didn't see any problem with that, so they watched local and then international news without comment. When it was over, Aunt Ruby shook her head sadly and said, "There is so much to pray about," before asking if she could turn the television off. She mentioned that she wanted to do her daily devotion, and quickly explained what that was, ending with, "Would you like to join me?"

"No, thank you, Aunt Ruby. Maybe some other time, if we're both here."

Aunt Ruby smiled and tapped the cast again. "They said I'll be in here for another few days, at least. How about you?"

"I have no idea. They want to monitor the baby for a couple of days."

"The baby?" Aunt Ruby was surprised. It was clear that she hadn't known there was a baby in the picture.

"Yes," the young lady responded with a deep sigh, "it seems I'm pregnant, and I have no idea whose baby this is, or whose *I* am, for that matter!" She felt as if she was going to start crying, but with great effort she held her emotions in check.

"There, there, my dear. Don't you worry and put any additional stress on yourself or that precious bundle of joy. You may not know who you are or *whose* you are, but like I said before, God does, and that's the most important thing. None of this is coming as a surprise to Him. He will reveal everything at the appropriate time."

"How come you're so sure?" She brushed a stray tear from her cheek.

"Because I asked Him to, and He almost always listens to me."

CHAPTER THREE

As a child, Daniel Donahue had been a huge fan of airplanes. Like many other boys, he liked to stand on the ground and watch them in the air, or run around with his arms outstretched, buzzing like a B-52 bomber. But he'd outgrown all that. Now that he was an adult, he'd decided he wasn't such a huge fan, after all.

He wasn't all that concerned with the fact that the plane was moving at hundreds of miles per hour, and several thousand feet above-ground, to boot; it was really the confinement he hated. He just didn't like the fact that he had to stay in that relatively small space, in close proximity with people with whom he was unfamiliar, breathing the same recycled cabin air, while everyone made strategic decisions that they hoped would get them out of the airplane and off to their final destination with the least hassle.

Today, he would gladly hand over his credit card or sign a blank check for some undisturbed time under exactly those circumstances. Since arriving in England a couple of weeks ago, he had been pulled in a hundred directions. Everyone wanted him to dine with them after his lectures at the various universities. Everyone wanted to show him the sights of their respective cities and campuses. Everyone wanted to take him to their favorite pub for a meal and a drink, though he wasn't a habitual drinker. He had been checking only his work email because he simply had no time to do anything else. He hadn't even had a chance to call Aunt Ruby, his mother's sister, since her return from her cruise. The fact that they were in different time zones didn't help, either.

She would have landed in Miami several days earlier, and there had been arrangements for her to take a chartered bus from there to St. Augustine since he wouldn't have been available to pick her up. His friend and her neighbor Ryan should have picked her up from the bus station and taken her home to Alistair Bay. He hoped everything had gone as planned. As he made his way back to his hotel room, he resolved to call her as soon as he got the chance.

Later that night, he finally had the opportunity to make a phone call. He'd misplaced his cell phone during his traversing back and forth across the United Kingdom, so he used the phone in his hotel room. He hadn't spoken to Aunt Ruby for such a long time—not since she'd left for her cruise—that he didn't think twice about the cost of the long-distance call. He dialed her number and listened to it ring: three times, four, five. Strange. She was always home between lunch and 3:00 p.m. He double-checked his watch, counting backwards to Eastern Standard Time. It was just about 2:15 there. When her answering machine picked up, his message was one of calm concern, "Hello, Aunt Ruby. How are you? I've lost my cell phone but I'll try to call you again this evening, around eight o'clock your time. Will you try to be home? It's so out of character for you to be out at this hour. Talk to you later!" He knew she didn't usually have any meetings at church on Monday nights. At least, not unless she'd started going to the singles' mingle. He smiled. He didn't think she was in the market for a new husband after twenty-odd years of being a widow, but anything was possible.

That night, he asked the receptionist at the front desk to give him a wake-up call at 8:00 EST. Again, his aunt's phone rang unanswered. Rather than get overly concerned, he called Ryan's house next door. The phone was answered on the first ring. Ryan's new bride Jasmine, who was four months pregnant, immediately told Daniel about Aunt Ruby's accident and that she was in hospital in Miami. She had the number at hand, so Daniel was able to call right away.

"I'm coming home." Daniel stated authoritatively after hearing what had happened.

"You'll do no such thing." His elderly relative was equally authoritative.

"But, Aunt Ruby...."

"No buts, Daniel." She was firm. "You have four days of lectures left, and I won't be able to leave for another couple of days anyway. Why interrupt this incredible opportunity just so you can come have a pity party with me at the hospital?"

"But, Aunt Ruby...."

"No. Buts." They were both starting to sound like broken records. "You're staying until Saturday, and that's that. If I'm still in the hospital then, you can fly into Miami International instead of Jacksonville and drive me home when they release me. If I'm discharged earlier, I've already made arrangements with Ryan to come get me. He'll only have to take one day off work and Jasmine will be fine for a day on her own. Didn't he tell you we'd decided on this?"

"No. I spoke with Jasmine."

"I see. Well, now you know, and I'm sure you'll agree that both Plan A and Plan B make perfect sense."

"They do," he smiled into the receiver of the hotel's telephone. What was it about Aunt Ruby that always made him pander to her? If his students at the college could only see him now! Professor Donahue of the History Department, who could silence them without ever opening his mouth, had just been put in his place by a woman who was almost a foot shorter than his six feet and just about twice as old as he was.

"Now, I imagine this call has already cost you two arms and your right leg. Believe me when I say that I don't want to hear from you again until you've found your cell phone. Come to think of it, you ought to look in your laptop case. That's where you'd left it the last time you lost it."

As she spoke, her nephew reached for the bag, fishing around in the outside flap on the underside of the case. As his fingers closed around his smartphone, he couldn't help but laugh out loud. She was always right. He knew it and she knew it. He didn't need to say a word.

"You're welcome."

He could hear the smile in her voice. "I love you, Aunt Ruby. Thanks. Now that I've found my phone, please call me when you know anything. Barring that, I'll call you tomorrow evening, UK time."

"Good night, Daniel. I love you, too. God bless and keep you."

"You, too," he said before hanging up. Her voice had, as usual, brought calm to his soul.

Daniel leaned back onto the crisp, white pillows. It wasn't easy imagining the woman who'd always been such a vibrant participant in his life lying in a hospital bed with a broken leg. Aunt Ruby meant more to him than anyone, with the exception of his own parents, may they both rest in peace. She was his friend and his confidante, the one he'd always gone to for advice and support. He smiled as he remembered how much he would look forward to visiting her every summer as a child. She wasn't his only aunt, but she had always been his favorite, so much so that they now shared a home in Alistair Bay when he wasn't teaching. Even before the death of his wife, Victoria, he had placed a high premium on those he held nearest and dearest, and he would do whatever he could to ensure that his beloved aunt was safe.

CHAPTER FOUR

"What are you watching?" the young woman inquired of Aunt Ruby early that Tuesday afternoon, the day after they had first talked.

"It's called 'Marathon Praise.' It's a fund-raising campaign this particular Christian television channel presents four times a year. It helps them to raise the necessary funds to keep broadcasting and bringing the gospel to the world."

Before the younger of the two could respond, Aunt Ruby went on to share the message of the gospel with her. She had never been ashamed of her faith, and was eager to usher as many people into the Kingdom of God as she could.

None of it sounded strange to the young woman who had no idea who she was; however, she had been doing a lot of pondering, and was full of questions that day. "I've been listening to the speakers you've been watching, and I can't help but wonder what God thinks of me. I mean, why would He allow me to be in this situation? Why did I have to fall out of the car? Why did I bump my head? Why can't I remember who I am? Whose baby is this I'm carrying? What's going to become of us? Where's my family?"

Aunt Ruby lowered the volume on the television and looked across the room into eyes full of questions. "The truth is, my dear, as old as I am, I don't know the answers to any of those questions, but there's a scripture that reminds me that God has a different outlook on life than we human beings. It says His ways and thoughts are higher than ours, so it's difficult for us to know exactly why He does the things He does and why He allows the things He allows." She took a deep breath, "I want to point out that if you hadn't fallen out of the car, you would have been caught in the fire, so that's a reason right there," the young lady wrinkled her brow as Aunt Ruby continued, "and the question I would ask you under other circumstances would be, why *not* you? But I understand that you might not be able to figure that out in your present state.

"I'd ask you, would you prefer for all these things to happen to someone else so that you could just live a comfortable life?"

The woman's eyes fell as a feeling of guilt invaded her mind. Aunt Ruby had a point there. She might not know who she was, but she hoped she wasn't selfish.

"All right. I concede that if it has to happen to someone, then there's probably no reason it *shouldn't* be me. But if it *had* to happen, why now?" She was nowhere near out of questions, "Why during a pregnancy? How do I bond with a baby, or even accept that I'm pregnant, if I can't remember the joy of learning I was pregnant, or the circumstances under which it happened? Whose baby is this? Where's my husband? Are we even married? Why hasn't he found me yet? How come no one has come to this hospital looking for me? Isn't that something a concerned family would have done by now?" She looked at her flat tummy, "All of this anxiety and uncertainty can't be good for a baby. Why would your God allow this to happen at this time?" She looked at Aunt Ruby as if she thought the older woman would be able to give her concrete answers.

"I have no idea why this would happen during your pregnancy. But I do know that God *can* use these circumstances for your good. Has it ever occurred to you that maybe you need to be going through this at *exactly* this time? Maybe there are things He wants you to learn before you have the baby. I think that's a possibility, and even if there couldn't be a worse time—and I can't imagine a time that could be worse—you can still *choose* to turn this into a learning experience. You can try to take the situation into which you've been thrust and make something positive out of it."

"How can I?" she returned. "How can I find the positives in this situation when I don't know what would *be* positive for me?" she added dejectedly, eyes downcast and full of unshed tears, "I don't even know what to call myself."

Aunt Ruby's response was quick. "Why don't we come up with a name, then?"

"Really?" Her roommate looked at her with something that resembled light in her eyes.

"Yes. It would be my honor and privilege to help you. My Bible tells me that faith comes by hearing God's Word. I firmly believe that if you speak God's Word over your life, your spirit—which lives on the inside of you—will begin to believe it and it will shape your life. When you call yourself a name, you are declaring something about who you are. You should have a name that speaks beauty and light every time you say it. When people speak about you, they should always be using a positive word, so that even malice directed in your direction will be cancelled out by the positive meaning of your name."

The young woman was intrigued. As she listened to her older counterpart, she was beginning to feel a little lucky to be able to be choosing a name for herself as an adult.

Aunt Ruby continued, "If I were in your shoes, I think I'd like to be called *Hope*."

"*Hope?*" she queried, puzzled. "Why Hope? I'm not exactly hopeful right now."

"*Hope*, because everything is ahead of you; there's nothing about your past holding you back. You're free of all those challenges and possible burdens. All you have are your present and your future. *Hope* should fill you up right now. *Hope* is the best way to move forward, regardless of—and perhaps *because of*—your circumstances. Yes, I think that's what you should call yourself."

Before the young woman could respond, there was a brief knock on the door and a nurse came in with an aide. She explained that they were going to take the young woman to another section of the hospital for a while. The aide helped her to get into one of Aunt Ruby's robes and the wheelchair. As she was leaving, she smiled gratefully at Aunt Ruby, "Thank you." They both knew she wasn't just talking about the item of clothing.

"You're very welcome, my dear," Aunt Ruby replied with her characteristic smile.

CHAPTER FIVE

When the young woman—*Hope*—arrived at her destination in another wing of the hospital, she was a bit surprised and uncomfortable to learn that she was to meet with an OB/GYN for an ultrasound. She had met Dr. Chelsea Roberts before, since the redhead had been one of the many medical professionals who had filed behind the privacy curtain around her bed at one time or another over the past few days. Dr. Roberts had already examined her internally, but it had not gone well. She was extremely uncomfortable during the very short internal exam, to the point where she'd almost had a panic attack. Dr. Roberts had been surprised by the response but had tried to make her comfortable, with negligible success. This would be her first ultrasound since waking up. She was not looking forward to it.

She listened to Dr. Roberts' preamble as she was being prepped for the scan, but she didn't really pay attention. She wasn't sure what to expect or how she would feel. At least the exam would be an abdominal one instead of the frightening internal check she'd had before. When the doctor placed the cold gel on her abdomen, she shrunk back in apprehension, but the doctor ignored the slight physical reaction and placed the scanning device on her. The patient turned her attention to the monitor, but she couldn't figure out what she was seeing.

Dr. Roberts was quiet as she moved the device over the young woman's abdomen. Then she began to point out various things on the monitor. Much of what she said sounded like gibberish to Hope, who was fixated on what she *could* identify on-screen. She could definitely see a head and something that appeared to be the baby's spine. She was fascinated, but she still found it difficult to believe that the baby she was looking at was growing inside her. And had been for the last twelve weeks or so. Again, her mind wandered to the father of this baby, to her family. Were they looking for her? Why hadn't they found her yet? She felt as if her mind were a broken record, thinking the same thoughts, asking the same questions over and over.

The doctor's voice droned on and on and Hope made a concentrated effort to focus on what was being said. "So I know it's not very clear to you right now, but the baby is doing well. He or she has met all the expected developmental milestones and you're about twelve weeks and three days along, as we told you before. Now, it's up to you to eat healthily, exercise, take your prenatal vitamins, and get the necessary health checks to ensure that the baby continues to develop. Regardless of the prevailing conditions, this baby's health and wellbeing has to be a priority for you and those around you."

Hope couldn't help but wonder who would be around her, and how she would provide for herself and this child if her memory didn't return or her family didn't find her.

After the exam, she was taken to do a scan to determine if the swelling in her brain was going down. She was told afterwards that Dr. Fields would let her know the results later that day.

Before she was taken back to her room, she was introduced to a psychiatrist, Dr. Roland Sharpe, who interviewed her and tried to make an assessment about her amnesia. At the end of the thirty minute-session, he told her that he would write a report stating that it appeared her amnesia was genuine and that she had lost all memory of her life before the injury. He explained that there were measures that could be taken to help her recoup her memories, but that none of them was guaranteed to work. He mentioned hypnosis, but told her that her memory could be triggered at any time, and by almost anything of significance to her former life. She might wake up one morning and remember every detail, or she might still be having challenges in a year's time. He advised that, difficult though it may be, she should try her best to remain as calm as possible and not to spend a lot of time trying to 'force' the memories back to the surface. In a fatherly voice, he said, "I probably shouldn't tell you this, but sometimes our brain closes the door to a particular set of memories for our self-preservation. It's called emotional amnesia. I'm not saying that's what you have," he removed his glasses and looked across the table and directly into her eyes, "but I'd recommend you let it happen naturally."

She nodded, shook his hand, and waited for the aide to appear (as he always did at the appropriate time) to whisk her away. Having endured a psychiatric evaluation after an unexpected ultrasound and a brain scan, she was relieved to be heading back into her room, where she promptly fell asleep without updating her roommate.

∞

The next time the woman woke up, she found Dr. Fields standing by her bedside reading her chart and a nurse preparing to remove the IV line. As the nurse carried out her tasks, the doctor explained to the patient that the swelling of her brain was receding. He was pensive.

"In cases like these," he explained, "we just can't say when your memory will return. I'm not a specialist, but after all those years of med school, I do have some familiarity with the brain," he chuckled to himself, "and I haven't been able to pinpoint any specific area of your brain that has been severely impacted by the accident."

Hope wasn't nearly as amused as he was. "So what does that mean for me?"

He suddenly became serious again. "Well, it means that we are basically playing a waiting game until your memory comes back."

She took a deep breath as despair threatened to overtake her, "But what if I don't remember who I am by the time I'm well enough to leave? Will I have to stay in the hospital forever?"

"We're hoping it won't come to that, but the worst-case scenario is that we'll introduce you to a social worker, and they'll take over and find placement for you. The police actually fingerprinted you while you were unconscious, but we haven't heard anything from them. I guess that will be between you and them and the social worker, if you end up needing one."

"I see." She subconsciously looked at her fingers, expecting them to be black with fingerprinting ink.

"But I'm hoping your memory will return before you're ready to leave in a few days and that none of that will be necessary."

"I hope so, too."

The doctor excused himself, leaving Hope to ponder her uncertain future. She realized that she was making a deliberate effort *not* to think about the pregnancy at all. She didn't think she could handle that reality just yet.

She had forgotten she wasn't alone until Aunt Ruby cleared her throat.

"Oh! Aunt Ruby, I'd completely forgotten you were there." She managed a weak smile.

The older woman smiled in return. "I can't say that has happened to me a lot, even in these my so-called 'twilight years,' but I know you've got a lot on your mind."

"Do I ever!" Hope noticed Aunt Ruby struggling to swing her legs over the side of the bed. "May I help you with something?"

"Well, I need to use the bathroom, and I'm tired of having to call somebody to help me." Aunt Ruby reached for the crutches she was just learning to use. "I'm a grown woman, not a baby, and I'm not used to needing help." As she started to slide off the bed, Hope hopped out of hers and hurried across the room.

"Here, let me help." It was the first time she was standing unassisted, and she felt a little dizzy, but she pushed past the feeling and quickly slipped her hands under Aunt Ruby's underarms to help support her. Slowly, the two of them made their way to the bathroom door. Afterwards, Hope helped Aunt Ruby into bed before wandering into the bathroom where, with the door open so she could hear Aunt Ruby, she stared at her reflection in the mirror. The woman staring back at her was effectively a stranger. She hadn't had the chance to be alone since first waking up, and having been untethered from the IV line, it was the first time she had seen herself in a mirror.

The stranger looking back at her had a warm, tawny complexion and curly, dark brown hair that someone had carefully braided into cornrows that ended with tiny rubber bands just above her shoulders. The area around each of her dark brown eyes was black and blue, her face a bit bruised. Her cheeks were full, and she imagined she was pretty enough behind all the discoloration. Raising her hand to her head, she could feel the tenderness of her scalp, and she couldn't help but wonder what memories were being suppressed there. She slowly shook her head from side to side and moved back into the bedroom and sat in a plastic chair close to Aunt Ruby's bed. She was tired of lying down.

"Thank you, my dear. I'm sure that given enough time and practice with these crutches, I'll be able to handle them on my own."

Hope smiled, but the image of her own face was seared in her mind and it took a great effort for her to concentrate on what her roommate was saying.

"You know, my dear, I couldn't help but overhear your conversation with the doctor. I want you to know that if the circumstances were different, I wouldn't hesitate to have you stay with me. But you're probably from the Miami area, and I'll be going back to North Florida soon. It probably wouldn't be wise for you to be too far away from here. In any event, my house would be a bit crowded. I live there with my nephew Daniel, and my neighbors Ryan and Jasmine have already made arrangements for someone to stay with me to help me out for a while, till I can get back on my feet. There's another bedroom, but…."

"Thanks for that, Aunt Ruby," Hope cut her off, "but I'm sure I'll remember who I am soon enough." She doubted the words even before they came out of her mouth, but she didn't want any charity from the elderly woman. There was no way she could stay with her and be unable to offer her something in return. She might not remember who she was, but she didn't want to be a burden on her new friend. Something would work out.

She hoped.

 config

The next morning, Hope found herself alone in the bedroom while Aunt Ruby was taken for a scan. As she stared out of the window, she found herself wondering, not for the first time, if she had a family in the area, or even in the state. Wouldn't they have found her by now? Her accident had happened several days ago, and still… nothing. It would soon be time to leave the hospital, and then what would she do?

She remembered Dr. Sharpe's advice and tried not to think too much about details that could cause her additional stress and frustration.

Her fears were somewhat allayed when a nurse came in, closely followed by a young brunette wearing a red suit and impossibly high heels. She introduced herself as "*Miz* Justine LaHaye, MSW," and she was the case worker who had been assigned to the case. As the nurse left, Miss LaHaye promptly took a seat close to Hope's bed. After five minutes of tapping on the screen of her tablet and organizing the leather portfolio on her lap, she suddenly made eye contact for the first time and then began to interview Hope as if her life depended on it.

"All right, Miss..., Miss...," her eyes rapidly scanned the tablet until she remembered why the necessary information was missing, "I'm sorry; you're the first client I've had who doesn't have a name."

Hope smiled uncomfortably, "I understand. People here have begun to call me Hope. You can use that, if you like."

"How appropriate, I suppose," the social worker tapped on her tablet a few times and continued. Hope wondered if there was a reason she was avoiding eye contact or if there was simply something too fascinating on her computer to miss.

"Well, Miss... *Hope*, the fact of the matter is that our office has never had a case like yours. Most amnesiacs are identified within hours of being admitted into hospital by family members who search for them and have conclusive evidence that they are who the family says they are, but in your case, no one has called this hospital or any other in the state—I've checked—trying to find an African American female in her late twenties to early thirties who is five feet nine inches tall, weighing 135 pounds, with dark brown natural hair and eyes. It's understandable that no one might know about your..." she paused as her green eyes wandered in the direction of Hope's abdomen before continuing, "... condition, because it's relatively early, so that detail has not been mentioned on your description."

She looked up. "In the absence of any kind of precedent, therefore, we will simply have to make this up—I mean, *figure this out*—as we go along." She made another notation before looking at Hope with what seemed to be a mixture of pity and annoyance.

"Well, first things first, as soon as you are released, we will go to the police precinct to meet with the detective who is investigating your case and find out if there are any leads. Normally, they would have come to interview you, but you're not a suspect in a crime, and they've already spoken with your primary physician here at the hospital—Dr. Fields, is it?—who has assured them that you have no memory of the accident. I'm not sure if you're aware of this, but the detective already came and took your fingerprints and entered them into databases for convicts, criminals and suspects, as well as missing persons." Hope could not miss the order in which the possibilities had been listed, but she said nothing.

"That turned up nothing, so the next thing to figure out would be your placement. I've spoken to Dr. Fields myself, and he has indicated to me that you are just about ready to go home—I mean, *leave.* The question arises, therefore: where are you going to go?"

Before Hope could open her mouth—not that she had anything to say—the other woman continued speaking, "Women in your state..." again, her eyes wandered to Hope's non-existent baby bump, "... who cannot be released into the care of loved ones, are usually placed in a state-funded halfway house, where they remain until they are able to find a job and make alternative arrangements." Hope opened her mouth, but Miss LaHaye kept talking, "However, that may be a challenge for you because, well, no one is likely to hire someone with no past, no name, no Social Security number." Hope closed her mouth.

"Nevertheless, with great difficulty I have found a place in a facility close to this hospital that is willing to house you until you can find somewhere stable to move to. It wasn't easy, because places in these state facilities are few and far between. Budgets have been cut, and fewer businesses and individuals are willing to put their hard-earned dollars into homes that welcome prostitutes, drug addicts and runaways."

As Hope imagined the kind of women with whom she would be placed, she felt fear and discomfort rising within her. She took a few deep breaths to keep them at bay; after all, who was she to judge these women she'd never met? For all she knew, she was one of them!

Miss LaHaye continued speaking as if she never needed to take a breath herself, "If no one comes forward to claim... I mean, *identify* you, your care will be funded until after you have the baby; however, you can imagine that the state would not be able to support you indefinitely, and after a period of no more than three months after the birth, you would be expected to have found yourself a job. I mean, we're talking about next year, so you should have had the opportunity to establish yourself as a useful member of society with a lot to contribute. It goes without saying that we will give you as much support and guidance as we possibly can." She looked up from the tablet, "Any questions?"

Hope figured she had hundreds of questions, but she knew it would be useless to ask most of them to this woman who looked like she had just graduated from high school but apparently had multiple degrees hanging on a wall somewhere.

"Yes. Do you know when I have to leave the hospital?"

"You mean they haven't told you?" Miss LaHaye's eyes widened.

"No."

"Tomorrow, Miss..." she quickly scanned her tablet again, "... *Hope*. You're being discharged tomorrow morning."

Hope felt the blood drain from her face. "Tomorrow?" She had hoped to have a little more time within the closed environment of the hospital to get used to the idea that she was pregnant and to see if her memory would return.

"Yes, Miss..." her eyes found the tablet again as she looked for the appropriate word, "... *Hope*. You're in great physical shape, at least as far as the medical professionals are concerned, so there's no need for you to be in the hospital. Let's not forget, Miss... *Hope*... that valuable public resources are being used to take care of you here."

Hope was beginning to feel like a real burden on the state and the country, but before she could wrap her mind around the latest development, Miss LaHaye continued, "So, I'll be here tomorrow by ten o'clock to pick you up. I'll bring you some clothes and other necessities. What are you? About a size eight to ten?" Hope didn't answer; she didn't need to. Miss LaHaye didn't even pause for a breath, "I'll bring you some size eight and ten clothes and sandals, and we can go down to the police precinct to talk with that detective. Then, after that, it's to the state facility for you to settle in. Or would you prefer to go to the facility first?" Hope opened her mouth, to no avail.

"Never mind, we'll see the detective first and then do all that afterwards, maybe even go shopping—how exciting—okay?" She didn't wait for a response before making a final swipe on her tablet, then standing and putting her things into her stylish leather portfolio. Hope had effectively been dismissed.

As the social worker was leaving, an aide was wheeling Aunt Ruby back in. As soon as she and Hope made eye contact, the young woman burst into a flood of tears.

"What's the matter?" Aunt Ruby gestured for the aide to wheel her over to the side of Hope's bed.

"I have to leave the hospital tomorrow, and I have nowhere to go!"

Aunt Ruby was silent as Hope sobbed. The faithful aide looked awkward standing there waiting for the wheelchair, so Aunt Ruby allowed him to help her onto her bed before waving him away with thanks and a grateful smile.

Hiccupping all the while, Hope moved across the room and fell into Aunt Ruby's open arms, barely managing to share the whole story—the state-run facility, the prostitutes and drug addicts, the detective, the police station, everything came tumbling out. She laid her head on Aunt Ruby's shoulder and cried until she had no tears left. Aunt Ruby smoothed her cornrows and whispered comforting words until the sobbing subsided.

"Sweetie, don't be afraid, God will provide for you and your baby. I'm sure that before you know it, your memory will be back, and you'll be in the embrace of your loving family. No matter where you are, sweetie, I will be praying that God will keep you right in the palm of His capable hand." Hope was neither convinced nor comforted. Vaguely aware of Aunt Ruby watching her as she crossed the room, she got into bed and, without saying another word, fell into a fretful sleep.

CHAPTER SIX

Thursday dawned bright and sunny. It was the complete opposite of how Hope felt on the inside—cold and dreary. The day had come for both she and Aunt Ruby to leave the hospital—the only home she could remember.

She knew Aunt Ruby was happy to be going home, and a big part of her was thrilled for her new friend, but an even bigger part was anxious—maybe even downright afraid—about what lay ahead for her. She may not remember who she was, but she instinctively knew that she would not be comfortable surrounded by the kind of women she expected to meet in the state-run house. Nevertheless, it was up to her to begin figuring out a way to take care of herself and the child she was trying hard not to think about, and she knew she couldn't remain in the hospital forever. Hospitals were for sick people, and she was in great health. If only she could remember who she was!

Since there was no likelihood of change on the horizon, she tried to resign herself to the fact that she had little control over what was happening to her and to just go with the proverbial flow.

Both Aunt Ruby and Hope were up early that morning. Hope put on a brave face she hoped would hide her anxiety and volunteered to help Aunt Ruby pack. The older woman still had her luggage from the cruise she'd been on, so Hope took out the clothes Aunt Ruby wanted to wear home and folded her other clothes and placed them lovingly into the suitcase. As she did so, Aunt Ruby would instruct her to take out a few items of clothing for herself, like two new pairs of white socks, and a couple of souvenir T-shirts and a floral dress that had originally been intended as gifts for some of the young ladies Aunt Ruby had befriended back home. Hope wanted to decline the offer, but she knew she couldn't. After all, she had nothing of her own, and she needed clothes. Who knew what she and Miss LaHaye would be able to find?

Aunt Ruby gave Hope her home phone number and told her that she should call as soon as she was settled in so that they could keep in close contact.

That morning, Hope agreed to join in Aunt Ruby's devotion, not so much because she was interested, but because she wanted to spend as much time with her as possible. She and Aunt Ruby had been roommates for more than a week, and they really enjoyed each other's company. Hope felt like in the dying hours of their relationship, she needed to sit at her friend's feet, listen to her stories and partake of her wisdom. Instead, she moved a chair close to the older woman's bed.

That day, Aunt Ruby's devotion centered on the theme of the fruit of the Spirit. After singing a couple of worship songs while Hope awkwardly twiddled her thumbs, Aunt Ruby read the scripture from the fifth chapter of Galatians and then took some time to explain her interpretation to Hope. The fleshly nature, she told her, caused people to become immoral, corrupt, short-tempered, selfish and a host of other things Hope absent-mindedly wondered if she was. Aunt Ruby explained that the spiritual nature, on the other hand, encouraged people to become loving, peaceful, patient, kind, good, faithful, gentle and able to control themselves. Again, Hope's mind was assailed with questions about the type of person she had been before the accident.

"Hope, you are at a particularly important junction in your life. You are at a place where you are unfamiliar with your past and uncertain about your future." Ruby put her books down and held Hope's hands in hers as she looked directly into her eyes. "Until you regain your memory, you have what so many adults wish they could have—a clean slate. Now is the time for you to invest in yourself and your baby. Take this dubious opportunity to choose the characteristics you want to have. Meditate on the fruit of the spirit: love, joy, peace, patience, kindness, goodness, faithfulness, gentleness and self-control. Make an effort to put on these characteristics, to make them a part of your everyday life. When you are caught in situations where you are tempted to succumb to the fruit of the flesh, exercise self-control instead. Be loving and peaceful. Be patient. Be kind and good, faithful and gentle. It might be difficult sometimes, and there will be people who exasperate and frustrate you, but try to take the high road and eat spiritual fruit."

Hope drank in every word Aunt Ruby was saying as if it were water and she were dying of thirst. She wasn't particularly interested in what she considered the 'religious' aspects, but she could see no harm and a myriad of benefits in adopting the characteristics Aunt Ruby was discussing with her. Even if one wasn't particularly religious or even spiritual, she couldn't imagine that it would hurt to be loving, peaceful, kind, gentle, patient, self-controlled, or even faithful. She didn't necessarily need to be faithful to the Christian God Aunt Ruby worshipped. No, she could be faithful to herself and her child. She could be faithful to their wellbeing. What could it hurt?

As she sat there meditating on the words, she didn't hear the older woman calling her. "Hope? Hope?" It finally dawned on her that she was being addressed. She was still getting used to the name.

"Yes?"

"I was asking if it would be okay for me to pray with you."

"Of course." Again, what could it hurt? And it would make Aunt Ruby happy.

Aunt Ruby bowed her head in reverence to the Lord. Hope knew she believed He was with them in that very hospital room, and that He would attend to every word of her petition to Him.

"Father, I come to You in the name of Your son, Jesus Christ, on behalf of this young woman. I come to You giving thanks. I thank You for Your many blessings upon us."

Hope tried not to scoff. She didn't feel very blessed at the moment. Aunt Ruby continued, "Lord, You have blessed her with life when she could easily have died. You have blessed her with good physical health, despite the circumstances that brought her here, and You have blessed her with a strong, healthy child."

Hope began to feel slightly uncomfortable. She supposed she had a lot to be grateful for. She just hadn't thought about it before. To be honest, thanksgiving wasn't high on her list of priorities just then. She was more concerned with where and how she would live.

"Father, You know her circumstances better than she knows them herself. She doesn't know who she is, but You know. You know the plans You have for her, ones that will bring her ultimate prosperity and not harm. Such was Your plan for Jeremiah, and such is Your plan for Hope. Make a way where there seems to be no way. Open doors for her that no man can shut, and close doors for her that no man can open in order for her to walk in Your will. I know You have already prepared a suitable home where she can take care of herself and her unborn child until her memory returns at the appointed time. Reveal that place today, I pray in Jesus' name. Amen."

Ruby then released Hope's hands and placed both of her own hands on top of Hope's head. "And now, may the Lord bless and keep you and make His face shine on you and your child."

☓

All too soon, *Miz* Justine LaHaye, Social Worker Extraordinaire (at least as far as *she* was concerned) gave a peremptory knock on the door and entered the room that was the only home Hope could remember. She was carrying a medium-sized paper shopping bag and was much cheerier than either Hope or Aunt Ruby felt at that point in time.

She was in a bit of a hurry, so she left the bag with Hope and went to take care of whatever paperwork needed to be done while Hope got ready.

In the bathroom, Hope unpacked toiletries and a pair of dark blue jeans with a flexible band that Hope assumed would accommodate an expanding tummy when the time came. She wasn't surprised that it fit. With her perfect gray pantsuit, red accessories and red five-inch stilettos, Miss LaHaye looked like she could have been a stylist in a former life.

Hope liked the loose see-through floral top with its attached white lining. Miss LaHaye had even included hair accessories, so she quickly undid the cornrows and combed her messy hair. She would need to get some kind of product to keep those curls in check. She gathered her curls into a ponytail and assessed herself in the mirror. She wondered where she had gotten that one-inch scar on her forehead. It looked much older than the fresh one on her right cheek, clearly from the accident. Her teeth, with their slight overbite and gap between the two front ones, looked like they could have benefited from braces as a child. Maybe her family wasn't very well-off. Her cheekbones were high, and she imagined many a well-meaning adult must have pinched her cheeks a lot when she was younger. Her face was dotted here and there with what looked like acne scars. Perhaps from the chicken pox? There was so much she didn't know.

She sighed. Her face was still discolored, and she was especially grateful for the oversized sunglasses Miss LaHaye had thoughtfully dropped into the bag. Hope didn't imagine she was the type of woman to wear a lot of makeup and spend a lot of time fussing with her hair, so she looked away from the mirror as she slipped her feet into the girly white sandals.

Despite the anxiety that had become part of her, she felt like a new person. She couldn't remember wearing anything other than the hospital gowns and slippers she'd been stuck in. Still, she wasn't happy about leaving Aunt Ruby. She had begun to lean on the older woman for strength and support and would miss her wise words, and even the Christian programming she watched on TV.

In the bottom of the shopping bag she found a small box containing a prepaid cell phone. Miss LaHaye had thought of everything. She stepped out of the bathroom and went over to Aunt Ruby, who was sitting with her journal and Bible on her lap.

"The good news is, I seem to have a phone number to leave with you. There was a phone in the bag. Here, the number was on the box." She showed it to Aunt Ruby, who wrote it down in the journal.

Miss LaHaye came back into the room and announced chirpily, "All set, Miss... Hope. We're ready to go. I have a home visitation to do early this afternoon, and we have quite a bit to accomplish before then. Are you ready?"

"I suppose I'm as ready as I'll ever be." She stooped in front of Aunt Ruby and gave the older woman a long hug. "Thank you so much for everything. I'll miss you, but I'll try to keep in touch."

"Don't worry, dear, I have your number now, so I'll definitely give you a call every few days and keep in touch, if you don't mind. I'll also keep you at the top of my prayer list."

"Thank you." Hope knew prayer was important to Aunt Ruby, so she didn't argue. Besides, she figured it couldn't hurt anyway. As she was standing up, Aunt Ruby pressed some money into her hand. She opened her mouth to protest, but Aunt Ruby wouldn't hear of it.

"Consider it a loan, dear. Keep it until you're back on your feet; then you can return it to me. It will give us an excuse to keep in touch." Hope nodded and slipped the money into the pocket of her jeans without counting it.

They said their goodbyes, and the next thing Hope knew, she and the medium-sized shopping bag with all her worldly possessions were being ushered into an elevator and then out of the building and Aunt Ruby's life.

૦૩

Miss LaHaye's car was nothing like Hope had expected. She was sure she would have had a shiny red convertible or something similar, so she was quite surprised when they got to the huge parking lot and a tiny blue car that could only be described as a super compact chirped and flashed its lights in response to Miss LaHaye's pressing of a button on her stylish remote control. The car had no back seat, but Hope wasn't bothered; it wasn't like she had a ton of stuff.

"Okay," Miss LaHaye began as they got into the tiny vehicle that resembled a clown car, "from here, we'll head to the police precinct and afterwards, we'll do a little shopping. Then we're off to the halfway house before it's time for my visitation this afternoon." She shifted the car into first gear and moved out of the parking space.

Before long, they were in the middle of Miami's mid-morning traffic. Miss LaHaye tried to make small talk, but Hope was more interested in the sights she was seeing outside. She hoped she would recognize a street, a business, maybe even one of the hundreds of people she saw as they passed by. Nothing seemed familiar to her, and she wondered if this city was her home.

Miss LaHaye soon pulled into a municipal parking lot and parked neatly. Hope realized they had arrived at the police precinct. Her stomach fluttered with nerves about what could possibly lay ahead for her.

Soon, she and the social worker were ushered to the desk of a big teddy bear of a man masquerading as a detective. He was round-faced and big-bellied and bore a slight resemblance to Santa Claus. Hope absentmindedly wondered if he could chase a criminal if he had to.

He was familiar with Hope's case, having seen her in the hospital shortly after the accident. He spoke to her in a manner that was gentle and respectful as he confirmed what Miss LaHaye had told Hope the day before. He would have returned to the hospital to interview her after she woke up, but the doctor had told him the extent of her amnesia. He also explained that Miss LaHaye had made contact and promised to bring her as soon as she was released. She already knew that the fingerprint search had revealed nothing, but he added that there had been no reports within the state of missing women matching her description. The next step he would take would be to take her photograph and run it through local and national databases to see if they could find a hit.

While the computer was doing its search, Miss LaHaye suggested that it should be fairly easy to find Hope's family by posting her photograph on various social media websites and asking the general public to circulate it. She explained that she had seen dozens of missing persons' photos being posted on her friends' pages, and she had certainly re-posted her fair share; however, Detective Sherman explained that it would be better to avoid social media in Hope's case.

"Human trafficking and exploitation are on the rise, so we have to be careful who has access to her image. Because of her amnesia, just about anyone could come and claim to be her relative or boyfriend, and for all we know, we could be releasing her into the hands of a pimp or drug kingpin or one of their henchmen. It would be better for us to wait and see if her memory comes back before we go that route. That way, she'll be able to identify whoever it is."

Hope's level of anxiety increased a notch or two, but she remained calm. She remembered Aunt Ruby's admonition to practice patience. She was trying.

In the meantime, the search of facial recognition software had turned up empty. The confirmation that she wasn't a convicted criminal gave Hope some measure of relief, but the fact remained that she still had absolutely no idea who she was.

Arrangements were made for the ladies to keep in contact with Detective Sherman, and they left the precinct with his business card next to the money from Aunt Ruby in Hope's pocket. The next stop was a strip mall where Miss LaHaye promised Hope she would find great bargains. Hope remembered the money Aunt Ruby had given her, but she was determined to keep as much of it as she could and one day return it to her generous benefactor. Before she could remind Miss LaHaye that she had no money of her own, the social worker handed her a prepaid credit card, which she had bought in a national superstore chain. She explained that it could be loaded with money from anywhere and that she had earlier loaded it with money that was Hope's to use to cover some of her needs. It would continue to be loaded every two weeks until she was able to find steady employment or until she was identified and returned to her family. When that happened, they would make arrangements for her or her family to repay the amount. "The problem, Miss... Hope, is that without an identity, without a Social Security Number, there are roadblocks everywhere as it relates to getting you the help you need from the state. This money is courtesy of a private charity with which I have some connections. I'll give you the details, and you can send them a thank you note or something."

Hope was beyond grateful. She had not anticipated having any kind of income, so she was overwhelmed with gratitude. At the same time, she was slightly embarrassed at having to receive what she considered a handout. Despite her discomfort, she knew she had no real choice at the moment.

"Now, I don't expect you to be the type of person to use this money as an excuse not to look for some meaningful way to spend your time, Miss... Hope, but I do understand how difficult it would be for someone to hire you with no background. In any event, use the money that's available wisely. While you're at the halfway house, your room and board will be taken care of, but if you choose to move out, you will have to pay for those things yourself."

Hope nodded and accepted the card. "You mean, I don't have to stay there until I regain my memory?"

"No, not at all. You're free to look for alternative housing. Just don't leave the state, and always make sure I know where you're staying. At the outset, I will be in touch with you almost daily."

Hope was relieved. She didn't know where she would go, or how she would manage it, but she knew she didn't want to stay in a halfway house for an extended period of time.

They didn't stay in the discount department store for long. Hope purchased what she considered to be immediate necessities: underwear, two more pairs of maternity jeans, a few loose-fitting feminine tops, two light floral dresses, a neutral cardigan, yoga pants, sweats, a pair of sneakers, a pair of black sandals and a small black bag that could fit a wallet and a few personal items. This left her with about half the money from her prepaid credit card and all of the cash that Aunt Ruby had given her. She was pleased with the purchases, as was Miss LaHaye, who mentioned how pleased she was that Hope didn't go overboard in the store.

There was a small supermarket on the same strip mall, so Hope also bought a few protein bars, snacks and bottled water. She wondered if she had always preferred salty treats, or if this was because of the pregnancy. She supposed she would be able to tell... *someday*.

As Hope settled into the car for the journey to the halfway house she would soon be calling home, Hope's new cell phone rang. Surprised, she answered it cautiously, "Hello?"

"Hope!" She immediately recognized Aunt Ruby's voice, and was pleasantly surprised.

"Aunt Ruby!" She smiled into the device. "Are you on your way home?"

"Not yet. I'm still at the hospital. You'll never believe what happened."

Hope tried to ignore Miss LaHaye's obvious eavesdropping. "What do you mean?"

"My neighbor Ryan is here, but he has some bad news... well, it's not really bad news, as it turns out."

"Oh?"

"Well, it so happens that Audra, the lady from our church who was supposed to stay with me and help me out... well, she had a family emergency, and she might not be available for weeks."

"Oh, Aunt Ruby, I'm so sorry to hear that." Hope commiserated, but vaguely wondered why Aunt Ruby was calling to report to her. "What are you going to do?"

"I'm going to have you come stay with me, of course!"

"What's that?"

"Don't you see? It's perfect! I prayed that the Lord would find you the perfect place where you would be safe and the baby would be taken care of, and He has. You're coming to Alistair Bay with me!"

Understanding dawned in Hope's mind. "I am?"

"Of course! You need a place to stay, and I need someone to come stay with me. It's the perfect solution. I *told* you God always pays attention to me!"

"Umm... let me run it by Miss LaHaye. I'm not sure...." She tried to tamp down the feeling of hope that was starting to rise in her chest.

"Go ahead, hon. I'll hold the line. I'm going nowhere fast anyway." Hope heard her chuckle.

"Problem?" Miss LaHaye inquired as soon as Hope moved the phone away from her ear.

"I'm not sure, actually." She relayed the information.

"Hmm." Miss LaHaye looked at her watch as she thought about what Hope was suggesting. "Where does this Aunt Ruby live?"

"Umm... in a place called Alistair Bay. Up north."

Miss LaHaye tapped her scarlet fingernails on the steering wheel in thinly veiled annoyance, "We're in South Florida, Miss... Hope. Just about everything is 'up north.'"

Hope smiled, determined to practice the same level of patience she would expect from a social worker dealing with an amnesiac. "North Florida."

"Oh," the smile that graced the other woman's face was unexpected. "You mean she's not going out-of-state!"

"No, she's not."

Hope could almost see the wheels turning in the other woman's brain before she said, "Well, let me just check in with my immediate supervisor." She pulled into an available parking spot on the side of the street and whipped out her cell phone in its sparkling case. Hope focused on the buildings outside as she made a real effort not to eavesdrop.

When the call was over, Miss LaHaye made a second phone call without updating Hope. When she disconnected, she gave a look that Hope could almost believe was joyful as she smiled, "Wonderful! I had to check with Detective Sherman, too, and he's fine as long as you don't leave the state. I just have to discuss a few things with your friend, and everything should be in place. This works out great," she confided as she pulled the tiny car back into the traffic. "To be honest, I wasn't looking forward to leaving you at that halfway house in your... condition. Some of those women can be brutal."

Hope shivered, grateful that she would never have to find out what that meant. Before she knew what was happening, she found herself whispering a prayer of thanksgiving, "Thank You, Jesus." She had done it without thinking about it, as if it were the most natural thing in the world.

଼

Back at the hospital, Hope and Miss LaHaye went directly to the room she had shared with Aunt Ruby. Having knocked and been told to come in, they were confronted with a giant of a man standing close to Aunt Ruby's bed. He had to be six feet five inches tall and was easily 300 pounds in weight. He looked at Hope curiously, but upon seeing Aunt Ruby's smile, he relaxed somewhat. She couldn't help but notice how handsome he was.

"There you are! This is my neighbor, Ryan Phillips. Ryan, this is the young lady I've been telling you about."

The two shook hands. Hope had expected Ryan's grip to be painful, but he held her hand with only the slightest of pressure. She suspected he had learned to control the inevitable power that went with his considerable size.

"And I'm *Miz* Justine LaHaye, her case worker." Miss LaHaye shook hands with Ryan.

"Aunt Ruby, I just don't know what to think. I don't want to intrude. I mean, you don't know me—"

"Nonsense!" The older woman interrupted her. She stretched her hands in Hope's directions and the young woman placed her own hands in Aunt Ruby's wrinkled ones. "You'll be doing me a great favor, Hope. I need someone to stay in the house with me so that I'm not alone, and you need a home until you can find yourself again. I shudder to think of you in a halfway house. We may not know exactly who you are, dear, but I'm sure that wouldn't have been a suitable place to prepare to bring a child into the world."

Hope looked at Ryan to see if he was surprised, but he was not. Apparently, Aunt Ruby had told him the whole story—or as much of it as anyone knew, at least for now. She wasn't perturbed. Her pregnancy would show eventually.

Miss LaHaye asked, "Where is it that you live?"

"Less than half an hour outside of St. Augustine. It's a small town called Alistair Bay."

"Well, that works out fine, then, doesn't it? I don't want her to leave the state, and St. Augustine, as far away as it is, is still in Florida." She was pensive. "The halfway house is really just that—a place to stay while sorting out a permanent home—and I wouldn't want her to be there for the remainder of her pregnancy. Just go ahead and leave me your contact information, ma'am, and I'll arrange for someone from the St. Augustine Department of Family Services to come and verify your address as soon as possible. But all that can wait a day or two, I guess." She waited while Aunt Ruby wrote down the details and then she waved goodbye and practically ran out of the room, stilettos and all. Just like that, Justine LaHaye disappeared, and Hope and Aunt Ruby found themselves roommates again.

CHAPTER SEVEN

Daniel had called Aunt Ruby's room to get an update on how she was doing and to find out exactly when she was going to be discharged, only to find out then that she had already been released. He was annoyed that no one had called to tell him she was on her way home, but he knew she was in good hands.

He would be finishing up his lecture tour of England on Friday and was scheduled to fly back into Jacksonville via Washington, D.C., early the next morning. With the time difference and a six-hour layover in D.C., he would be landing in Jacksonville somewhere around 7:00 p.m. Then he would pick up his SUV and be in Alistair Bay in less than an hour.

Ryan had actually made it a lot easier for him. If he had been the one to pick his aunt up from the hospital, he would have had to cancel speaking engagements, pay to change his flights, and rent a car in Miami. Then he would still have to go to Jacksonville International Airport to pick up his own SUV. He conceded to himself—but not to Aunt Ruby or Ryan—that the right decision had been made, even without his input. He silently acknowledged, however, that the control freak in him was not pleased with being informed after the fact.

He was glad that Audra, a forty-something-year-old member of their church, had agreed to stay with Aunt Ruby during her period of convalescence. Audra worked in home healthcare and was between jobs, so they had arranged, through Ryan, to hire her. He was pleased to know that someone would be there with his aunt to do the little tasks she might otherwise force herself to do. Equally important was the fact that Audra was someone he knew and trusted. His trusting nature had died with his wife, and he would rather take unpaid leave from the university than leave his aunt in the hands of a stranger. He would never allow anyone to take advantage of her the way Victoria had taken advantage of him.

It was late Thursday night, London time, so he asked Ryan to send him an email later to let him know they had arrived safely. He thought he heard someone else's voice in the background, but concluded that it must have been the radio. Jasmine had been too sick during the pregnancy to travel, and he couldn't imagine who else would be making the trip with them. He relaxed a little. He knew Aunt Ruby was in good hands. Ryan had been his best friend and confidante since they had met working construction the summer before their senior year in college. Later, Ryan had been instrumental in Aunt Ruby and his mother Emmy's decision to purchase a home in Alistair Bay. Ryan had worked as part of the architectural team that had conceptualized the quaint-looking neighborhood. They had designed it so that it would look as if the homes were from the eighteenth or nineteenth centuries, but inside, they were quite modern and spacious. There could be no question that Ryan would protect Aunt Ruby with his life, if he thought it necessary. Daniel drifted off into a deep, dreamless sleep.

ೞ

The five-hour journey to North Florida was quite uneventful. Ruby regaled Ryan and Hope with stories of her childhood in the nearby scenic town of St. Augustine. She then began talking about Alistair Bay, the town to which she had moved with her sister Emerald a few years before Emmy's death. She described it as a family-oriented neighborhood of fewer than 5,000 residents somewhere to the northwest of the historic town of St. Augustine.

She explained that it was a beautiful community in its own right, but did not have St. Augustine's distinction of being the U.S. town continuously occupied by Europeans for the longest period of time. Unlike its more prestigious neighbor to the northeast, Alistair Bay had not been settled in the late sixteenth century; in fact, up until the end of the 1900s, it had been 20 acres of agricultural land where cattle had grazed and rows and rows of corn had flourished. Then it had been bought by a real estate developer, who had built 300 Victorian-style homes that surrounded a large rectangular park. Close to the park were a few quaint shops and a community center, and forming an external rectangle were the municipal buildings, three schools sharing a single compound, a medical center, two shopping malls, a twenty-four hour grocery store, the library, three churches, and a few other buildings.

Despite its misleading name, she told Hope, Alistair Bay was not by the sea; in fact the developer, Ryland Bay II, had named it in honor of his parents, Ryland Bay I and Margaret Alistair Bay. The closest thing to the sea in Alistair Bay was a huge fountain in the middle of the park. The Atlantic Ocean was half an hour's drive away.

Eventually, she stopped speaking and Hope realized that she had fallen asleep. It wasn't long before she did the same.

ಌ

Jasmine Phillips was sitting on the porch of the Victorian-style home she shared with her new husband, Ryan. She smiled as she reflected. It had been only five months since their wedding day—and night— and she was already more than four months pregnant. She supposed all those years of celibacy had resulted in their being more fertile than expected. Truth be told, she hadn't really been happy about getting pregnant on their honeymoon, but there was nothing she could do about it now.

She was thinking about the day she and Ryan had gotten married. Since they were both Jamaican, they had had a small destination wedding on the North Coast, close to Ryan's home town but a couple of hours from hers. The ceremony and reception had been intimate, perfect, with only their families and closest friends in attendance. Daniel and Aunt Ruby had made the trip, as had Jasmine's best friend, Holly, who had recently moved to Atlanta. She had just hung up the phone from talking to her.

She thought for a few minutes before beginning to write in the brand-new journal she was holding on her lap.

April 9

This pregnancy has been harder than I could ever have imagined. I believed all the books that said the first trimester would have been the most difficult, so much so that on the first day of the second trimester, I'd kind of expected to wake up feeling perfectly fine, with no more nausea, no more tiredness, no more bags under my eyes, and maybe even a little weight gain. Boy, was I wrong! I'm kind of glad I quit my job a few months ago, because I don't think I could have gone to work every day, feeling the way I've been feeling.

I guess, looking back, it should have been obvious at the time that I was pregnant. I don't know how I could have missed it. I mean, I know my cycle has always been unpredictable, but I should have figured it out.

We always knew we wanted children, but neither of us had expected them so early in the marriage; I'd wanted to enjoy some alone-time with my new husband a little bit more. I guess it might have been different for him at his age, always knowing he wanted kids. I've always been kind of on the fence about that myself, like if I have them, I have them. But getting married to Ryan, I knew kids were going to be on the agenda someday. 'Someday' came really quickly for us, though. When I found out that I was six weeks pregnant, we had only been married for two months. To think we spent all that money going to that all-inclusive, yet we hardly ever left the room that first week! It makes me blush just thinking about it.

I kind of feel guilty now, but I wasn't exactly thrilled when I took that pregnancy test and it came up positive. I didn't believe it at first, and even when we went to the doctor and he confirmed it, I was still in denial. I refused to take any prenatal supplements. Taking supplements meant this was really happening, and I wasn't ready for that. I regret it now, but I claim a perfect child, in the name of Jesus.

Besides, Sister Claire has prayed over the baby and anointed my tummy. When your pastor's wife prophesies that, "This baby will touch people and change lives for Christ without having to say a word," you sit up and take notice. I can't wait to see it being fulfilled.

I've been really, REALLY sick, though. At first, when I began feeling ill all the time, I blamed it on some Thai food I had. But it lasted too long. Then I began to wonder if it was the long commute from Alistair Bay to my job in Orlando. I was just so tired all the time. By the time Ryan would get home at nights, I'd be fast asleep on the sofa. What a way to start a marriage.

So we discussed it, and I left my job with the intention of finding something closer to home, or if all else failed, starting my own accounting firm. I'd start small, of course, perhaps working from home in the early stages and going out to clients instead of having them come to me. I guess I can still do that someday.

When I actually took the pregnancy test, it was kind of a joke—I was trying to eliminate pregnancy as a possible source of my symptoms. When those two lines turned pink, I thought it was someone's idea of a sick joke, so I immediately went out and bought two more tests. Both of them were positive. The next day, Ryan took me to the doctor, who examined me, asked some questions, made me take another test and confirmed the results. I was six weeks along. Right now, it seems like a lifetime ago, but it's only been about ten weeks since then.

So much has changed. I've had to learn to depend on Ryan a lot more than I probably would have. My stomach has been so unpredictable; I can't cook or even tolerate the smell of meat. At first, I was surviving on cereal and milk, and then thankfully, Aunt Ruby started to make me some veggie broth almost every day. She saved my life! Since she's been away on the cruise and then in the hospital in Miami, Ryan has been a real gem, bringing me vegetarian Sui Mein from my favorite Chinese restaurant. It's the only thing I feel like eating. We even call the baby Sui Mein, sometimes, although Sister Claire's nickname for him or her is Little Praise, and it's starting to stick.

I've basically had to forget about cooking, which really bothers me because Ryan always enjoyed the meals I'd prepare for him. He especially loves my spaghetti Bolognese, but I just can't *handle the smell of the ground beef these days. He has been living on Chinese and Thai takeout, pizza and hamburgers eaten before he gets home or out on the patio. That man is a real sweetheart.*

At first, he thought I was faking being sick all the time. No one he knew had that kind of response to pregnancy. He even called Mommy in Jamaica, and she confirmed that every pregnancy is different just as every woman is different and that some women really do have a tough time of it. His own mom believes that pregnancy is a condition, not an illness, but she knows me well enough to know that I wouldn't be faking this. Since speaking with Mommy, he has been really supportive despite his long work hours overseeing construction sites. Thank God for his job, too, that allowed him to be in the right place at the right time to buy this house at a discount when one of the purchasers backed out after construction had already started. God just has a way of stepping in and making a way where there seems to be no way.

I am grateful to the Lord for my husband, for our relationship and for the child He has blessed us with. I am super blessed, and I know with everything within me that Romans 8:28 is definitely true. In everything, my God is working for my good because I love Him and I am committed to walking in His path for me.

J.

❃

Hope woke up when she heard the unfamiliar sound of a man's voice talking quietly and that of a female responding. She realized Ryan was on the phone with someone, whom she assumed to be his wife Jasmine. He was using a hands-free device, so Hope could hear Jasmine's tired voice as she spoke. According to Ryan, who was trying not to disturb his passengers, they had just left St. Augustine and were heading to Aunt Ruby's. They'd be arriving there in around twenty minutes. Jasmine told him she'd use the key Aunt Ruby had left with them to open the house and turn some lights on.

Hope remained quiet as the lights by the side of the local road whizzed by. She had very little idea of what was ahead for her, and as they added miles and miles to their journey, she couldn't help but feel a little anxious. She knew she was in great physical health now, but would she be able to give Aunt Ruby all the assistance she needed, especially as her tummy grew, without jeopardizing the baby's health? She really hoped so, but she supposed only time would tell. The last thing she wanted to do was disappoint Aunt Ruby or inconvenience her.

She couldn't help but wonder, too, what would happen if her memory returned tomorrow. She'd no doubt be returning to her family, assuming she had one, and if she did, she would be leaving Aunt Ruby in the lurch, wouldn't she? Then again, she didn't get the impression that Aunt Ruby *couldn't* hire a private nurse, but that the hiring arrangement they'd made earlier had fallen through.

She and Aunt Ruby hadn't spoken of payment, but she knew room and board would be adequate remuneration for her. She couldn't thank Aunt Ruby enough for her generous offer, and hoped her benefactor wouldn't live to regret it.

಄

When they arrived at Aunt Ruby's house, it was already after nine o'clock. A beautiful young woman with shoulder-length hair was sitting on the porch of the home Hope assumed to be Aunt Ruby's. It was fairly dark, but Hope could see that the house was a beautiful one. The porch stretched almost the entire width of the building, and to the right was a room that was probably a formal living room or dining room that projected forward, beyond the front steps of the porch. The driveway was to the right of the yard and went all the way past the house. Hope would later learn that the garage, with its automated door, was to the rear so as not to take away from the authenticity of the house's Victorian look.

Aunt Ruby woke up as the large SUV stopped, and expressed genuine pleasure at being home after a few weeks away.

Hope helped her out of the vehicle and onto her good foot before handing her the pair of crutches she had acquired in Miami. Through the corner of her eye, she noticed Jasmine's questioning look at Ryan as she watched Hope with Aunt Ruby. She realized Ryan hadn't told his wife about the new addition to their little community. Hope hung back as Jasmine came forward to give Aunt Ruby a hug that was necessarily awkward because of the crutches.

"Jasmine!" Aunt Ruby's greeting was warm and motherly, "Let me look at you," Jasmine stepped back. "You've gained a little weight since I left, but you're still way too thin." Hope could tell the older woman was at least a little bit concerned.

Before Jasmine could respond, Aunt Ruby gestured to Hope to come forward. "Jasmine Phillips, this is our new friend, Hope. She's here to help me until I can get back on both feet again. Hope, this is Jasmine, Ryan's blushing bride. You're going to be the very best of friends, given enough time."

Jasmine gave Hope a welcoming smile and shook her hand, "Welcome, Hope."

Hope's smile was tentative. "Thank you."

Aunt Ruby smiled in Jasmine's direction before saying loud enough for Hope to hear, "Yes, there's a story here, and yes, it's quite interesting, but your hubby will share all the details with you when you both get home. Until then, can one of you please help me to the house?"

Ryan, who had already taken Aunt Ruby's luggage and Hope's shopping bags into the house, easily swept Aunt Ruby into his gigantic arms and headed towards the right side of the house instead of up the porch steps. It was only then that Hope noticed a wheelchair ramp at the side of the porch. It was cleverly obscured by the shrubs that had been planted beside the wide staircase with its five steps. Aunt Ruby started to protest at first, but then she flung her arms around Ryan's neck and began to giggle like a school girl, to everyone's amusement.

The house was gorgeous on the inside. It had a spacious open concept floor plan from the comfortable living room through to the kitchen with its stainless steel appliances, but the room that Hope had originally thought was a dining room or formal living room was separated by a wall; its door was closed, and Ryan had placed Aunt Ruby's luggage beside it. She would learn later that the formal dining room had been converted to a wheelchair accessible bedroom. Shiny hardwood covered the floors and went all the way up the stairs to the floor above. Hope's shopping bags were at the foot of the stairs.

Ryan placed Aunt Ruby, who was by now blushing through her giggles, into an overstuffed sofa, and Hope placed her crutches beside her.

The doorbell rang, and Jasmine headed towards it, explaining as she went, "I figured you'd all be hungry, so I took the liberty of ordering delivery from that Chinese place. Besides, I felt like having some of their Sui Mein."

Ryan joined her at the door, and they soon headed to the kitchen with their bags. Hope was comforted by how at home the couple was in Aunt Ruby's kitchen, even though they didn't live there.

"I hope you don't mind; I ordered vegetarian for you, Aunt Ruby. I just can't stand the smell of meat these days."

Aunt Ruby smiled knowingly, "That's fine, dear."

"I didn't know you were coming, Hope," Jasmine looked pointedly at Ryan, "but they always send way too much, so we should be fine. We have vegetarian fried rice, pot stickers and Lo Mein, as well as Singapore noodles with tofu and eggs. Or you could have some of my vegetable Sui Mein, if you prefer."

Hope joined them in the kitchen. She had a little of the Lo Mein but she really enjoyed the Singapore noodles. They were spicy, but she didn't mind at all. According to Jasmine, the very thought of having anything curried gave her indigestion, but she had ordered them because of how much Aunt Ruby liked them.

They all sat at the dining table that took up the space between the kitchen and the living room. Hope was impressed and slightly amazed by the amount of food Ryan consumed, but she imagined that his intake was proportional to his size. While Jasmine had soup and Aunt Ruby shared the mouth-watering Singapore noodles with Hope, he had a mound of fried rice, pot stickers and Lo Mein. He washed it all down with a bottle of iced tea from the fridge. Hope couldn't help but stare at him as he made his way through what appeared to her to be a giant meal while Aunt Ruby answered Jasmine's questions about the cruise.

When she caught the way Hope was surreptitiously eyeing her husband, Jasmine smiled knowingly at her, "Believe me, you get used to it! By next week, you won't think anything of it. Wait until you see him put away a plate of ribs!" At the mention of the meat, Jasmine looked slightly nauseous, but Hope could almost see her determination to plough her way through the feeling.

Before they knew it, it was eleven o'clock, and the couple got up to leave.

"Jazz, before you go, could you show Hope up to the Lilac Room? And could you bring me a couple of towels and such from upstairs? I'm going to stay in Emmy's room for a while."

Jasmine indicated for Hope to precede her up the stairs before she gingerly made her way up behind her. Ryan brought up the rear, carrying Hope's shopping bags and ensuring that his wife and their precious unborn cargo were safe. He stopped at the top of the stairs and put the bags on the floor of the landing. As Hope reached the top of the stairs, she took note of a door to her right and a set of bi-fold doors facing her. To the left, there was a long hallway with two doors on either side. The passageway ended at a doorway that was straight ahead once you turned left at the landing. Jasmine headed down the hallway, opened the first door on the left and ushered Hope inside.

"This is your room, Hope. Daniel's is one of two master suites; it's at the top of the stairs on the right. The one across the hall is now Daniel's office, and the bathroom is next to it. The washer and dryer are behind the folding doors. You'll find the linen closet next door to you. Aunt Ruby's bedroom is the other master suite, at the end."

Hope looked around the beautiful room decorated in various shades of purple accented with white. There were a full bed, two nightstands and a dresser, all painted in brilliant white. In one corner of the room was a sitting area with a white rocking chair and beside it were a small antique escritoire and a white ladder-back chair. Hope gasped with pleasure. She couldn't imagine what the alternative—a place in a state-run facility—would have been like.

"I'll just leave my things here and go help Aunt Ruby get ready for bed." Hope put her shopping bags inside the Lilac Room and closed the door. If Jasmine wondered why all her things were in those kinds of bags, she didn't ask any questions. Hope knew her husband would fill her in later. She wondered how Jasmine would respond to her the next day.

Ryan had waited on the landing, and after Jasmine had retrieved the linens Aunt Ruby had requested, he preceded the two women down the stairs. Hope could see that he was very protective of his pregnant wife. She couldn't help but wonder if the father of her own child had been equally protective of her. She supposed that as long as she was here, her interactions with Jasmine would raise even more questions about her own pregnancy and her own family. She might as well get used to the idea that until her memory returned, there would be hundreds more questions than answers.

Downstairs, Ryan and Jasmine said good night to Aunt Ruby and Hope with promises to check in on them the next morning. There were more hugs between Jasmine and Aunt Ruby, and Hope could see that there was genuine affection between the two. She wondered if there were anyone with whom she had been that comfortable in her old life. She certainly hoped so.

She locked the front door before helping Aunt Ruby into the room that would be hers for the foreseeable future. The room was decorated in a muted shade of yellow interspersed with green. The furniture was antique, and Hope sensed that the pieces had been chosen with care. She helped Aunt Ruby over to the bed and then brought in the suitcases one at a time. Aunt Ruby insisted that she leave them by the antique dresser with its oval mirror until the next day. She directed Hope to the toiletries and other things she would need, and then Hope helped her to prepare for her bath in the accessible bathroom.

Afterwards, Hope helped Aunt Ruby to prepare for bed. They talked about Aunt Ruby's sister, Emmy, who, though fiercely independent, had developed Multiple Sclerosis later in life and had reluctantly agreed to live with Ruby. Hope learned that the dining room had been converted to a fully accessible suite for Emmy, who had passed away a few years earlier.

Aunt Ruby admitted that she had been much closer to her older sister Emerald than to either her younger sister, Sapphire, or her younger brother Garnet, who were living in New York and New Mexico, respectively. Their parents had named them after precious stones, but Emerald had despised her unusual given name and had preferred the moniker Emmy, given to her by Ruby when she was just learning to talk.

According to Aunt Ruby, Emmy was brilliant. She had excelled in mathematics and physics and had become a successful teacher of both. She had married her colleague Abel Donahue, who taught chemistry and biology, when they were both 23. Their son Daniel had come along a few years later and was the light of their lives. No one was surprised when he chose to become a teacher himself, although he had the mental fortitude to become a success in any area he chose. Several of his own teachers had suggested that he study to become a lawyer, but he had no interest in the law. Instead, he'd fallen in love with history and had eventually become a history professor at a private university in St. Augustine. Aunt Ruby beamed with pride as she explained his reasons for traveling to England.

In response to her new friend's questions, Aunt Ruby, who rarely discussed her own achievements, explained that she had been a health inspector and had worked with the city of Jacksonville for most of her career. She had married in her early forties, having met her husband Howard Crawford at church. He had passed away of cancer during their seventh year of marriage. She had never had any children of her own. She was particularly close to Daniel, since all her other nieces and nephews lived quite far away.

By the time Aunt Ruby finished telling Hope about Emmy and her family, she was lying under the covers with the lamp on. She directed Hope to the suitcase with her Bible and other books.

"I can't fall asleep without spending some quality time with the Lord," she explained, "and especially on a day like today. There's a song that says, 'Through many dangers, toils and snares, I have already come; 'tis grace that brought me safe thus far, and grace will lead me home.' We have no idea what could have happened to us today, travelling as far as we did, but the Lord took us all home safely and I'm grateful.

"Even more than that, though, I have been praying that He would open doors for you to end up exactly where you were supposed to be after you left the hospital, and here you are. I don't know if I could have slept tonight with you in a halfway house, but instead, you are with me in my own home, which is something neither of us could have predicted. Yet it is the best thing that could possibly have happened for you other than the return of your family or your memory. Perhaps you should also whisper a word of thanks tonight." She didn't pressure Hope to join her, she only asked if she would be okay upstairs and, after Hope assured her that she would, told her good night. As Hope left the room, she could hear her singing the same words she had just mentioned. Hope would later learn that the song mentioned earlier was the very popular hymn, *Amazing Grace*.

After checking that all the doors were locked as if she were on auto-pilot, Hope went upstairs, where she gathered a few things and headed into the shower. She had a lot on her mind as she reflected on Aunt Ruby's parting words. She wondered if the Lord had, indeed, had a hand in her ending up in the guest bathroom of Aunt Ruby's house tonight. Perhaps it wasn't just a great coincidence. She supposed that, as with much of the rest of her life at the moment, only time would tell.

That night, before she fell into a deep sleep in Aunt Ruby's Lilac Room, she wondered what the next day would hold for her.

CHAPTER EIGHT

Saturday morning dawned bright and clear. The air was crisp as Hope took her cup of honey lemon tea out onto the patio to do some quiet reflecting before it was time to help Aunt Ruby prepare for the day. On Friday, she had helped Aunt Ruby unpack her luggage, and had managed to do all of the laundry that had piled up during the older woman's time away from home. She had also gone with Jasmine to do some shopping in order to re-stock Aunt Ruby's pantry and refrigerator. Ryan had, as expected, filled Jasmine in on who Hope was, and Jasmine had a lot of questions. Despite being given the third degree, Hope had enjoyed the outing with Jasmine and really felt like they could become good friends if they had the opportunity.

Alistair Bay was large enough to have everything anyone really needed but small enough that the neighbors knew one another by name. Hope enjoyed seeing the children on their way home from school and wondered what kind of homes they hailed from. Jasmine showed her various points of interest on the drive and was sure to tell Hope which bus stops she would need to use if she were running errands on Aunt Ruby's behalf. As they passed the low-key medical center where Jasmine's beloved Dr. Elaina kept an office, Jasmine explained that the lowest floor consisted of a small emergency room and an area where various free clinics were hosted on a periodic basis. The second floor hosted several general practitioners and specialists, including an OB/GYN, a cardiologist, a pediatrician, a dentist and others. Many of the doctors had practices elsewhere and came to Alistair Bay only once or twice per week since the town did not need full-time medical specialists. The top two floors constituted a small private hospital with twenty-eight private rooms and two operating rooms for optional surgical procedures. She explained that most serious emergencies were treated in St. Augustine. The patients at the free clinics were attended to by the same doctors who had their practices in the offices above as part of their community outreach efforts.

Jasmine also shared some of her challenges with her pregnancy with Hope. Having heard Jasmine's stories of nausea, excessive vomiting and fatigue practically since the beginning of her pregnancy, Hope felt quite lucky to have none of those kinds of symptoms. Nevertheless, the fact that she was expecting a baby in a matter of months was never far from her thoughts. She supposed if she was going to live next door to a woman who was only a few weeks more advanced than she was, she would be even more aware of the pregnancy than she had been before. She hoped that Jasmine's symptoms would subside soon. According to her new friend, the days she felt well enough to drive were few and far between, and she couldn't remember the last time she had felt so... well, not *good*, exactly, but not *as bad* as she usually felt.

Today, she and Aunt Ruby had no plans but to stay home and rest a bit. Aunt Ruby was still recovering from the past two weeks or so, which had been a bit of a challenge to her seventy-three-year-old body. She was also expecting her nephew Daniel that night, and she expected that they would have a lot to talk about.

Hope was looking forward to meeting Daniel. He sounded so responsible and accomplished. Aunt Ruby had told her he was trying to turn his lectures on Caribbean studies into a book, and she would love to get the chance to speak with him about his work. She wondered what she did for a living, or if she even had a job. If she did, shouldn't her colleagues and employers be looking for her, too?

As she sipped her tea and waited for some kind of indication that Aunt Ruby was awake, she wondered if there were posters showing her likeness in some small town or large city somewhere in the United States. Still, doubt assailed her; if anyone out there were searching for her, wouldn't she be in the missing persons database by now? How could it be that nobody had noticed she was missing yet? And what about the father of her child? What kind of relationship could they have had if he wasn't searching high and low for her? Shouldn't the whole country know she was missing by now?

CR

Aunt Ruby sat at the kitchen table and gave Hope clear instructions for making her famous chicken soup. She had done a lot of the preparations, such as dicing the pumpkins, carrots and potatoes, herself, and then she had outlined the procedure for Hope to follow, since it would be difficult for her to manage with the crutches. She told Hope that she wanted to make sure that her favorite nephew could have his favorite meal when he got home after several weeks away.

"There's going to be enough for you to take some over to Jasmine, too. That girl is way too thin for someone almost halfway along in her pregnancy." She fussed, "I don't care what the doctor says about 'healthy weight gain'; Jasmine needs some fattening up. And quick. Make sure to take all the chicken out of hers," she instructed Hope. "Maybe that will be okay."

As Aunt Ruby sat there flipping through the pages of a magazine that had arrived in the mail, she said, "I should tell you, Hope, that I haven't mentioned you to Daniel just yet. If I know him, he's not going to be very happy about me allowing someone he doesn't know to stay here, but I'm a grown woman, and I have the right to make my own decisions. And I've already decided that you *will* be staying here." She stomped her one good foot down, making Hope jump at the same moment that the now-familiar feeling of anxiety once again reared its head.

CR

Daniel Donahue had never been more grateful to see the Jacksonville International Airport. As the plane touched down, he felt extremely blessed and grateful, because he knew he was another step closer to seeing his aunt and making sure she was okay.

Even before his parents had died, Daniel had been close to Aunt Ruby. As a child, he had loved visiting her in St. Augustine. While his classmates and friends had clamored for the bright lights of Miami or South Beach, even as a university student he had been more comfortable in the historic town, riding the trolley cars and seeing the sights over and over again with his beloved companion.

He had grown up with his parents in Jacksonville and had gone to university there. After working for a few years, he had gone to graduate school in St. Augustine, and that was where he had met Victoria, the woman he had married and with whom he had planned to spend the rest of his life. He had been offered a graduate assistantship while studying and had been hired upon his completion of his Ph.D. He had spent some time teaching in St. Augustine before moving to Lake Butler five years ago. Now a tenured professor and would-be author, he still enjoyed the time he got to spend with Aunt Ruby. He regretted not being able to live with her—and keep a watchful eye on her—full-time, but the commute between Alistair Bay and Lake Butler was almost ninety minutes, and it was just more efficient for him to remain in the housing the university had provided for him close to the campus. He went home to Alistair Bay every weekend that he was able and never went more than a day or two without talking to his 'favorite girl.'

He hadn't spoken to her yesterday, though, because he had been so busy wrapping up his tour and turning down invitations for his last night in England. He had received a text message from Ryan, albeit very brief in typical Ryan style: *Home safe. All's well.* Still, he was a bit anxious. She had not disclosed to him why it had been considered necessary for her to remain in hospital for such a long time if her broken leg was the only thing wrong with her. He wondered if there was something more serious going on, which only made him more anxious to get home.

At around 7:40 p.m., he finally pulled his SUV into the driveway at Aunt Ruby's house and drove around to the garage. From there, he had direct access into the kitchen by way of the small mud room, and if he knew his aunt, even with her leg in a cast, she was definitely somewhere close to the place she called the heart of any house.

He thought of the two-bedroom town house he occupied in Lake Butler. He had moved out of the home he had shared with Victoria a couple of months after her death, and as far as he was concerned, his current abode served its purpose—it was somewhere he could lay his head at night. He reflected on its sparse decorations—the décor was contemporary and, he could admit to himself, cold, with lots of glass and stainless steel everywhere. It had no heart, and it wasn't really his style, but he just wasn't interested in the whole 'making your house a home' spiel. Aunt Ruby was distressed to know that he rarely used the kitchen other than to make himself a cup of coffee. He was happy to survive on the wide variety of takeout that was available nearby.

Daniel stepped through the garage door into the mud room and wasn't overly surprised to hear Ryan and Jasmine's voices coming from the kitchen. He had not, however, expected to be greeted by the unmistakable aroma of Aunt Ruby's rich chicken soup, not when she was nursing a broken limb.

As he stepped into the kitchen, he saw Ryan standing at the stove ladling out a bowl of soup, and he noticed Aunt Ruby, Jasmine and a woman he didn't recognize sitting at the island in front of steaming bowls of their own. His stomach growled. He hadn't eaten much all day, and the aroma of the soup was causing all sorts of things to happen inside him. He wouldn't be surprised if everyone could hear its complaints from the doorway.

There were loud greetings and welcome hugs from Jasmine and Aunt Ruby, and lots of back-slapping shared between Daniel and Ryan. As he made eye contact with and nodded to the stranger in their midst, he was aware that everyone had stopped talking in order to observe their meeting.

"Daniel, this is Hope. Hope, meet my nephew Daniel Donahue," Aunt Ruby made the introductions.

"Hello, Hope." He extended his hand to the woman, who was looking at him with noticeable apprehension. He searched her face— her unsmiling pink lips, dark brown eyes and high cheekbones—for familiarity, but could find none. He figured he would probably have remembered her unruly dark brown curls, but he couldn't tell if they were natural or store-bought. He was too tired to try and figure it out.

"Daniel, it's nice to meet you. Aunt Ruby talks about you all the time." She looked up at him with her eyes wide, as if she were frightened of him.

Daniel was at least three inches taller than Hope, and was light-skinned with dark brown eyes, high cheekbones and a slight cleft in his chin. He wore his black hair close to his scalp and was clean-shaven. He wasn't surprised at the way her eyes quickly swept over him. With his slightly bowed legs and medium build, he had attracted the attention of many women, although over time, he had perfected a disinterested look that made them think twice before making any advances. Tonight, he was tired, and his shoulders stooped slightly from the weight of his travels.

Daniel was not perturbed that this woman — *Hope* — had used the familiar term with his aunt; he knew that most people who met her called her by that name. He was, however, mildly surprised that she was sitting at the kitchen island. Aunt Ruby rarely invited people inside her home, and even though she had plenty of visitors, she liked to entertain them on the porch, reserving the 'inner sanctum' for family and the closest of her friends.

He moved to the cupboard, took down a bowl and began to serve himself. Afterwards, he looked at Aunt Ruby with a quizzical expression on his face, but before he could voice his thoughts, the older woman answered his unasked query, "Hope is going to be staying here for a while and helping me around the house."

In response to his raised eyebrows, she continued, "Audra was called away on a family emergency, and Hope was in the right place at exactly the right time, so here she is," Aunt Ruby smiled tentatively.

"What right place was that?" Daniel asked as he walked to the dining area, sat at the large circular table across from Ryan and began to consume the soup as if he hadn't eaten in days. Ryan, Jasmine and Hope were watching the interplay between nephew and aunt as if it were a tennis match.

"She was my roommate in the hospital in Miami."

"She was?" Daniel gave the young woman a quick once-over as she sat at the island across the room. He skimmed her slim figure and took in her roomy T-shirt and stretchy Capri-style yoga pants. "If you don't mind my asking, what were you being treated for, Hope? You look perfectly fine to me."

Ryan chuckled at his choice of words. Hope looked uncomfortable.

He noted his *faux pas* and corrected himself. "I mean, you look quite healthy!"

Hope did not respond, but looked at Aunt Ruby instead.

"She was in a terrible car accident," Aunt Ruby volunteered. "She was thrown from the vehicle and sustained head injuries. The car burned to a crisp, and the driver didn't make it, but thankfully, she survived."

"Head injuries? I'm sorry to hear that," he was looking at Hope again. "They weren't serious, were they?"

Again, Aunt Ruby stepped in. "Serious enough. Her brain was swollen and her memory has been affected."

"Her memory?"

"Yes."

"How so?" He looked into the bowl at how little soup was left. Despite the on-going conversation, he was enjoying the meal immensely.

"She has amnesia, Daniel. She has no memory of who she is or where she's from. She had nowhere to go."

Daniel raised his eyebrows in Ryan's direction and his friend nodded. Daniel took a deep breath and pushed the empty bowl away. "Folks, can you give us a few minutes?" He looked in the direction of Hope and his friends. They obliged, placing empty bowls in the sink before filing out of the kitchen and onto the patio at the back of the house.

"So, let me get this straight," Daniel got up from the dining table and stood across the island from where Aunt Ruby was sitting with her crutches leaning beside her. He looked at Aunt Ruby, "You meet this woman in the hospital. She tells you some story about having amnesia; you believe her and invite her to live in your home. With you. Alone. Am I getting that right?"

Aunt Ruby looked at him with determination stamped on her face, "Yes."

"Aunt Ruby, you have got to see that this is an ill-advised idea at best and downright dangerous at worst!" He was trying very hard to maintain his cool.

"Daniel, I understand you might think I'm putting myself at risk, but I believe she really does have amnesia."

"Auntie!" Daniel threw his hands up in the air and turned his back for a moment.

"Daniel, we shared a room in Miami. I was there when the doctors were examining her while she was unconscious. I was there when she woke up completely disoriented. More than once. I was there when she couldn't remember her own name. I was there when the doctor explained what part of her brain had been affected by swelling and how it could result in long-term amnesia. I believe her."

"Aunt Ruby, you can't expect me to allow this!"

"Daniel, I do not expect you to *allow* anything," her face was set. "I am an adult, and I am ultimately responsible for my own life. My leg may be broken, but my brain and, more importantly, my *spirit* are fully functional. Helping her is something I feel led to do. You will *not* change my mind."

"Aunt Ruby, I understand you feel sorry for her. You've always had a soft spot for anyone who's down and out, but times are different now; you can't just trust people. You have no idea who this woman is or what her motives are."

"Daniel," Aunt Ruby's voice was measured, "I may be old, but I am not naïve. I know that we are living in dangerous times, but I also know the Lord. I don't have to trust people, so long as I trust Him. When I found out about Audra, Hope had already been discharged from the hospital and was with a social worker. I called and invited her to come and stay with me. I need a caregiver, and she needs a safe place. The Holy Spirit told me that this woman needs to be in a place where her spirit can be nurtured while she heals, and this is a place where that can happen. I could not have slept at night, knowing that she was in a state-run halfway home, sharing her space with prostitutes and drug addicts and God-knows what other women. How could her spirit be nurtured there?"

"Her spirit is not your responsibility."

If Aunt Ruby could have stood, she would have jumped to her feet in determination. "Of course, it is! You've known me your whole life, Daniel, and you of all people should know that I don't believe in coincidences. I don't believe it was happenstance that caused me to have my accident in Miami instead of any of the ports of call we visited, or that she had her accident when and where she did. I don't believe we were roomed together by chance. I believe the Lord led us to the same room there in that hospital in Miami because He knew that she needed me. And that I would need her."

"The next thing you're going to say is that the Lord broke your leg so you could be in the hospital, too!" He slammed his hand on the island.

"No, Daniel. I don't think the Lord *broke* my leg, but I think He allowed it to be broken. As a believer who has submitted myself to God, I agree to be used by Him in any way He sees fit so that His ultimate purpose will be fulfilled. I thought you understood that," she shook her head in disappointment and continued without allowing him to respond. "It isn't as if she hasn't tried to find her family, Daniel."

"Oh, she told you she's been trying, did she?" Daniel was doubtful.

"I told you—she has a social worker. They went to the police station and searched for her face among people who have been reported missing across the country. They even checked her fingerprints, Daniel. She's not a criminal, and she hasn't been reported missing."

"You mean she's never been *arrested*. She could still be a criminal, Auntie."

"That's a chance I'm willing to take."

"Hmm," Daniel was pensive, "what about social media? Have they been posting her face on any websites, trying to get her image out there so that people can identify her?"

"You know I'm not into all that Internet stuff, but no. I heard her telling Ryan that the detective thought it was a bad idea. If people know she doesn't know who she is, they can come and claim to be her family, even if they aren't. They're not willing to take that risk. They think she would be in a better position if she waits till her memory comes back or someone starts looking for her."

"What if she's not *missing*, Auntie? What if she simply wanted to say goodbye to her old life, and this story about amnesia is just an excuse to do that?"

"I don't think so, Daniel. Besides, she's pregnant," she waited for his outraged response. It came immediately.

"Pregnant!" He jumped to his feet. "You've taken some strange, *pregnant* woman into your home?! Clearly she has some kind of ties to someone, somewhere. What if she's run off and left her husband and family?" He ran his hand over his face. He was tired.

"Daniel. Not everyone is Victoria," Aunt Ruby spoke quietly. "I know you had a very difficult experience. I know it has caused you to look at things and people through warped lenses. But there is still a lot of good in the world. There are good people who do not lead deceptive double lives. God is still good. He is still in control, and I still trust Him. And because I trust Him, and have asked Him to order my steps and direct my path, Hope will be here until He sees fit for her to leave.

"I will not allow you or anyone else to force me to put that woman and her unborn child out onto the streets or send them to a halfway house. That, my dear nephew, is that." She closed with her signature statement, the one that signaled that, at least as far as *she* was concerned, any discussion on the matter had been closed.

This time, however, Daniel did not allow her to have the last word. His tone was even, "I respect your wishes, Aunt Ruby; this is, after all, your house. But I *will* be doing everything I can to gather information on this woman. I will not allow her to take advantage of you in any way. And if I do find that she is not the person she claims to be, I will not hesitate to eject her from this household—unborn child or not."

With that, Daniel gathered his suitcases from the mud room and took them upstairs. He did not return downstairs for the rest of the night, and when Aunt Ruby awoke the next morning, he had already left for Lake Butler.

CHAPTER NINE

Hope was very disturbed when she realized that her presence had caused a rift in the relationship between Aunt Ruby and Daniel. The last thing that she had wanted to do was disrupt anyone's life. She tried to express her regrets to Aunt Ruby the next morning when they realized that Daniel had left, but Aunt Ruby shrugged it off.

"Daniel means well," she defended her favorite nephew, "and I can't say I'm surprised at his response. I suppose if he had told me that he had invited a total stranger to come and live with him, I'd be just as concerned about it. And as if that isn't enough, he's also had some experiences that have really affected his ability to trust others. I wouldn't worry about it if I were you, Hope. Daniel and I will sort it out soon. You can count on that."

The two were sitting at the kitchen island having breakfast. Hope had made Aunt Ruby her customary cup of coffee, and, since she'd already been up for a couple of hours, was having her second cup of tea—peppermint this time. Aunt Ruby had given Hope clear instructions about how to make scrambled eggs just the way she liked them: with diced turkey breast, onions, green peppers, tomatoes and a dash of milk, but no salt and no pepper.

Hope was having a healthy portion of eggs and toast herself. Having spoken to Jasmine about the challenges her new friend had been having with her pregnancy, she was glad she had none of the usual complaints. She didn't remember her first trimester, but she was feeling perfectly fine, with no nausea, backache, swollen ankles or general feeling of malaise to report. She had a robust appetite, though, and wondered if that was something that had developed as a result of the pregnancy or if she had always eaten a lot. Having lots of questions and no insight into what her life had been like only a matter of days before was becoming familiar to her.

CB

That night, Jasmine sat in the recliner with her feet up, writing in her journal while her husband watched two grown men attack each other in a highly-anticipated prize fight.

April 12

Today was another fairly good day. Things have really been looking up recently with respect to my symptoms. Even though the nausea persists, I haven't been throwing up as much, thank God! The baby's movements have become more noticeable, and sometimes I'm sure I can identify a tiny foot or elbow pressing against my skin.

This baby has become so important to me. He or she and Ryan really are the best things that have ever happened to me, but generally, I just feel so blessed these days.

I've been thinking about Hope's situation, and it has really helped me to feel much better about my own challenges. Although physically I've been very sick, emotionally, I couldn't have asked for more support. Ryan has been beside me just about every step of the way, and even though Mommy is far away in Jamaica, she's really been there for me, too. She calls as often as she can, considering her busy life with the grandchildren there. I don't know why I thought she would have been getting a lot of rest as a retiree. I should have known better! Despite the arthritis and other medical complaints, she is perhaps more up and about now than she has ever been. Thank goodness that we can talk as much as we do. I'm so grateful to have her as a source of wisdom and advice, even though her old Jamaican bush remedies haven't always worked!

I remember the day she told me that if I wanted to relieve the nausea, I should keep a quarter of a nutmeg in the corner of my mouth, between my back teeth. Although it did give me a little bit of relief for a couple of hours, I threw up as soon as I got rid of it. I can't walk around with something like that in my mouth all day! Then there were the ginger candy, peppermints, the minty gum, the gallons of peppermint tea... I could go on and on. Nothing has helped for long, except the medication I was trying to avoid. Still, Mommy's really trying to help, even from a distance, and I feel closer to her than ever.

She's already assured me that she'll be coming around the time of the baby's birth to give Ryan and me a hand until we settle into some kind of routine. I love her and Daddy so, so much. They're such awesome grandparents, and I know even though he doesn't say much, Daddy can't wait to have the baby come visit so he can show him or her all around their little farm. I remember watching him and my youngest nephew playing Ring around the Rosies in the garden. Priceless! They all have their grandparents wrapped around their little fingers, and I know my child will be no different. It's a pity they live so far away.

Ryan has also been really great, now that he realizes that this pregnancy has really been rough, and I haven't been making things up. He's accepted all the changes in our lives without complaint, and I'm really thankful for that. I'm sure when we got married, he thought he'd be coming home to a sexy wife hanging from the chandeliers in nothing but a negligee, and that just hasn't been happening. He'd probably like to have a home-cooked dinner when he gets home, but that's not happening, either. Still, he's been eating takeout and Aunt Ruby's cooking and hasn't said a word. I feel so blessed that he's my husband. Sure, we argue every now and then, but in the grand scheme of things, there's nobody I'd rather be arguing with, and we always resolve it quickly. What a great hubby he's been! I love him more now than I did the day we got married. And that's saying a lot!

And then there's Aunt Ruby. I cannot imagine where I'd be in this pregnancy without her. She's been so kind and has always over-extended herself. Now that she's incapacitated, I really want to do as much as I can to help her. Since I'm feeling well enough to drive, I can take Hope to the supermarket or wherever, so that will work out well. I know she'll take the bus if she has to, but since I have the time and—these days—the energy, I'll volunteer as much as I'm needed.

Hope is really in a bind. I hope she knows how blessed she is to be here, regardless of Daniel's reaction to her presence.

Where would she be without Aunt Ruby? I mean, that just has to be God right there! For her to have been placed in a room with Aunt Ruby, and for Audra to have been called away, making way for Hope to stay in Alistair Bay.... I mean, none of that can be coincidence! I hope Daniel can see that.

I can't really blame him for being apprehensive. I was, too, at first, but after knowing her for just a couple of days, I can say that Hope just seems like such a genuine person even though she's clearly having a lot of self-doubt and questions. I pray that God will use all of us to lead her into a closer relationship with Him. I know He's already using Aunt Ruby. What an awesome, mighty, caring God we serve! He's aware of everything that concerns us, and He really does make a way where there seems to be no way. As we say in church just about every time we meet, He is good all the time, and all the time, He is good!

J.

ᙣ

Daniel sat at the glass-topped kitchen table in his town house, literally twiddling his thumbs as he let his third extra-large cup of coffee for the day get cold. He was anxious. He still couldn't believe his aunt had taken in a complete stranger. And a pregnant one, at that! Knowing what she did about Victoria, he'd have thought she'd have been more careful. Pregnant women were not always as harmless as they appeared.

He understood that she thought she was doing God's work. He even understood that she may have thought the Holy Spirit had led her to welcome this woman into her life and her home. He remembered being sure that he should marry Victoria; he remembered feeling like he was being led in that direction, yet look where he had ended up: used and taken advantage of. He couldn't—*wouldn't*—let that happen to the woman who'd helped raise him.

He leaned back in the chair with his hands clasped behind his head and considered his next move. He wondered what his options were.

He needed to call in a favor or two. He picked up his cell phone and scrolled through the numbers until he found the one he was looking for. He stared at the name before taking a deep, steady breath. He dialed and listened to it ring once, twice, three times, before it was answered.

"Hello?" The voice on the other end was confident.

"Detective Henlin? It's Daniel Donahue. How are you?" He forced himself to sound more cheery and light-hearted than he really felt.

"Daniel!" He could hear the smile in the detective's voice, "It's good to hear from you. How are things?" Her voice took on a deeper tone than when she had answered. Now, she sounded almost sultry.

"Things are going fairly well, Detective Henlin."

"I'm sure I've asked you to call me Frances more than once, Daniel." Her tone was now one of chastisement, as if she were talking to a naughty child and trying her best to be patient.

She would never understand how difficult it had been for him to call her. She had been one of the investigators who had looked into Victoria's death, and the fact that she knew all the details would have been reason enough for him to avoid her. If that wasn't enough, since a few months after the end of the investigation, she had made no secret of her desire to make their relationship a more personal one, so to speak, despite the fact that she was at least ten years older than he was. And despite the fact that eight years had passed.

"Okay, Frances."

"There you go. Was that so hard?"

He ignored the question, giving a nervous chuckle instead, "I had a quick question, Detec—... uh... Frances."

"Yes?"

Without giving too many details, he asked how she would handle an amnesia case.

She instantly took on a more professional tone, "Well, the first thing I would do is check the national database of missing persons and do a fingerprint check and see if anything comes up that way. I'd also run facial recognition software in the hope that I'd get a hit."

Those were the things Aunt Ruby had reported to have already been done.

"And if all that turned up nothing? Would you involve social media? Perhaps put the person's image on the news?"

"Actually, that's not advisable these days because of the rate at which people are being exploited. Human trafficking is real, you know."

He sighed.

"You're not thinking of going missing, are you, Daniel?" Before he could answer, she added, "Because you know I'd find you!"

"Yes, I'm sure you would." He quickly made an excuse and ended the call before she could invite him for coffee, as she often tried to do. He sighed again. It seemed that he had come up against a brick wall. He had to find another approach.

The problem was, his mind was blank. He couldn't think of anything else to do to help determine whether or not she was being genuine. After all, he wasn't a medical professional.

Then another idea occurred to him: he may not be a medical professional, but he was sure the Internet could shed some light on the condition from which Hope claimed to suffer.

He was disappointed when he could find nothing definitive online. It seemed that a traumatic brain injury really could lead to the type of amnesia the woman claimed she was having, and like Aunt Ruby said, there was no way of predicting when her memory would return. Of course, being the skeptic that he was, he was fully aware that she could also have done an online search and found out exactly how to present herself as a retrograde amnesiac. There were just so many possibilities and too little information.

The situation was untenable; he would have to do something about it. And fast!

He considered calling Aunt Ruby. As stubborn as they both were, he wasn't comfortable with the way he had left things. Couldn't Aunt Ruby see that this woman was already impacting on their lives in a negative way? He couldn't remember a time when he and Aunt

Ruby had clashed wills like that. He picked up the phone to dial her number, then put it down again. For the first time in his life, he didn't know what to say to her. Nothing had changed since their last conversation. He still felt the way he had felt then, and he was sure her opinion hadn't changed, either. Why call her when they had nothing to say to each other?

He wondered if Aunt Ruby had gone to church, but suspected she would wait another week, when she had gotten enough rest and was better able to manipulate the crutches. He knew it wouldn't do for him to suggest she use his mother's wheelchair. Aunt Ruby would *never* agree to that if she had a choice. Determined, he picked up the phone and dialed, refusing to allow a stranger to compromise their relationship.

The phone rang twice before an unfamiliar voice picked up, "Hello?"

He hesitated before responding, "Hello. May I speak with Aunt Ruby, please?"

Hope recognized his voice instantly. "I'm sorry, she's resting right now. May I take a message?"

Daniel looked at the clock on the wall that was otherwise quite bare. It was barely eleven o'clock. "Resting? At this hour?" He wasn't sure he believed her.

"Yes. Resting. At this hour." Her tone reflected his—impersonal.

"That's quite out of character for her."

"Perhaps," there was a pause before she added, "in fact, she said as much; but she was in a bit of pain this morning, so she took two painkillers and went to lie down. She's been sleeping for twenty minutes. I'm supposed to wake her for lunch."

He still wasn't convinced. "Oh? And what will that be? Takeout paid for with cash from my aunt's purse?"

He heard her take a deep breath before she responded evenly, "No. We're going to be having some more of the chicken soup I made yesterday."

"The chicken soup *you* made?" He was surprised she had the nerve to say that. That soup had been made by his aunt, and he should know. She'd been making that soup once a week for as long as he could remember. He didn't believe Hope, and wondered why she would lie about something so simple. She just couldn't be trusted!

"Yes. I made the soup while she supervised. She would have found it too difficult with the cast and crutches."

He hadn't thought about that. Now he felt a bit stupid. He should have known that it would have been not only impractical, but also *impossible* for her to cook something that labor-intensive. So Hope had been telling the truth.

"I see." The simplicity of his response belied the raging internal dialogue he'd been having. "Well, please tell her I called."

"I will. Goodbye." Her farewell was stiff and formal.

"Goodbye." He ended the call and sat there, drumming his fingers on the table. He considered calling Ryan or Jasmine to ask them to drop by and make sure Aunt Ruby really was okay, but decided against it. Weekends were sacred for those two. It was the only time they had to spend more than an hour or two of uninterrupted awake time with each other. He didn't want to intrude, especially now that Jasmine was feeling a little better. They were still newlyweds, after all.

He looked at the time again. He didn't have any classes to teach until the middle of the week. He'd been representing the university in England, so they had given him three extra days off before returning to work. He didn't actually *need* to be in Lake Butler until Thursday morning. He hurried into his bedroom, put a few things into his bag, packed up his laptop and all the papers he'd need to work on for the next few days, and jumped into his SUV. He needed to resolve things with Aunt Ruby, and it wouldn't hurt to be there to observe Hope first hand. Now that he thought about it, he'd been a bit reckless to leave Aunt Ruby there with her in the first place, especially when Hope knew he was suspicious of her. If she was some kind of scammer, she would probably make her move sooner than planned. If she wasn't, he figured in a few days he'd be better able to make some kind of accurate judgment about the woman who was invading their lives.

CHAPTER TEN

Aunt Ruby and Hope had just sat down to their lunch of re-heated soup and crackers when they noticed the maroon-colored SUV passing the kitchen window on its way to the garage in the rear. Aunt Ruby raised her eyebrows at Hope, whose heart fell to somewhere below her knees. She had wanted to be well-prepared before facing Daniel again. She didn't like the way he had looked at her when he learned who she was and why she was there, as if she were the scum of the earth, and he was making it his personal duty to rid the world—or at the very least, his aunt—of her. She sighed and took up her spoon.

Daniel came through the mud room and into the kitchen, where he gave Aunt Ruby his customary hug before greeting them both, "Good afternoon."

Hope muttered a response without looking up from her meal, but Aunt Ruby's smile was genuine, "Daniel! I didn't expect to see you again so soon!"

ଔ

Daniel was pleased by Aunt Ruby's response to his unannounced arrival. Since they hardly ever argued, he wasn't sure how she would have taken his decision to depart the house before sunrise in order to avoid her. At least he was here now.

"I decided to take the university up on their offer to take a few days off after the tour," he looked in the direction of the stove, "Something smells good."

Hope stood to her feet, "May I offer you some soup?" She asked without making eye contact.

"Sure, if there's enough."

He sat next to Aunt Ruby and asked, "Didn't you get my message?" He looked in Hope's direction with annoyance on his face.

"Asking me to call you? Yes, but I only woke up fifteen minutes ago. I decided to have something to eat first. I didn't realize it was urgent."

"It wasn't *urgent*, necessarily. I just expected to hear from you."

"Well, you certainly must have driven like the wind to get here. I barely went to sleep two hours ago. Did you call from the road?"

"No, I called from home, but then I decided to come spend a few days with you."

"Um-hmm," Aunt Ruby's response said she knew exactly why he was there, but she didn't elaborate.

Hope placed a steaming bowl of the pumpkin-based soup with crackers on the side on the island in front of Daniel. She didn't smile. She wasn't hiding the fact that she resented Daniel's presence.

ରେ

As Hope sat at her own place setting, she decided to take the high road and try exercising the fruit of the Spirit again. Today, she suspected she would have to employ all the self-control, patience, kindness and goodness she could muster up, "So, can you tell me about your work?" Her question was meant to deflect any queries Daniel may have posed to her, and she figured he suspected as much but was willing to play along.

"What would you like to know?" he asked.

"Oh, I don't know. I guess I'm interested in finding out what you do. I mean, I know you teach, but Aunt Ruby said you're also doing a lot of research."

"Yes. Well, first things first, I teach history at a small, private university in Lake Butler." As he continued to talk about his work and his interest in the Caribbean, he seemed fully focused on his lunch. "At the moment, I'm doing research into the lies told by the Europeans who settled in the Caribbean."

"Lies?"

"Yes. Lies. Author Chinua Achebe said something along the lines of, 'Until the lions have their own historians, the history of the hunt will always glorify the hunter.' You see, the recording of history has always been done by those who have the power to do so—the ones who produce written accounts of an event are those whose versions tend to be given the greatest credence. The truth is, a lot of what we believe to be true now was actually created in the minds of those with the power, and they wrote whatever they could to present themselves in the best possible light."

Hope found herself genuinely interested in what he was saying. "What do you mean by that?"

That simple question led to a detailed discussion that gave Hope an idea what it would be like to sit in one of his lectures. He was informed, of that there could be no doubt, but he was also very passionate about what he was discussing, and it was a bit contagious. She didn't have to feign interest, although Aunt Ruby's eyes glazed over a time or two.

Hope nodded. "Wow. I can tell this means a lot to you, but why? You sound so passionate about it. Do you have Caribbean roots?" She looked from him to Aunt Ruby.

"Not that I know of," Daniel excused himself and retrieved his bowl and that of Aunt Ruby from the table. Hope hadn't touched her own soup since she had sat down again. He went on, "Growing up in this state, there are so many Caribbean people around me, so I've always felt drawn to the region. When I went to teach at the university, I realized that most of my students had absolutely no interest in what I was sharing with them. Most of the classes I teach are compulsory: if students don't pass them, they can't graduate. So, they were sitting in those lecture halls because they had to, not because they wanted to. I figured one way of getting them interested was to actually make it relevant to them. Many of my students are actually from the Caribbean or are close to someone who is. It seemed like a no-brainer: if I wanted to interest the students, I had to give them a focus they would actually be interested in. It's been working so far. I still teach all the other stuff, but knowing the Caribbean inside-out like I do—even if I do say so myself—their grades have improved, and the students seem genuinely interested and motivated."

Hope imagined they were. She wondered if she had gone to college and whether she had enjoyed her classes or simply endured them, "Yes, I can see why."

"I hate to interrupt, but your soup is getting cold, Hope. Why don't you finish up before you find yourself having to re-heat it again. Remember, you're eating for two. You shouldn't allow yourself to get too hungry."

Aunt Ruby's gentle reminder seemed to snap Daniel back to the present, and Hope noticed through the corner of her eye that he was trying to look at her abdomen without being too obvious as she stood by the island.

"So, how far along are you?"

She almost choked on her cracker. It took her a few moments and a sip of water before she could recover sufficiently to answer, "Thirteen weeks."

"I see. So you're due ... when, exactly?"

"October."

"Ah. And are you planning to be here until then?" His eyes were boring into hers. She felt extremely uncomfortable. She had a feeling it was a look he reserved for errant students, and she felt like she would have squirmed in her seat if he were her teacher.

"I'm not planning anything. I have no idea what's going to happen to me from one day to another. I could wake up and remember everything tomorrow, or my memory could stay gone for years." She closed her eyes against the unexpected tears, "I can't plan six months ahead. I can't even plan six *hours* ahead."

"Hope, don't you worry about a thing. If you need to be here for months and months, there's room," Aunt Ruby looked at Daniel with that familiar determination in her eyes, "and as long as this is my house, nobody but me has any voting rights about who stays here and who doesn't."

Daniel put his hands up in a defensive stance, "Not to worry, Aunt Ruby, I know this is your home, and you're queen of the castle. You make the decisions and we, your humble servants, abide by them. So, Queen Ruby, am I allowed to stay for a few days? I have some writing to do, and I may as well do it here, away from the distractions at the university."

Aunt Ruby smiled, and Hope detected blatant sarcasm in her voice as she responded, "Of course, Daniel, of course. We wouldn't want you distracted by all the *noise* in that gated community you live in, what with all those other *loud* professors and their loud *parties*, would we?"

ೞ

Over the next three days, the occupants of the house settled into some kind of pattern. Hope would get up first and prepare breakfast, and about an hour later she would be joined by Aunt Ruby. Daniel, who worked in his office till the wee hours of the morning, rarely got up before ten o'clock, and by that time, Aunt Ruby and Hope would be sitting on the porch.

Hope was impressed by the number of visitors dropping by on a daily basis. Many of them were retirees who lived in the same neighborhood. Others were members of the same church. All had heard that Aunt Ruby was back and that she had been hurt, and everyone just wanted to come and say hi. Several of them brought casseroles with them. Hope was introduced as a friend who was staying with Aunt Ruby for a while, and everyone was quite welcoming. Hope was feeling less and less intimidated as the days went by. She wished she could say the same concerning how she felt about Daniel, but she simply couldn't wait for him to leave. His presence made her extremely uncomfortable. It was as if he were waiting for her to slip up and make some huge error that would expose what he considered to be her façade of amnesia. Whenever they were in the same room, she could feel his eyes following her around in a way that made her feel... well, not threatened, exactly, but uncomfortable and self-conscious. She wished he would just go back to work.

At around noon each day, Hope would prepare a light lunch of sandwiches or soup. She was lapping up Aunt Ruby's culinary knowledge, and she suspected she rarely cooked. Nothing came naturally to her except making coffee, although she never drank it. Everything else she did in the kitchen felt unfamiliar, and hadn't Dr. Shields said she should remember habitual actions? Wouldn't her family be surprised when she returned to them with a repertoire that included several different types of soup and a collection of healthy entrees!

After lunch, Aunt Ruby would rest until around three while Hope did the laundry or cleaned the house one room at a time—without going into Daniel's rooms, of course! Then she would take a walk around the neighborhood or settle down to read for a while until she was needed again.

In the evenings, Aunt Ruby would instruct Hope in the kitchen. Hope had already learned how to make stir-fried chicken with vegetables, baked spaghetti and seasoned, buttery fish fillets steamed in aluminum foil with sautéed spinach or some other green, leafy vegetable. After dinner, Daniel, who surfaced on an unpredictable basis except at meal times, would retreat to his office for several hours, and Aunt Ruby and Hope would sit in the living room and watch religious or family programming on television. Hope particularly enjoyed a good movie, but Aunt Ruby usually fell asleep before the end and had to be awakened so she could go to bed by 10:00 p.m.

Aunt Ruby's sister Emmy had had a wide selection of novels and non-fiction books, and Aunt Ruby had encouraged Hope to borrow any of the titles in which she was interested. Reading… now *that* was a habit that came back to her. She would get so involved in whatever she was reading that she would become absorbed for hours if she didn't have something specific to do. She found herself gravitating towards biographies and autobiographies. Perhaps because she was seeking her own personal history, she found herself drawn to the details of other people's lives.

She was particularly intrigued by the autobiography of Nobel Prize-winning author, Gabriel García Márquez. The writer's account of growing up at the feet of his grandmother in a small coastal community in the South American country of Colombia resonated with Hope, and though it was quite a thick volume, she read it in just a few days. She thirsted after similar pieces, and during a discussion with Aunt Ruby about her interest on Monday, the day after Daniel's surprise re-appearance, the elderly woman encouraged her to visit the local library, where she could probably find some of the author's titles.

Of course, she couldn't actually get a library card, since she had no last name, no identification, no date of birth, and no permanent ties. It was then that Aunt Ruby suggested that Daniel accompany her to the public library to see what could be done. Neither Daniel nor Hope was happy about the suggestion, but neither of them wanted to be the one to cop out, so they hopped into Daniel's SUV that Tuesday afternoon, and off they went on the longest twenty-minute drive in world history.

ॐ

Daniel got the feeling he was being set up and there was nothing he could do about it. He had happened to walk into the kitchen for an ill-timed afternoon coffee break just as Aunt Ruby and Hope were discussing the younger woman's desire to read some of an author's fictional work. It was then that Aunt Ruby had suggested that he take Hope to the library. She would have asked Jasmine, but she hadn't been feeling well for the past day or two and probably wouldn't be up to driving.

He had acquiesced without much of an argument. He desperately needed a break from writing and thinking anyway. He had been watching Hope and her interaction with Aunt Ruby for two days and couldn't find anything to complain about. She was caring and attentive toward his aunt and was never far away from her for too long unless Aunt Ruby was asleep. She did housework, she cooked, she did the laundry and she basically filled in wherever Aunt Ruby needed her. There could be no complaints there.

Daniel still wasn't happy with the domestic arrangement, but he had no reasonable cause to demand that Hope leave. He could see that Aunt Ruby genuinely liked her, but he couldn't be absolutely sure that she wasn't just pulling the wool over everyone's eyes. Hadn't he had that experience before?

As Hope climbed up into the SUV, Daniel could sense her discomfort, which mirrored his own. Up until now, she had gone to great lengths to avoid making eye contact or conversation with him, and now they would be forced to spend the next hour or so together, this time without Aunt Ruby as a buffer between them.

The first few minutes were spent in awkward silence. Both Daniel and Hope stared at the road ahead as if their lives depended on it. Hope eventually shifted position, and Daniel was surprised when after a couple of minutes of staring out the window, she commented, "Isn't it a bit strange to build an entire neighborhood of Victorian-style houses in the twentieth or twenty-first century? I mean, why didn't the developers use more contemporary styles?"

"You don't like the look?" Daniel asked.

"Love it. I just find it odd."

"I suppose it's different where you come from?" Daniel asked casually.

"I don't know," she answered just as casually. She was staring intently at the homes that were flying by. She was so intent on what she was looking at that Daniel knew she had missed his attempt to catch her in a lie. "I guess they wanted to remind people of a simpler time, when life was not so complicated."

"Is your life complicated?" Daniel was embarking on another fishing expedition.

"It is beyond complicated." She was still staring out the window, and he suspected her thoughts were miles away. "I mean, here I am in this place I've probably never heard of, living with a woman I hardly know, pregnant with a child I think I'm in denial about, and I have no idea who I am, whose child I'm carrying or where I'm from. I don't know where my family is or if I even *have* one. Am I married? If not, what kind of life could I be living where I end up pregnant and alone? Where was I headed to in that taxi? Where was I coming from?"

After a few more minutes, Daniel asked, "So, what kind of books are you thinking of checking out?"

"I'm not sure. I read Gabriel García Márquez's autobiography, and I think I want to read one or two of his books."

"Okay. He died recently, you know?"

"Really? Oh, that's too bad. If his memoirs are anything to go by, he was a gifted writer. He definitely chose the right profession!" He could tell that her mind had begun to wander again when she said out loud as she stared out of the window, "As for me, I have no idea what kind of profession I'm involved in or if I even *have* a profession. For all I know I could be homeless, or a prostitute or a thief. But the biggest question of all is: why isn't anybody looking for me? I mean, contrary to how it may appear, I didn't just fall from the sky—or an overpass, as the case may be. I didn't just appear out of nowhere!"

Daniel found himself chuckling against his will. He knew she wasn't trying to be funny, and laughing was probably inappropriate, but in his mind's eye, he was looking at an image of Hope fluttering from the sky and falling gently onto the soft shoulder of that Miami thoroughfare. He knew nothing could be further from the truth.

"What's so funny?" she asked, clearly annoyed that he could find humor in her obviously distressing situation.

"You are!" He couldn't seem to stop laughing, "I mean, what if you *did* just appear out of nowhere? Maybe you're an angel, or some kind of ghost from the spiritual underworld." He was almost roaring with laughter now. She wrinkled her brow. She was not amused.

"I'm glad you find my life to be a source of comic relief."

"I'm sorry. I really am, but I just can't get the picture of you appearing out of thin air out of my head. I'm starting to believe it's a possibility."

Hope scoffed, "So am I, Daniel. So am I."

By the time they arrived at the public library, Daniel had composed himself. He was beginning to think the wrinkle in Hope's brow would be a permanent feature of an otherwise attractive face, but he caught himself before he could even complete the thought. *Attractive?* He thought to himself, *Now, where had that come from?*

Inside, they realized that perhaps the best thing to do would be for Daniel to use his library card to borrow several books on Hope's behalf. She found an entire catalog of novels by García Márquez, and was delighted to borrow his most renowned novels: *One Hundred Years of Solitude* and *Love in the Time of Cholera.* They both agreed that she would ask Jasmine to facilitate her for any future library visits. As they left the building, her smile was so genuine that Daniel wondered if it was possible that she was being sincere and not trying to scam his aunt... and him.

The drive back to Alistair Bay was less tense than the trip to the library. Hope and Daniel were able to have a normal discussion about books he had read and which ones he would recommend to her. He hadn't read anything by García Márquez, but he recommended Caribbean authors such as the Nobel Prize winner and Trinidadian native V. S. Naipaul and Jamaican writer Anthony C. Winkler. She made a mental note of their names, and told him the next time she went to the library, she might try and borrow a couple of their books.

"No need. I have a few of their books in my office. Maybe tomorrow you can come have a look."

Hope's raised eyebrows suggested that she was somewhat surprised at the invitation, but Daniel had an ulterior motive. He would not allow their temporary cease-fire to blind his judgment about the reason he had stayed in Alistair Bay. He wanted to see how she would react in his well-equipped office. If she really had evil intentions, he was sure they would make themselves known as soon as she stepped into what was undoubtedly the most valuable room in Aunt Ruby's house.

CHAPTER ELEVEN

It was already Wednesday afternoon and Daniel had very little time with which to work. He had invited Hope to come to his office to select a few books, but he had yet to put the necessary plans in place; he had gotten caught up in his writing and had only just surfaced. Now that he was aware of the time, he needed to move, and *fast*.

The converted office he maintained at Aunt Ruby's house was his home away from home as it related to getting his work done. It looked like a regular bedroom from the outside, but inside was equipped with the latest electronic equipment, which served him well on the occasions that he found it necessary to work from Alistair Bay. In addition to an up-to-date desktop computer with its two side-by-side nineteen-inch flat panel monitors and built in webcam and microphone to facilitate recording lecturers and broadcasting them as part of the university's open campus facility, he had a state-of-the-art multi-function printer/scanner/fax; a forty-two-inch flat panel television; a Blu-Ray player and a stereo system with built-in surround-sound speakers. He had also brought along his laptop and his ten-inch tablet computer. He loved technology, and if Hope somehow passed this test, he was going to suggest she upgrade her cell phone to a smartphone that would allow her to download electronic books from various online sellers. She could use the prepaid credit card Aunt Ruby had told him about to purchase them, and there were lots of free downloads available if you knew where to look.

Since he didn't know exactly when Hope would be dropping by, he needed to put his plan into place without delay. The desktop monitors were on a computer desk facing the door, and he placed the laptop on an adjacent desk that was at right angles to the first. He hid the tablet behind objects on a wall shelf. Each and every computer had its camera activated and feeding to a website that would store all the information for a couple of days. The entire room was covered. No one who entered his office could make a move without it being recorded and stored somewhere in the ubiquitous 'cloud' everyone was talking about these days.

He sat in the recliner in the corner of the room to read an instant message a colleague had sent to his smartphone. At around two o'clock, there was a hesitant knock on his door. It was so quiet that he thought he had imagined it.

He set a timer on his phone and opened the door. Hope was standing there looking almost fearful. Had the circumstances been different, he might have been sorry for scaring her.

"Hello."

"Hi, Daniel. I wanted to look at the novels you offered to lend me," she shuffled from one foot to another. As if there could be any other reason she would turn up at his office.

"Sure. Come on in," he stepped back.

Hope gave the office a quick once-over, but her eyes immediately zeroed in on the stylish bookcase that took up quite a bit of the wall on the left. She didn't wait for instructions to go over and have a look. It was as if she was drawn to the books by an invisible force. He began telling her about the different authors and the types of books on the shelf. He had a wide range of thrillers and a few sci-fi pieces, but he favored fictional works from the Caribbean.

She was so engrossed that she didn't even hear when Daniel's phone rang. She eventually noticed that he was talking to someone other than her, and when he made eye contact and indicated that he was stepping outside of the office to take a call, she nodded her head.

Daniel was outside of the closed office door for almost ten minutes, pretending to talk to someone on the phone. In reality, when she had come in, he had set the timer to alarm and had only pretended to talk to someone else for a few minutes. As he continued to pretend he was deep in conversation, he prayed the phone wouldn't actually ring while he had it to his ear. He wanted to give Hope enough time to do anything she felt she needed to do. When he was about to re-enter the office, he made quite a production of bumping into the door so that she would know that he was coming.

When he came back in, she was standing directly in the middle of the room, looking at him nervously as if he had caught her in the act of committing a dreadful crime. She had a novel in her hand, and there were at least four others perched on the very corner of the computer desk. His quick eyes noticed that the keyboard had moved and that the desktop PC he had left in sleep mode had come on and was showing the home page of his web browser. He almost smiled. He knew she would not have been able to resist temptation once left alone in the well-appointed room.

As he surveyed the room to see if anything else was amiss, he casually asked if she had found anything of interest.

"Yes, I wondered if I could borrow these titles," she showed him several titles by V. S. Naipaul. "I figure if he's good enough to win a Nobel Prize for Literature, then he should be at the top of my reading list. I also picked out *I, Tituba, Black Witch of Salem* by Maryse Condé and *The Manley Memoirs* by Beverley Anderson-Manley. I've enjoyed the memoirs your mother had," she smiled. Daniel couldn't help but notice her beautiful smile with the gap between her teeth and how it lit up her usually stoic face. For a moment he regretted the fact that he hadn't seen that smile often. Still, he told himself that it wasn't his fault. He had been placed in an awkward position—that of keeping his aunt safe—and he would do so even if it meant he had to keep her safe from herself and her own questionable decision-making regarding this woman. The way he saw it, time would tell if she was being sincere or not. He'd probably know in just a few minutes.

"Of course. I keep my office door locked when I'm not here, but you can just leave them in the living room, and I'll pick them up when I come back on the weekend."

"Oh, you're coming back this weekend?" The question sounded casual, but her eyes looked a little wild, as if she might fear his answer.

"Yes, I'm usually here every weekend. Do you have a problem with that?" He asked, tilting this head.

"Not at all. I just figured since you'd be here until tomorrow, you'd probably be gone until next weekend instead."

"Well, I haven't quite decided yet." His decision would ultimately be guided by what he saw on the videos he would watch as soon as she left the office, but he couldn't tell *her* that. Depending on what he saw, he might not leave at all. At least, not until after she did.

"Well, thanks for the loan. I'll take good care of them and return them as soon as I can." She stepped through the office door.

"No problem. Take your time," he said, as he closed the door behind her.

○ঙ

Inside the office, Daniel took a deep breath. He carefully took the tablet computer from its precarious perch on the shelf and turned all the cameras in the room off. Then he logged in to the website and began to watch the recordings his electronic devices had just made. The tablet on its high perch would have had the best view of the office, so he watched that video first. He wondered what he would find and how his aunt would react when he told her that her new 'friend' was most likely an opportunist and a scammer.

As he watched the video, he fast forwarded through images of himself sitting in the recliner reading until he saw himself get up and go to the door. There was no audio on the tablet, so he could only watch. When Hope entered the room, she settled her gaze on the bookcase. He saw himself step out of the room with the phone to his ear. He fully expected to see Hope trying to turn either the desktop or laptop computer on, lift the cover of the scanner, open the desk drawers, even move the two pieces of wall art to see if there was a safe hidden behind either of them. Instead, she remained in her position in front of the bookcase on the far side of the room from the surreptitious tablet and its camera. While standing there, she chose several books and placed a stack of them beside the printer on the desk. He noticed the top one fall onto the computer keyboard, shifting it slightly and causing the machine to wake up. She retrieved the fallen book and placed the entire stack closer to the edge of the desk. Then, without looking at the monitors, she went to sit in his recliner as she read the back cover of one of the books. Suddenly, she jumped from the seat and moved quickly to stand in the middle of the office, looking around nervously. It was then that he had walked in.

As he clicked on the tab to stop the video, he found himself slightly disappointed. There was no need to watch either of the other videos. This one showed it all, every single detail of what Hope had done—or rather, *not* done—while he was outside of the office.

The moment was rather anticlimactic for him. He realized that he had almost been looking forward to exposing the woman. Instead, there was nothing to expose. She hadn't even looked around the office. He suspected that if there had been a gold nugget sitting anywhere except among the shelves of books, she would never even have seen it. He paused for a moment, his brow wrinkling. What was it about him that caused him to assume the very worst of people? He thought about his aunt, who was the diametrical opposite of him in that regard. She automatically thought the best of people and claimed that it was her Christian duty to do so.

As Daniel sat there reflecting, he remembered that his own mother's favorite Bible verse had been Philippians 4:8. Throughout his life, she had entreated him to think of that which was true, noble, right, pure, lovely, admirable and generally praiseworthy.

He could hear her voice now, "Meditate on the positive things in life, Danny Boy. Too much of our precious lives are wasted worrying about things that will never happen and being upset about things that have happened that we have no hope of changing. Accentuate the positive, Danny Boy, and eliminate the negative."

Daniel sighed. He missed his mother. Despite her sage advice, it was not in his nature to only find the positives in situations. In fact, since his experience with Victoria, he had doubted every single individual who came across his path. The only persons he trusted implicitly were Aunt Ruby, Ryan and their pastor Robert Marsden, who had been a childhood friend of his. He had known all of them before he had even met Victoria, and he nourished his relationship with them to the exclusion of all others. He could put confidence in no one he had met since the death of his wife; he'd even given Jasmine a hard time. It was he who had originally suspected that Jasmine was exaggerating her morning sickness, and he supposed he was the one who had placed doubts in Ryan's head. He regretted it now, and decided to make an effort to apologize to Ryan.

He leaned back in his recliner and clasped his hands behind his head. He wondered if he would ever trust anyone again. Would he ever form new, lasting friendships? Or would his life revolve around those people he already knew? He led a pretty good life when he was here in Alistair Bay, but at the university, he kept himself closed off from just about everyone. He hardly ever accepted invitations by other faculty members, and certainly had not dated anyone seriously since Victoria had died. Everything was just too raw, and he couldn't imagine ever putting himself back in a position to be hurt the way Victoria—his *wife*—had hurt him. He had given her everything he had; he had given her *who he was*, and she had trampled on him. He told himself he would never get over it. Life was fine the way it was. He was just fine.

Chapter Twelve

Jasmine sat at the island in her well-appointed kitchen with her journal open in front of her, a cup of steaming chamomile tea and a bottle of honey within arm's reach.

April 18

I almost can't believe how much better I've been feeling lately. Even though I haven't been well enough to drive for the past couple of days, I really am feeling a lot better than I have felt since before I knew I was pregnant. At least the last couple of days, I've been down because I have a cold and can't take too much medicine, and not because of the nausea and throwing up I've been dealing with for the past few months.

I feel like I've returned to the land of the living. And just in time, too, because Mommy is coming to visit in a few days, and we're going to be doing all the shopping for the little one. We'll also decorate the nursery while she's here. She's so good at that kind of thing. Not like me. I wouldn't know what colors to use. I'm glad I'm not her only daughter, or I'd probably be a huge disappointment to her. At least my two sisters know what colors match and what colors don't! Hopefully, the baby will inherit her sense of style instead of my color-cluelessness.

And then there's these two black thumbs of mine! When I think about Mommy's garden back home in Jamaica, I can see all the different flowers that flourish under her green thumbs. Roses, hibiscus, orchids, chalice vines, yellow shrimp and, of course, night jasmine all prosper in her front yard. Yet I can't even keep an herb garden healthy out on our patio. I really am a lot more like my father in many respects. Yet I know it doesn't really matter to Mommy. She loves us all and doesn't treat Rose and Orchid any different than she treats me. Our brother Reed is no different. We all bask in our mother's love, and all of us feel like we're her favorite. Even Ryan has told me he feels that way when she comes to visit and fusses about him just like any of her biological children. I can't wait to watch her fuss over our baby in much the same way. She's already a wonderful grandmother to all five of my nieces and nephews, and she is so looking forward to this arrival.

When she comes on Sunday, she'll stay for two weeks, and then she'll come back again just before the baby is due. What a date to be expecting a baby: 10/10. And coincidentally, it's the date of the Fall Festival, so everywhere I turn, I see the reminder. I couldn't forget that date if I tried! It's like God's little way of telling me that no matter how sick I feel, there is an end in sight. I'm working towards a goal, and for Ryan and me, it's the best goal of all: the best of him and the best of me all rolled into one beautiful little bundle. Our Little Praise. I'm feeling more excited every day. I can't wait till Mommy gets here!

I'm so grateful to be feeling better and looking forward to great things that are just beyond the horizon for us. God is so good. I can feel His love and presence all around me these days. People are even starting to say I'm glowing, even though very few know that I'm expecting. At eighteen weeks, I'm not even showing yet!

J.

၈

For the first time all week, Daniel joined Hope and Aunt Ruby for breakfast, since he was going to be leaving early in order to make it to his afternoon class. Hope served Aunt Ruby her usual cup of black coffee with just a little salt, "to cut the bitterness, dear," as the older woman had explained. Daniel got his own coffee, and Aunt Ruby scoffed as Daniel spooned three heaping teaspoons of sugar and added a dash of Irish-flavored creamer into the extra large travel mug he always drank from, even when he wasn't going on the road.

"Daniel, you haven't joined me for my devotions all week," Aunt Ruby commented without criticism. "Maybe today would be a good day. We could do it before we eat."

"Of course, Aunt Ruby. I'll go get your books." He put down the travel mug and headed into the yellow bedroom.

"Thank you, dear. Maybe Hope will join us, too." Aunt Ruby called out to him as he went through the bedroom door. Hope nodded as she continued drinking her second cup of tea.

Daniel returned with the books: a dog-eared Bible, a devotional and a journal. They all put their cups aside as Aunt Ruby opened the devotional and the Bible.

"I want to start by singing 'Bind Us Together, Lord.' It's one of my favorites, Hope, and you'll be able to catch it pretty quickly." She closed her eyes and lifted her hands and head to the Lord as she began to sing a song about the Lord binding people together. Daniel, his own eyes closed, joined in. His voice was low and smooth, and provided the perfect complement to Aunt Ruby's higher tone. Hope was soon singing along, as well.

When the song had ended, Aunt Ruby read to Daniel and Hope from her devotional, which focused on Philippians 4:13. Daniel gave a quiet sigh of relief. For a moment, he'd thought she was going to say Philippians 4:8, which was the same verse on which he had been reflecting the previous afternoon.

Instead, Aunt Ruby read the devotional, which explained that Saul, after he had been converted on the road to Damascus and had become known as Paul, had been just as zealous *for* Christ as he had been *against* him earlier. He had even been arrested, and it was from prison that he had written of his determination to be content in all circumstances: whether he was rich or poor, free or in prison, hungry or full.

Daniel felt convicted during the devotion. He was sure Aunt Ruby was talking to him directly. Lately, he had been feeling more and more uncomfortable with his life, especially as it related to material possessions. He had been comparing himself to the Daniel he had imagined he would be, and he kept feeling that he had fallen short.

Certainly, when he was younger, there had been expectations of a wife and children, but those dreams had been abandoned with Victoria's death. Even outside of that, he had expected that by this time in his life, he would have had his own home. Instead, he lived in university housing. He had thought he would have published at least three books. Instead, he was just writing his first. He had thought he would have been a widely-known expert in his field. Instead, he was only just getting his name out there and had just completed his first lecture tour. Things were not going the way he had expected. He was behind his own schedule, and he had begun to feel more and more anxious about it.

He took a deep breath. It was time to focus not on where he had thought he would be, not on where he wanted to go, but on the fact that he had already come so far. He was glad Aunt Ruby had invited him.

慘

Across the table from Daniel, Hope felt as if Aunt Ruby were directing the admonition at her. She had been so uncomfortable inside her own skin, with so many questions she couldn't answer, and so much to think about. She had not taken the time to be truly grateful for what she had and where she had ended up, at least for the time being. She felt convicted that many persons were in a much worse position than the one in which she had found herself. In fact, had it not been for Aunt Ruby's generous offer, she would have been in just such a position herself. She endeavored to try to find contentment, and to take each day as it came, without worrying too much about what lay ahead for her. She took a deep breath and smiled, glad she had not declined the invitation to participate.

So it was surprising when Aunt Ruby shared that she was sure that the message of today's devotional was directed at *her*. She didn't go into the details, but she confessed that after walking with the Lord for so many years—so many decades, really—she was grateful to be able to do devotions and feel more and more in touch with the Holy Spirit every day. As the exercise ended, she prayed that each of them would learn to be content regardless of their circumstances, that they would all learn to put their trust in God, and that they would listen to the Holy Spirit. She prayed that Daniel would get back to Lake Butler safely and that he would have a productive week. She prayed for Hope's memory to return at the appropriate time and for her health and that of the child she was carrying. She also prayed for Jasmine and Ryan and other family members and friends.

Hope tried to stay alert during the lengthy prayer, but her mind kept drifting to other things. It was a real effort to concentrate, and she was glad when she heard the end of the petition.

They sat in companionable silence, each eating his or her breakfast and reflecting on the theme of the devotion. Then Daniel got to his feet and told them he was going upstairs to get his things. He soon returned with his computer bag and small suitcase. Hope told him a quick goodbye before excusing herself from the kitchen and heading upstairs to do a load of laundry. She figured they would like to be alone.

 જ

This time, Daniel didn't think too much about Hope's sudden flight upstairs, nor was he curious about what she was going to do. His little experiment had shown that she probably wasn't trying to steal information or possessions, at least, not now. He had wanted to talk privately with his aunt anyway, but she preempted him.

"So, Daniel, did you learn whatever it was you stayed here to learn?" She looked at him slyly.

"What do you mean?" He feigned innocence.

"Daniel, Daniel, Daniel," she shook her head, "you've never come to Alistair Bay to write, not with your quiet office in your quiet town house in your quiet college town. You're more distracted here than you are when you're in Lake Butler." She looked at him with disapproval written across her face.

He smiled. He never could fool her. "Okay, I stayed so I could keep an eye on Hope."

"That, my dear nephew, goes without saying. And...?" She was curious about what he'd discovered.

He sighed. "And as my students would say when they're staring at a blank answer script during their history finals, I got nothin'."

"I'm not in the least bit surprised, but you seem almost disappointed." Aunt Ruby had always been very intuitive concerning her sister's son.

"I'm not disappointed. At least, not in the way that you might think. I still feel like she's got to be hiding something, and I'm disappointed that I didn't find out what it is on this particular trip. But I'll be back. I will not leave you alone with a virtual stranger in the house. Not for an extended period of time. She's got to understand that I can—and *will*—show up whenever I feel like. I have no problem driving an hour and a half just to check on you if I'm uncomfortable. I did it on Sunday."

"I understand where you're coming from, Daniel, and I do appreciate your concern, but I trust the Holy Spirit implicitly, and if I were in any real danger, I believe He would let me know."

"I hear you, Aunt Ruby, and I can't argue there, but all I'm asking is for you to let good sense prevail, and if for some reason, this turns out to be a not-so-good idea, we'll have to make an alternative arrangement for your care."

"That's not an unreasonable stance to take, Daniel, and I agree. If for some reason, I live to regret this decision, then I'll allow you to provide an alternative. Who knows? Maybe Audra will be back soon. Do we have a deal?"

"Yes, we have a deal. Shake on it?" He chuckled and stuck his hand out, knowing exactly what was coming next. Aunt Ruby grabbed his collar, pulled him close, and gave him a peck on his cheek.

"We have a deal. I love you, nephew."

"And I love you, Aunt Ruby."

And with that, they bade each other farewell for the next few days.

CHAPTER THIRTEEN

For the next couple of days, things remained much the same for Hope and Aunt Ruby. There were a few changes to the pattern here and there, but there was nothing they couldn't handle together. Something came up for Daniel at work, and he decided not to return for the weekend, so Aunt Ruby went to church with Ryan and Jasmine while Hope stayed home and caught up on her reading. All three had encouraged her to come to church with them, but she declined and told them she would definitely join them the following week.

In the meantime, Hope had remained in touch with Miss LaHaye, and they had received a visit from a social worker who had come by from St. Augustine to verify Ruby's address and that Hope was, indeed, staying with her. There had been no changes to Hope's status. It appeared that no one was looking for her anywhere in the United States.

Still, she was determined to be content regardless of the circumstances, and every day she was forced to practice a little more patience. She had seen Jasmine a couple of times and had been encouraged to go to the medical center to register for the next OB/GYN clinic in another week. Jasmine was feeling better and volunteered to drive her. They decided to go see a movie, which was a really enjoyable outing for both of them. Jasmine even felt inspired enough to have some butter-free popcorn, which she hadn't done for months and months. Afterwards, Jasmine treated Hope to a pedicure and the two ladies went for a walk through one of the two malls. Jasmine couldn't remember the last time she had felt up to doing any of those things. They had a fabulous time but didn't stay out more than a couple of hours since Aunt Ruby had been left alone at home. Ryan was next door, though, so they knew if there were some kind of emergency, he would have been there to handle it.

Unfortunately, not everyone shared that opinion. When Jasmine pulled into her driveway and Hope walked across their respective lawns, through the opening in the hedge and in through Aunt Ruby's front door, Daniel was sitting at the dining table. His face reminded her of the sky just before a thunderstorm unleashed its dangerous energy into the atmosphere. She had intended to check on Aunt Ruby before heading into the kitchen to make dinner, but she slowed to a stop in the living room instead.

"Where have you been?" Daniel demanded. Although it was clear that he was upset, he had not raised his voice, which led Hope to believe that Aunt Ruby was still resting.

"Excuse me?" She was offended by his tone.

"You heard me. Where have you been?"

"I went out."

"Out? Out where?"

"Why do you want to know?" She demanded in turn. Mindful of the need to speak relatively quietly, she moved toward the dining table where he was still seated, but she remained standing.

"I want to know because I'm curious about what could *possibly* be more important than staying here and taking care of my incapacitated aunt. I've been here for almost two hours and you haven't even called to check on her once in that time."

"First of all, your aunt is not incapacitated. She handles the crutches very well, and most of the time, she only needs me to help out in the kitchen or if she needs something done upstairs." She folded her arms across her chest, "I saw no need to check on her."

It was his turn to be indignant, "Excuse me?"

"I said, I saw no need to check on her. I was only gone for two hours, so you must have driven in as soon as Jasmine and I left. We told her before we left that Ryan is next door in case she needs anything. He told us specifically that if we didn't hear from him, we weren't to worry. We didn't hear from him, so we didn't worry."

"Well, Ryan hasn't checked on her once in the entire time I've been here."

"Well, then, I think Ryan is the one you should be accosting, and not me."

"Accosting?" He stood. "Accosting?" His voice had become a bit louder, but Hope could see that he was trying to keep it under some semblance of control. "You—a complete stranger with no past and possibly no future—convinced my elderly aunt to take you in, you and your unborn child—if there even *is* a child, that is—under the guise that you would be some sort of caregiver. Yet as soon as my back is turned, instead of caring for my aunt, you go off all over the place when you should be here keeping an eye on her. You have a warm bed to sleep in, in your own room. You're eating food someone else has paid for, and sleeping under a roof that is someone else's responsibility, yet you're not keeping up your end of the bargain. You're trying to take advantage of Aunt Ruby's generosity, and let me tell you something, young lady, I will not have it!"

"'Young lady?' Who are you calling 'young lady?'" She drew herself to her full height. "I may not know exactly how old I am, and I may not know anything about my family, but I'm pretty sure that you, Professor Donahue, are *not* my father. And even if you were—which you most certainly are not—I'm guessing I'm over the age of eighteen, and therefore old enough to go where I want, when I want, as long as a contingency plan is put in place for your aunt." Her chest was heaving now. "If it is, sir, that you're looking for someone to parent, I suggest you go out and find a family with children of your own, and don't look in my direction. I certainly do *not* need you to parent me!"

She was just getting ready to dig her heels in and fight, but to her surprise, Daniel went completely pale and then turned around and headed upstairs without another word. Before she could even process the fact that their argument was over, she heard his bedroom door click closed at the top of the stairs.

She was standing there beside the dining table with her bag still over her shoulder, wondering what she had said to elicit that kind of response from him, when she heard Aunt Ruby's voice quietly say, "One day, Hope, you will understand exactly how low a blow that was." As Hope turned around, she saw her benefactor slowly shake her head and retreat into her bedroom.

ଔ

The next morning, Hope was downstairs early as usual. A glance into the refrigerator confirmed that neither Daniel nor Aunt Ruby had eaten any of the stir-fried chicken she had cooked the night before. She sighed. This morning, she would make the coffee as usual, and she would make the breakfast, as usual, but she doubted things would be the same as they had been before.

She still wasn't sure what she had said to make Daniel pale the way he had. She had played the conversation over and over in her head, and the only thing she could figure out was that what she had said about him needing to get his own family must have struck a chord with him. She still wasn't sure about Aunt Ruby's cryptic response. Either way, she needed to apologize to them both. They were extending the hand of generosity to her in a time of desperate need, and she should never have raised her voice in their house the way she had. She wasn't looking forward to it, though. She might not remember any of the details of her life before the accident, but she suspected she had hated apologizing even then.

That morning, it was Daniel who joined her in the kitchen. She was sitting at the kitchen island nursing her tea when he made his appearance.

"Good morning," she held the greeting out like an olive branch.

"Morning," came the bear-like reply as he poured his coffee into his travel mug and added his usual creamer. He sounded like he hadn't slept much at all.

"Look, I... I wanted to say how sorry I am about my behavior yesterday."

"It's no problem, Hope. I said a few things that were out of line myself." He sat at the dining table without making eye contact with her—not that he could have even if he had tried; she was sitting across the kitchen staring into her tea as if she thought she might find her missing past inside the cup.

"Perhaps you did, but two wrongs don't make a right. If I said something to offend you, I'm truly sorry." Hope moved from the island to the table in an attempt to mend fences, but instead of looking at her, he studied the steam rising from his travel mug. He seemed to have aged overnight, and Hope felt like she was somehow responsible.

"I'm sorry, too. I spoke with Ryan after I went upstairs last night, and he told me he didn't call to check on Aunt Ruby because she called and told him she was going to take a nap, and that she'd call him when she woke up. I should have checked with either one or the other. I didn't do that. I was only too happy to jump to unjustified conclusions about you, and it was wrong of me."

"Thank you." Now that *that* was over, she felt as if they had nothing to say to one another. The uncomfortable silence stretched interminably between them until, as if on cue, Aunt Ruby's door opened and she came hobbling out. Both Daniel and Hope rushed to her assistance.

"Good morning. I see you two have called a truce."

"I suppose." For the first time that morning, Daniel looked into Hope's eyes, "Truce?" He extended his hand to her.

"Truce," she agreed as she shook it.

"Now, Daniel," Aunt Ruby smiled, "suppose you tell me why you turned up in the middle of your work week?"

"I just wanted to check on you, Auntie." He looked at her with a mischievous twinkle in his eye.

"Check on me?" Aunt Ruby's twinkle mirrored his, "Don't you mean you wanted to check on Hope?"

He chuckled, "Yes, I suppose I did." He looked in Hope's direction, "No offense, Hope."

"None taken," she smiled in response. If Aunt Ruby had been her aunt, she would probably have driven ninety minutes just to come check on her, too.

೫

Daniel had returned to Lake Butler on Wednesday morning after their shared devotional exercise focusing on Second Corinthians 5:17, in which Paul admonished the Corinthians to forget that everything they had done in the past, because all things had become new.

Again, he knew he had a lot to think about. Chief on his list was finding an appropriate devotional so that he could once again spend some time communing with God before starting his day.

Daniel was a Christian, having been baptized at the age of seventeen; however, since his experience with Victoria, he had kept just about everyone, including the Lord Himself, at arm's length. Although he had maintained his friendship with his pastor, he had not entertained any of Robert's attempts to counsel him beyond the initial grief counseling sessions they had scheduled.

At first he had been angry with God for not allowing him to see Victoria for exactly who she was and what she was up to before he had married her. Then, after the initial anger, he had become indifferent to God. He still believed God was there, but it had been some time since Daniel had trusted Him blindly, neither did he spend any time in communion with Him. The past few days, however, had reminded him of the relationship he had once had with his Creator. The conviction he had felt at Aunt Ruby's table had reminded him of those times when he could feel the presence of the Holy Spirit with him throughout the day.

He remembered a time when he would wake up and thirst after his quiet time with God the way he now thirsted after his extra large cup of coffee. He remembered when he listened to Christian music in his car on the way to work and when he watched Christian programming on television. It had been a long time since he had done any of those things consistently. He missed them. He missed his fellowship with God, and he knew that it was time he did something about it.

So, despite having a busy day in Lake Butler running errands, late that Saturday night, he drove back to Alistair Bay with the intention of accompanying his aunt to church the next morning. Although he had taken her to church almost every weekend since a couple of months after Victoria's death, it was a long time since he had actually looked forward to it. He felt like a change was coming, and he was both excited and anxious about it at the same time.

03

The next morning, Hope was up even earlier than usual. A week earlier, she had promised Aunt Ruby that she would go to church with her this week, even though she wasn't particularly looking forward to it. She imagined the people staring at an unfamiliar woman in their midst, and she wasn't keen on being the center of their attention. Still, Aunt Ruby had given so much and asked for so little that it was the least she could do.

She prepared pancakes, eggs and bacon and brewed and poured Aunt Ruby's cup of coffee. She then tapped on her door and offered to help her get ready. Afterwards, she took her second cup of tea upstairs so that she could get dressed.

She hadn't heard Daniel come in the night before, so she was surprised to see him stepping out of Aunt Ruby's bedroom with a Bible and his aunt's bag in hand just as she was coming down the stairs. She felt a tingle of awareness run through her stomach as he took in her slightly rounded figure in the knee-length black, white and hot pink floral dress she was wearing. She knew he had never seen her dressed up before, and she couldn't help but notice his appreciative look as his eyes traveled from her bare ankles, up her exposed legs and all the way to her face. She even shocked herself by smiling as she greeted him.

"Daniel, hello, I didn't know you were here. I thought we were going with Jasmine and Ryan this morning."

"I came in late last night. Everyone had already gone to sleep. It's been a few weeks since I took my favorite girl to church." Aunt Ruby blushed prettily, having just come out of the powder room.

"Well, I'm glad you made it safely." Hope tried not to notice what a dashing figure he cut in his immaculate dark brown suit, light shirt and paisley tie. She wondered if she had ever noticed how broad his chest was. Reining her thoughts in before they wandered too far, she finished descending the staircase and took up her position by Aunt Ruby's elbow and wondered why the elderly woman was smiling so wistfully at the two of them.

On the way to the service, Aunt Ruby explained that New Covenant Christian Fellowship was one of only three churches in Alistair Bay. It was a non-denominational church with a varied membership. From the parking lot, Hope could see that the building itself faced the park and was simple, with a brick façade and white trim. It didn't appear to be very large from the outside, but inside had more space than she had imagined, since there was a balcony upstairs for seating. The service was just about to start when they got there, so Aunt Ruby, Daniel and Hope quickly entered a pew close to an exit at the side of the building.

The service started when a praise and worship team comprised of six young adults, backed by a live band, began to lead the congregation in a series of lively songs. Even Hope soon found herself joining in, since the words were being projected onto two large screens on either side of the wide stage. She noticed that even Daniel was clapping his hands and singing. Aunt Ruby looked like she was having difficulty remaining seated, but she clapped, sang and rocked in the pew.

After about twenty minutes of up-tempo singing, the team slowed the music and began to sing a song of gratitude to the Lord, their eyes closed and their faces pensive.

One of the worship leaders invited the congregation to take a minute to give quiet thanks to the Lord for all His blessings on them. Aunt Ruby, who was sitting between Daniel and Hope, began to pray silently, as did Daniel. Hope, for her part, hesitated. Here she was, pregnant and separated from her family members and friends. She had no idea who she was or where she belonged. She sat quietly and respectfully while the others around her whispered their thanksgiving to the Lord who had been so good to them, but she couldn't think of anything to say.

Afterwards, a few members of the worship team said prayers of thanksgiving into the microphones and most of those present said a loud "Amen!" after each one. Then the team left the stage, and a woman whom Hope later discovered to be the minister's wife stood behind the lectern.

"Good morning, brothers and sisters!" she said in a pleasant voice.

The response was loud and equally pleasant: "Good morning, Sister Claire!"

"Well, family, we as a church have a lot to be grateful for this morning."

Hope could hear several people agreeing, "Amen!"

"I said, we have a lot to be grateful for!" The woman dressed in a simple fuchsia suit and strappy high-heeled sandals gripped the lectern as if she might float away without it. "Is there any one of you out there who could not find a single reason to give thanks to the Lord today?" She didn't wait for a response. "I'm guessing only a few of you… and I want to remind you that God is good…"

"… All the time!" The church responded on cue.

"And all the time…" Sister Claire continued.

"…God is good!" came the unified shout, which was followed by a round of applause and head-nodding. Hope was quite entertained.

"Well, church, as most of you know, our dear sister Ruby Crawford had a terrible accident when she was returning from a recent cruise and broke her leg." Many of the congregants nodded their heads, and those who were aware of Ruby's presence turned to smile at her sympathetically. "She's been recuperating at home for a little while, and glory be to God, she is with us today, crutches and all!" The end of her statement was drowned out by loud hand-clapping and shouts of "Praise the Lord!"

"She's seated right over there with her nephew Daniel, whom we all know and love, and her caregiver, Hope," as everyone turned to look at the three, she continued, "in fact, this is Hope's first time here at New Covenant, so may I ask a few members to just extend a hand of welcome and fellowship to her?" She smiled in Hope's general direction before continuing, "Is there anyone else worshipping with us for the first time?"

Hope barely had time to notice if she were the only first-timer as so many hands came in her direction that she didn't even see whose they were. She was caught up in shaking them for a little while.

"We do welcome you to Alistair Bay and New Covenant and hope that you will enjoy the fellowship here. Please come as often as you can." Sister Claire sounded like she genuinely meant what she was saying.

Hope smiled and nodded in the direction of the stage as shouts of "Amen!" resounded in her ear. She suspected her hearing might never be the same again.

"Now that that's done, we're going to invite Sister Kylie up here to do a special song after praying for Aunt Ruby and all the other members of our church and community who are not doing so well."

The soloist walked onto the stage and took the microphone from Sister Claire. Her prayer was short and heartfelt, and she sang in a clear, beautiful voice in which the name of Jesus was compared to the fragrance after the rain.

While she sang, Hope noticed that many members stood with their arms raised, as if in reverence to God. By the time Sister Kylie reached the second verse of the song, many persons were singing along with her. To Hope, it was as if a wave of quiet reflection had overtaken the church, and she could see that many were touched by the song. When it was over, the young lady took her seat in the front row and though the church was filled with shouts of "Amen!" and "Praise the Lord!" there was very little applause.

Several other members of the church took to the stage during the morning's service, and when it was the preacher's turn, he took a moment to share a scripture. Reverend Marsden was roughly the same age as Daniel and wore a dark robe with a colorful stole over his suit. He had looked quiet and unassuming as he sat to the side of the stage during all the proceedings before he stood, but Hope could see that he had a quiet strength to him. As he stood in the pulpit, he opened a thick Bible and purposefully turned the pages. "I would like to add my greetings to those already extended here today and to give my own special welcome back to Aunt Ruby. We've missed you at our usual prayer meetings and Bible studies, but I'm sure you'll come back all rested and revitalized in a few weeks' time." Aunt Ruby beamed.

"Now, church, if you would all just turn with me to the third book of Colossians, I want us to spend some time meditating on this Word today." He gave the congregation some time to find the scripture, which Hope noticed was also projected onto the two large screens used earlier, before he began to read the chapter. He then continued, "Now, the Word is clear enough, but I want to break it down and tell you what the chapter is saying in layman's terms. I'm gonna give you the RMV—Robert Marsden Version, if you will." He smiled.

"What the Word is saying, as I interpret it, is this: you used to live a particular life 'back in the day.' You weren't acting right. Some of you used to get drunk; you used to smoke; you used recreational drugs; you slept with folks you weren't married to; you wanted stuff you saw other people with; you lusted after people. You know what I'm talking about!" Members of the congregation waved their hands as he said various things that resonated with them. "And I know some of you are still living like that!" He surveyed the entire congregation before going on. "And before you start trying to figure out what your neighbor is doing in his or her life, I want you to examine yourself.

"Are you greedy? Do you keep eating that lasagna even though you're full? And then you tell yourself your mama taught you to clean your plate and not to waste food. Uh-huh. You know what I'm talking about! Do you secretly wish your boss would keel over dead at his desk one day? Do you have fantasies about that church sister dying and you getting married to her husband and raising her beautiful children? Do you have impure thoughts? Do you find yourself thinking about someone in an inappropriate way? When you're channel surfing late at night and you see a music video or a love scene you know you've got no business watching, do you linger there a little too long? Do you get so upset at your children that you can't see straight? Do you curse when you think no one is listening? Maybe when you're in traffic and someone cuts you off? Uh-huh. You know that ain't right. Is there a church sister or someone at work you don't talk to? Do you harbor unforgiveness?" He paused for a while.

Hope could sense people in the congregation becoming uncomfortable. She looked around and saw several people examining the maps in the backs of their Bibles as if there would be a quiz after the service. A few squirmed in their seats, but no one put their hand up this time. No one said "Amen!" She was intrigued.

"Well, my brothers and sisters, I'm here to tell you today that there is hope! Not only does God forgive us our sins once we confess and repent… not only does He forget them, but He goes further. He shows us how to live the way He wants us to live. He tells us to put away certain behavior, certain ways of life, certain attitudes, and to put on others. In this chapter, we are told to kill those things that are not of Him: sexual immorality, lust, evil desires and idolatry in the form of greed. Put them away. Kill them! Make a conscious decision every day that you will not pick up those old clothes again. Instead, these are the things we should put on daily: compassion, kindness, humility, gentleness, patience, longsuffering, a forgiving nature, love, peace and thankfulness.

"Now when the Word says we should clothe ourselves, ladies and gentlemen, my brothers and my sisters, it means we have to do something *active*. Clothing ourselves is not passive. We have to *decide* to do it. Ladies, you know what I'm talking about now—you stand in front of that closet and you spend a lot of time deciding what to wear. If you're anything like my beautiful wife, you have a lot of stuff to consider, and you have to think about the pros and cons of every single piece." He paused for dramatic effect. "Every… single… piece." The congregation laughed. "We gentlemen, even though we don't take quite so long, also think about what we're going to put on. Is it right for the occasion? Does it accentuate our broad shoulders?" He squared his shoulders. "Does it minimize our paunch?" He stood straight and sucked in his stomach, puffing out his chest. More laughter from the congregation. "The point is, for most of us, getting dressed doesn't just happen." He made eye contact with a few congregants. "In the same way, our decision to put on compassion, kindness, humility, gentleness, patience, longsuffering, a forgiving nature, love, peace and thankfulness doesn't *just happen*. We have to think about it. Consider it. Weigh the pros and cons. Ask ourselves whether it's a good fit for us as God-fearing Christians. And after we've done all of that, my brothers and my sisters, we've got to step into these characteristics. Put them on, one by one, and make sure they fit the person we say we are."

There were a lot of shouts of "Amen!" and "Preach it!" from the group. Hope could see that the message was hitting home for many of them, and the truth was, it was resonating with her, too. As the minister continued to preach, she began to feel varying emotions. She felt as if he was looking straight at her, talking directly to her, and giving her clear instructions on how to proceed with her life going forward. His message was taking what Aunt Ruby had told her about the fifth chapter of Galatians to a whole new level. She felt like if she followed the reverend's instructions, she would be well on her way to living the kind of life she wanted to live. Mostly, for the first time since she had opened her eyes in the hospital, she felt more than just a little hopeful.

ଔ

It was clear to Hope that Daniel was glad he had gone to the service. He and Aunt Ruby discussed the sermon, but she remained quiet and pensive in the back seat. She had a lot on her mind. A lot of what the pastor said had stuck with her. They stopped at a restaurant for lunch, but even while they were there, she said very little. She was thankful that Aunt Ruby was not trying to draw her into their conversation like she normally would and that Daniel had no questions for her today.

Now was the perfect time for her to do all that Reverend Marsden had implored them to do. Now was the time, when she had no history hanging over her and her whole life ahead of her, to clothe herself in the characteristics that were desirable whether or not one was a Christian: compassion, kindness, humility, gentleness, patience, longsuffering, a forgiving nature, love, peace and thankfulness. Some of them were identical to the fruit of the Spirit she had already been trying to incorporate into her life, and the others were definitely complementary.

The sermon was something of an eye-opener and a turning point for Hope, but unlike many of the persons in the congregation that morning, she did not feel led to respond to the altar call issued by Reverend Marsden after his soul-stirring sermon. It wasn't that Hope didn't believe in God; she absolutely believed that there was a God and that He had created the world. She believed He had sent His son Jesus Christ to redeem sinners, saving them from their sin; however, she did not feel as if she had a personal, one-on-one connection with Him.

Despite feeling a little bit distant from Him, she felt like there was a lot to learn from the Bible, and she had been reading one that she'd found on the nightstand in the Lilac Room, but she didn't feel an unction to become a Christian the way Aunt Ruby, Jasmine and Ryan were.

She felt each of them had a personal relationship with God, and both Aunt Ruby and Jasmine had explained that they felt that Christ was not only the Savior of the world but their *personal* Savior and Lord. To Hope, it seemed as if Aunt Ruby, for one, couldn't start the day without setting aside some one-on-one time with the Lord. She was yet to have a conversation with Jasmine that didn't end up with Jasmine professing her love and gratitude to Him. She couldn't ever imagine living her life like that; she just didn't think blind faith was for her. Still, there was no harm in adopting the positive principles found in the Bible, so until and unless she was led to do something more, that is what she would do.

Chapter Fourteen

The day of Hope's visit to the OB/GYN clinic had finally arrived. She had not been examined or seen by a doctor in the weeks since she had left the hospital in Miami, and she was a little bit anxious about what would happen. Jasmine had promised to accompany her, and she was looking forward to spending some time with her new friend. Jasmine's mother, Hyacinth, was visiting from Jamaica, and she and Jasmine had been spending the past few days shopping for the baby and decorating the nursery. Hope was thrilled for Jasmine, but she couldn't help but feel a little bit jealous about the relationship Jasmine and Hyacinth shared. Surely, if she had a mother that was anything like Hyacinth, she would have left no stone unturned in her search for her daughter and her unborn grandchild... if she even knew about that grandchild. This mother-to-be, despite her moniker, was beginning to lose hope, but she was determined to try and find a way to be content, regardless of the circumstances.

Jasmine had been having quite a busy day, but she had promised Hope that she would take her to the clinic, and although she was a little bit tired, she managed to keep her promise. Besides, she told Hope, she wanted to personally introduce her to Dr. Elaina and tell Dr. Elaina her story so that she would be quicker to believe Hope's questionable explanation for not knowing the exact details of her pregnancy.

They arrived at the clinic a full hour before it was scheduled to start, but even so, there were at least four people ahead of Hope.

Since they had a little while to wait, they decided to go to the library, where Hope returned a couple of the books she had borrowed using Daniel's library card and borrowed more using Jasmine's. She may not know much about herself or who she was, but she knew without a doubt that she had a voracious appetite for reading. Afterwards, they still had some time to spare, so they ended up sitting outside a café near the clinic, having ice cream and watching people go by. They spoke about many things, but mostly about Jasmine's relationship with Ryan and how it had come about.

"So, Jasmine, tell me about you and Ryan." Hope was truly enjoying her sundae. She would gain too much weight if she kept eating like this!

Jasmine sighed as she smiled around her mouthful of mango ice cream. "You mean my gentle giant? We met at a singles' social at church around seven years ago. I was twenty, he was thirty-three, and we never gave each other a second look. We'd say hi at church and that was that." She looked off into the distance.

"Back then, he would never have dated a woman under twenty-five anyway, so I couldn't have gotten his attention even if I'd wanted it. Not that I wanted it. I was very 'into' a bad idea named Stephan, whom I dated on and off for years. Eventually, Ryan started bringing an executive assistant named Melinda to church, and it was pretty obvious that they were heading for marriage. They seemed perfect for each other. Then for some reason, they both stopped coming to church. I didn't even ask what had happened at the time. It just wasn't that important to me. I had Stephan."

She wiped a trickle of the sweet treat from her wrist as she continued. "But then the week before I turned twenty-five, I bumped into Ryan at the supermarket, and in the course of conversation, my birthday came up. When he learned that I didn't have any plans — Stephan was out of town for a few weeks—Ryan insisted on taking me to dinner and a movie to celebrate and within a few months we were dating.

"I was pretty sure we were going to get married. I mean, he started coming back to church, so we were both Christians. We had similar backgrounds—we even came from the same country. We had a major hiccup and stopped dating for a while, but we found each other again, and after another year, we got married in Jamaica. That was just six months ago, and here I am five months pregnant." She smiled wistfully as she rubbed her tummy.

As she spoke, Hope couldn't stop herself from wondering—as she often did—about the father of her own baby. Did they have a beautiful love story? Had they wandered away from each other and then found each other again? How long had they been together? Were they blissfully happy? She had to make a deliberate effort to focus on what her new friend was saying.

Hope smiled. She reflected on her pregnancy and wondered if she and her baby's father had had a similar story. Had they been friends before they had become a couple? Were they married, as she hoped? Had they been together for a very long time? These days, she was more and more able to ask the questions she couldn't answer without becoming anxious about the responses that would not come from her own memories. She was learning to take one day at a time and wait until everything that she needed to know would become clear to her. She hoped one day it would.

ႚ

When they returned to the doctor's office, Dr. Elaina had started seeing patients. After a further wait of half an hour, they were ushered into the examination room, where Hope was invited to climb up onto the examination table. Dr. Elaina was a redhead with glasses so oversized that she almost looked laughable. Hope liked her immediately, and once Jasmine explained Hope's memory loss, all three were soon chatting like old friends.

The doctor's examination of Hope was brief. She allowed her to hear the baby's heartbeat, but explained that there was no need for an ultrasound at that stage. If Hope wanted to know the baby's sex, she could make an appointment for the twentieth week of pregnancy, otherwise, she should continue to come to the clinic once per month until the seventh month, at which point she would need to begin seeing a doctor once every two weeks.

Hearing the baby's heartbeat was a very emotional experience for Hope. Although she had seen ultrasound images of the child she was carrying, being able to hear the strong, rhythmic beat of a heart inside of her own body almost reduced her to tears. She felt like crying for her baby and the father who must be wondering what had happened to them. She felt like crying for herself and for the future and the past. She felt like crying for the time she was losing with her family, and for the fact that they had already missed so much of the pregnancy.

Yet she refused to actually cry. She had not had a good cry since being released from hospital, and she felt like allowing a single tear to fall would be akin to opening a floodgate and allowing a rushing river to engulf her. She supposed a time would come when her tears would overflow, but for now, she tried to remain stoic and smile through the bittersweet experience.

ଓଃ

Late that night, Jasmine yawned as she made an effort to stay awake long enough to record the day's events in her journal.

April 24

Having Mommy here has been such a blessing. I cannot thank her enough for coming to be with me. We've done quite a bit of shopping for the things the baby needs, and it's been quite a challenge leaving any of those cute items on the store shelves. As I write, I'm sitting in the rocking chair in the room that's going to be the nursery, and I'm surrounded by so many things. Everywhere in the room, I see the cutest little onesies, booties, socks, mittens and knit caps. There are receiving blankets separate from regular blankets, hooded towels and tiny little washcloths in a rainbow of pastel shades. We even bought several dozen cloth diapers, at Mommy's insistence, of course! I'd planned to use the disposables, but she insists that the cloth ones are better for both Little Praise and the environment. I've learned to compromise rather than enter into prolonged differences of opinion with my mother—especially in areas such as this one where she considers herself to be something of an expert—so I've agreed that we will use them so long as she is here to wash them, and I'll try to use them as much as possible after she goes back home. We do have a fully functional washing machine, after all, and if all else fails I'll use a diaper service. She couldn't believe such a thing existed.

There's just so much stuff that they are beginning to get underfoot, so I've decided to pack them away in suitcases until we can get the furniture put in. This baby hasn't even been born yet, and already he/she has more clothes and accessories than I do!

Another thing I've really enjoyed doing this week is shopping for maternity clothes. Before now, I was still losing rather than gaining weight. I'm just beginning to show and gain healthy weight now, and I finally feel comfortable and confident enough to wear maternity dresses and blouses. After all, there is no shame in my being pregnant. Ryan and I did the right thing—we each had our own histories of physical relationships before becoming Christians, but once we got saved, we repented from those sins. We put away those fleshly desires, and even when they were overwhelming—as they can be for any normal, red-blooded adult—we chose to ignore them until we were legally and morally free to engage in a physical relationship. Even after we got engaged, we made sure we were never alone in enclosed spaces where we might have been tempted. It was difficult, but so worth it!

Our baby is a product of not only our love, but that special relationship ordained by God and sanctioned by society—although even THAT is changing more and more these days!

So I finally bought some flowing maternity tops, and I plan to debut a cute polka dot dress I got on sale when I go to church this Sunday. I can't wait! It'll be like making an announcement without saying a word, and I know everyone will be thrilled for us.

Wow, things have changed so much over the past couple of weeks. Oh, what a little time can do! A couple of months ago, I was so insecure and self-conscious about being pregnant and becoming a mother, but with the love and care of my husband, our respective families, and our neighbors, I have crossed over into a place of acceptance, contentment and joy.

Thank God, the worst is now behind us. That alone is something I could rejoice about for days.

J.

120

April 30

I know that if I say the things that are on my mind, people will think I'm crazy, that I've lost my mind or that I'm having a crisis of faith or whatever, so I'm writing this rant down. If I ever let it get out of my mouth, they'll have me committed, I just know it.

I can't believe it. I still can't believe it. How could this have happened? I thought that when you did exactly what you were supposed to do, your outcome had to be great. I thought that if Ryan and I waited until we were married to consummate our relationship; if we did all the right things, and if we prayed all the right prayers, and sang all the right worship songs and gave God all the glory, then He would give us the fervent desires of our hearts. Isn't that what the Bible says?

And after we did all that, and I got pregnant, we dedicated our child to the Lord. And even then, I was so sick. I mean, I spent months feeling sick all day, every day. And now that I've finally crossed over into feeling good physically, emotionally, and mentally, <u>this</u> happens?! How could this happen? How could the Lord allow this to happen to US? I really thought for a while that I was His favorite child; didn't Ryan and I always say we felt like the apple of His right and left eye? So how could we—a man and woman of God, a couple who praise Him and lead others to the throne of glory through my praise and worship sessions and Ryan's devotion to the youth ministry—be going through this?

On Thursday night, I felt great. Little Praise was extremely active, though, and I remember asking Ryan to put his hand on my tummy and feel all the movement that was taking place. Then we slept. The next morning, I woke up and all was well—or so I thought. Mommy and I stayed home all day and she washed some of the maternity clothes. We both took great pleasure in hanging them on the line outside in the backyard and watching them flutter in the breeze.

And then late in the afternoon, I noticed that I had not felt the baby move all day, so I consulted the pregnancy guide and followed the suggestion to have a glass of milk and then lie down and count the kicks for the next hour. Nothing.

I called Ryan and put the phone on speaker. His voice always had a way of waking the baby up. Nothing.

So I called Dr. Elaina's office and asked Mommy to accompany me to see her. I was very nervous but I prayed nothing would be wrong. Mommy even asked Ryan to send a text message to our closest 'prayer warrior' friends and ask them to pray for Little Praise's health.

Ryan managed to get away from work and he met us at the doctor's office. After all the checks, I will never forget the words she said. "Jasmine, Ryan, I'm afraid today is not a good day."

The tears came. There was no need for her to explain. Little Praise was gone. I mean, he was still there, but he was gone.

Ryan gripped my hands and I could feel his strength leaving him. She gave us a moment before continuing. "I'm not seeing any signs of life. There's no movement, no heartbeat. I wouldn't be able to say what happened at this point, but please know that I'm terribly sorry for your loss."

She left us to pull ourselves together, and after a few minutes of silence and not touching, we joined her and my mother in her office. My mother, speechless for once, was sobbing uncontrollably, and when I finally looked into Ryan's eyes, they were bright with unshed tears. Neither of us had said anything up to that point. He was sitting in an oversized armchair, and I couldn't help but go and sit in his lap and give him a big hug. As he held me close and sobbed, I knew I couldn't cry. If I started, I'd never stop. Even Dr. Elaina looked a bit emotional.

When we learnt that I would still have to go through labor and deliver the baby.... How strong does God think I am?

All I was thinking was, How could this happen? How could this happen? I'm a Christian, God's child; how could this happen to me? This is supposed to happen to people who don't do things God's way, not to good girls like me!

Much of the rest of the day passed in a blur. I remember walking through the door and collapsing in a heap, and Mommy, *with the best of intentions, trying to console me by saying, "The Father above knows best, Jasmine. He knows best." I wasn't convinced. I still am not.*

That night, the dam broke when Ryan picked up the phone and called Daniel. When I heard him say the words, "We lost the baby," I wept and wept and wept, and then we all wept together— Ryan, Mommy and me. And when we were spent, my husband and I slept close. He hugged me and I snuggled against him, my back against his chest, and we both hugged our precious Little Praise. We both knew it would be our last night as a family.

Although I checked in to the medical center the next morning, it took two days for labor to begin. James Lucas Phillips was born in the stillness of the wee hours of the morning on Monday. It was very painful, but I was only in active labor for about an hour.

It was just the four of us: the midwife, her assistant, James Lucas and me.

The midwife asked if I wanted to call anyone, but I didn't. She asked if I wanted to see him, but I didn't. Ryan and I prefer to remember people when they are alive and well, and it was the same for our little child of love. However, Nurse Marilyn did take a photograph of him, which she will keep on my file until we decide whether or not we want to see what he looked like.

We'll have a memorial service, but I'm not sure I'll be able to go.

In the meantime, I don't want to see anyone. I don't want to hear the phone ring. I don't want to eat. I don't even want to see my mother. I just want my husband and the baby I was finally looking forward to. The days are running into one another now. I feel like I'm in an abyss. I wonder if the worst is yet to come.

I don't even know who I am right now.

J.

CHAPTER FIFTEEN

It was Daniel who called Aunt Ruby to let her know about Ryan and Jasmine's loss. He'd just fallen asleep uncharacteristically early that Friday night when his cell phone rang, and he was jolted out of his slumber. The minute he saw his friend's number on the phone, he knew something had to be wrong. Even though it was only ten o'clock, Ryan never called him that late.

In the split second before he answered the phone, a barrage of thoughts bombarded him. Was something wrong with Aunt Ruby? Had she fallen? Had she suffered some kind of delayed effect of the fracture? Was it a clot? Her blood pressure? Her blood sugar?

And then other thoughts assailed him. Was it Hope? Had she done something to Aunt Ruby? Had the house been robbed? And just when he was starting to feel comfortable about her being there, too.

When he heard what had happened, his heart broke for Ryan. He knew how much the baby had meant to him, how much having a family had always meant to him. Ryan had grown up in Jamaica without his father around to guide him, and as an adult, he had looked forward to the day when he would become a father. He had always told Daniel that he would be one of those men who stuck around. He would rise to the challenge of fatherhood and of being a husband. He would be a provider for his loved ones even while he made himself available to them, rearranging his work schedule, perhaps even leaving a job if necessary. Unlike his father, *he* would be what he considered a real *man*. He wouldn't run off to another country and create a whole new family.

Daniel had teased him about marrying a woman who was more than ten years his junior, jokingly accusing him of marrying her because she had many more child-bearing years ahead of her. In his typical, unassuming, gentle giant manner, Ryan had never confirmed Daniel's so-called theory, but he hadn't denied it, either.

Daniel was disappointed in himself when he remembered the way he had doubted Jasmine and kept on hounding Ryan about it. He had asked his friend repeatedly whether he was sure that Jasmine was all she appeared to be. He had wondered if she could be using Ryan in the same way that Victoria had attempted to use him.

Of course, Ryan had denied that any of these things could be true, and reminded Daniel that, unlike his whirlwind romance with Victoria, his relationship with Jasmine had taken years to cultivate, having started before she had even graduated from college. They had maintained a platonic friendship for years before he even began to consider her attractive, and he was sure that the same was true for Jasmine.

So, as he had done with Hope, Daniel had taken a step back to simply observe how Jasmine related to her husband. She always treated him with respect and never belittled him in public. Even when they had their private disagreements, Ryan himself had told Daniel that she never cursed him or used anything from his past against him, although she certainly knew enough about him to do so. After a couple of years, he was finally beginning to trust her almost as much as he trusted Ryan and considered his skepticism about her prolonged and exaggerated morning sickness to have been a momentary lapse of judgment on his own part that he had, unfortunately, allowed to contaminate Ryan's own view of his wife.

And now this.

Daniel had no idea what to say to Ryan except, "Darn, man, I'm so sorry." And like the typical man, he immediately asked, "What do you need me to do?" Not that he genuinely thought he could do anything to help.

He could hear Ryan sigh heavily as he thought about the question for a long time. Eventually, he replied, "Pray that we'll get through this. That's what you can do. I'll let you know what's going on."

"I'll drive over tomorrow."

"Thanks, man. And can you tell Aunt Ruby what's going on? I don't think I can deal with another woman's grief right now."

"Is Jasmine's mom still there?"

"Yeah."

Daniel was relieved; at least Jasmine and Ryan weren't going through this alone.

Ryan went on, "She's broken, man. We all are."

"I am, too, Ryan. I am, too," he shook his head as if the brisk movement would get rid of the bad news. "I'll talk to you in the morning. And I'll be praying for you all."

"Thanks, man," Ryan could be heard sighing again as they ended the call.

He supposed there was no way he could avoid telling Aunt Ruby. The families were too close for her not to know as soon as he did. He knew it was late by her standards, but he dialed the number and listened to Aunt Ruby's phone ring once, twice, three times before someone picked it up.

"Hello?" Hope's voice was sleepy and full of concern. He almost felt ashamed for having wondered if she had somehow harmed Aunt Ruby.

"Hi, Hope," his voice was quiet.

"Daniel? Is everything all right?" He could hear anxiety in her voice. Aunt Ruby's phone never rang this late, either.

He didn't answer her question, asking instead, "May I speak with my aunt?"

"She's already gone to bed."

"I know. It's important."

"Hold on, I'll wake her up."

Daniel waited. He could hear Hope descending the staircase. She must have picked up the extension on the wall in the hallway outside his office. A little while later he heard when she knocked quietly on Aunt Ruby's door. Her speech was muffled, but his aunt picked up the extension in her room.

"Daniel?" Another voice full of concern. He waited for the click that indicated that Hope had disconnected the extension she was using. When it came, he sighed heavily, "I'm afraid I have some sad news, Aunt Ruby." Without giving her time to speculate, he went on, "Jasmine has lost the baby."

"What? Oh, no! Oh, dear! What happened?" Aunt Ruby was almost distraught.

"They don't know yet. The baby stopped moving so they went to the doctor. I'm driving over in the morning."

"Okay."

"And... Aunt Ruby?"

"Yes, honey."

"Give them a little space. Don't rush over there tonight, okay? Just pray that they'll survive this."

"All right, honey. I'll be praying."

❣

Hope was in the kitchen stirring golden honey into two cups of chamomile tea when Aunt Ruby hobbled out. It wasn't necessary to ask Aunt Ruby anything; she could tell by the expression on the older woman's face that something had gone terribly wrong. She sat and took a sip of her tea. *What's going on?* She wondered. *Does it concern me?* Had Daniel found out something about her past that she was unaware of? Was she about to lose the only home she could remember? Until now, she hadn't realized how comfortable she had become with Aunt Ruby and how much she was enjoying the company of her new friends. Was she about to lose everything she could remember? She cupped her hands around the warm cup and waited, anxious but trying not to show it.

Aunt Ruby assumed her usual position at the kitchen island, and when Hope placed the cup of steaming liquid in front of her, she took a tentative sip before getting straight to the point.

Hope couldn't believe what she was hearing. How could this be happening? What had Jasmine done to deserve the loss of a pregnancy? She had already been through so much since becoming pregnant, and now this? Hope's mind was spinning. The inevitable question was whether the same thing could happen to her. *Would* it happen to her? If it happened to such a gentle soul as Jasmine, why shouldn't she expect the same kind of experience to come knocking on her own door, as well?

From across the island, Aunt Ruby put her wrinkled hand on Hope's, gently bringing her back to reality. "Before I talk to you about Jasmine, Hope, I want to focus on you for a little while," she looked into Hope's shining eyes. "I can imagine what you're thinking, and I want to share a scripture with you. It's from the tenth chapter and fifth verse of Paul's second letter to the Corinthians. In it, he highlighted their decision to 'cast down imaginations and every high thing that exalteth itself against the knowledge of God, and bring into captivity every thought to the obedience of Christ.' Now, I know that you may not have a personal relationship with Christ yet, but as with so many scriptures, this one can be applicable to your life whether you're a Christian or not.

"I know that almost as soon as the words left my mouth, you began to ask yourself if the same thing could happen to you, and there's no way to deny it—it could. But we can talk about that later. For now, I just want you to actively cast down those images and focus instead on what we can do to help Jasmine in this terrible time."

Hope nodded. A tear dripped from her chin and into her tea. It was followed by another. And then another. The next thing Hope knew, she was weeping. Weeping for Jasmine. Weeping for the baby Jasmine and Ryan had been calling Little Praise. Weeping for herself. Weeping for her own child. Weeping for her unknown family. Weeping for her lost past. Weeping for her uncertain future.

She wept until she had no tears left to cry. And then she found some in a secret reserve, and wept a little more. The floodgates had opened, and she wept until she had no more energy left.

Aunt Ruby had moved around to stand awkwardly beside her, and hugged her and rubbed her back until she stopped heaving. The older woman was crying tears of her own.

When the two of them composed themselves, Aunt Ruby returned to her seat and Hope went to freshen her tea. By now, it was almost midnight. The lights had finally gone out in the house next door, but Hope wondered if anyone would sleep. She knew she certainly wouldn't.

Aunt Ruby said, "The one thing Ryan asked was for us to pray that they would survive this tragedy, and that is what I'm going to do. Will you join me?" She stretched her hands towards Hope, who clasped them lightly.

"Father in Heaven, we come to You in the name of Jesus. We come to You with thanksgiving. We thank You because You are a gracious and merciful God, and even in the midst of such a tragedy as this, Your grace and mercy continue to flow. We thank You for the relationship we have with each other, with You and with Jasmine and Ryan, who have felt confident enough to share this experience with us and to ask us to approach You on their behalf.

"Father, You know the grief they are going through, the grief we are all going through at this time. You can relate, because You watched Your own Son die a terrible death on the cross. Now they have lost their first child, and they are hurting. Send Your peace to engulf them. Remind them that You are still on Your throne. Remind them that You can show up and show off even in circumstances such as these. Touch them in a special way, Lord. Put hope in their hearts and help them to exercise their faith even in this trial.

"Allow the process that now needs to take place to be a timely one. Provide Your healing for Jasmine's body, and for their spirits, hearts and minds.

"Help those of us who love them to give them the support they need. Help them to ask for it, Lord. Strengthen them and their relationship, because we know that this challenge can make or break their marriage that is so young, Lord.

"We offer this situation up to You and ask You to use it for Your glory. We pray in Jesus' name, amen."

Hope repeated the ending of the prayer, signaling her agreement with Aunt Ruby, but inwardly, her mind was racing with hundreds of questions. If the Lord loved Jasmine and Ryan so much, why had He allowed such a terrible thing to happen to them? Had He *allowed* it? Or had He *caused* it? What good did He think could come of such a loss? How could He use it for His glory? And why should He even want to?

She remained silent, however, not wanting to approach Aunt Ruby with all these questions now, when she already had so much on her mind. Instead, she went over and gave her benefactor a warm hug. "It's late," she said, "shall I help you back to bed? We'll probably be up early in the morning, trying to figure out what needs to happen now and how we can help."

"Yes, dear," Aunt Ruby agreed. Together they went to her room and Hope helped her to get back under the covers. They bade each other good night and Hope quietly closed the door. She sat at the kitchen table with her tea, thinking about the situation until she went in search of a book to distract her. Daylight found her in the same position.

෬

At the same moment that Aunt Ruby was breaking the news to Hope, Daniel was leaning against his pillows, which he had propped up against the headboard. He couldn't believe it. His friends didn't deserve this kind of grief. Nobody did. He wondered what kind of God allowed a couple to get pregnant, only for them to lose the baby months later. Was there some lesson they needed to learn that God was trying to teach them? Was there no other way?

It was his turn to sigh. He clasped his hands behind his head. This was what he didn't understand about God. It seemed as if the people who tried to do the right thing were the ones who always faced challenges that resulted in crises of faith.

He thought about Jasmine and Ryan. They had both been Christians before they fell in love, and even before their relationship, they had both decided that they would be celibate until marriage. They both admitted they weren't saints before becoming Christians, but even so, there were no divorces, no children born outside of wedlock, no skeletons in the closet. They loved the Lord and trusted Him with every area of their lives. And look what that had gotten them.

He thought about his own story. He had gotten saved as a teenager and had made one colossal mistake. He'd thought marrying

Victoria was the godly thing to do, and look where that had gotten him. He had lost everything—his wife and the child she was carrying, his faith, his hope—all in one day. Why would God allow that to happen to him? He'd only been trying to do the right thing.

He didn't often reflect on the details of that distant afternoon, but he allowed his mind to drift far away to a distant time he would rather forget.

ఇ

That morning, Daniel had returned home unexpectedly to retrieve his forgotten cell phone. He hadn't noticed the expensive coupe parked in the communal parking lot, but as he had stepped through the front door, he'd seen the keys that had been left on the entrance table, right beside a sophisticated gift basket featuring a teddy bear holding a baby blue balloon with the words, "It's a boy!" He'd wrinkled his brow.

Hearing voices out on the rear terrace, he had made his way in that direction, only to find his wife sitting with one of her former professors, a gentleman who was now Daniel's own colleague, in a manner of speaking, since they were both on staff at the nearby university—Professor Hargreaves a tenured professor and Daniel a mere graduate teaching assistant. As Daniel watched them from inside the town house, he couldn't help but notice that their body language gave away a relationship that was, from his perspective, a bit too intimate. Their heads were angled toward each other, their knees were touching, and Professor Hargreaves' large hands were enveloping Victoria's smaller ones. They didn't even see him, though he was standing close enough that he could touch them if it weren't for the glass sliding door. Their voices were low, but not too low for him to hear what they were saying.

"Does he suspect anything?"

"Daniel? No, he's basking in all of this. You'd think he was the first man to become a father. If it wasn't so pathetic, it would be cute." Victoria's voice was cold. Daniel briefly reflected on the fact that he had been hearing that coldness more and more often since they had married seven months before.

"Vixen, you know I had to do what I did. I couldn't go through this with you. You know the college's policy on faculty fraternizing with students."

"And let's not forget your wife," Victoria's voice was bitter.

"Yes. How could I forget about her?" Professor Hargreaves chuckled, "She never lets me forget that night I fell asleep in your apartment and didn't get home till daylight."

Daniel felt ill. He couldn't just stand there and listen while his world crashed down around his ears. He had thought Victoria loved him, had blamed himself for her pregnancy. His shocked intake of breath alerted them to his presence, and Professor Hargreaves had almost tripped over his feet in his attempt to stand.

"Donahue! So good to see you," he stretched his hand towards Daniel's for a handshake, but Daniel put both of his into his pockets and pursed his lips. After a lengthy pause, Professor Hargreaves continued awkwardly, "I just stopped by to congratulate you both on the impending arrival of your son." Through the corner of his eye, Daniel noticed Victoria wince at that last word.

"I would thank you, but I'm not sure I should," Daniel responded curtly. He was talking to the professor, but he was looking directly at his wife, who could not meet his eyes. "You see, Professor Hargreaves, my wife and I... well, we decided early in this pregnancy that we wouldn't tell anyone the baby's sex until he was born. Yet you've come bearing blue gifts."

Professor Hargreaves began to sputter a bit, but Daniel's attention was focused only on the woman he had promised to love, cherish and honor till death parted them. She had recovered from the momentary crack in her composure and was getting to her feet with great difficulty, considering her distended abdomen. Neither man offered to help her.

"Daniel, I don't know what you're insinuating here. You've always known that Professor Hargreaves was my mentor, so it came naturally to me to share our little secret with him. I don't know why you keep insisting that we not tell anyone we're having a boy." She strolled past him with as much grace as her protruding stomach and awkward gait would allow her to muster up, heading for the kitchen. Professor Hargreaves stared after her as if he needed her to defend him from her husband, who was several inches taller and a couple of decades younger than he was.

Daniel was pensive. He allowed his mind to wander through the memories of his relationship with Victoria—past their elopement at a small wedding chapel in St. Augustine; past their decision to wed; past the lunch date when she'd told him she was pregnant.

His thoughts settled on one fateful evening only four months after they had met at university. He had just started his Master's degree, having worked as a high school history teacher after graduation, and she was in her senior year. He had been attracted to her the moment he'd seen her browsing through the T-shirts in the college bookstore, and had asked her out immediately. Although he was a Christian and she wasn't, he ignored his own conviction that he should choose someone with whom he was equally yoked, as the Bible advised, rationalizing his decision to date her because she was from a godly home. She wore a lot more make-up than he liked and her taste in music wasn't what he would have preferred, but she didn't curse or go out clubbing, and he had to admit her figure was very pleasing on the eyes. Besides, she had seemed to be quite interested in him from the moment he had gone over to say, "Hi there."

Four months into their relationship, she had begged for him to take her to see a romantic comedy. He generally didn't watch R-rated movies, but her favorite actress starred in the film. Daniel didn't enjoy the foul language or adult scenes, and at the end he felt a bit overexposed, but they went out to dinner afterwards as planned. He had started feeling unwell, though, and they had left before dessert.

That night, Victoria had driven him to her apartment, something that had never happened before because he liked to be a true gentleman and had always been the one to take the wheel of his aged, very used sedan. When he had attempted to walk her to her door, she had invited him in to lie on her couch until he was able to drive himself home. There, she had begun a sinful seduction that had led to the bedroom of her small apartment and a morning of regrets on Daniel's part. Although he had felt remorseful for falling into the sin of fornication for the first time since becoming a Christian, he prayed about it and repented, turning from that kind of behavior, and was thankful that he had been forgiven. He had no intention of going down that road again. He knew better.

Victoria, for her part, hadn't insisted they marry at first, but when it was clear that she was pregnant, she had told him through bountiful tears that her sanctimonious family would disown her if she had a child out of wedlock. It was on that lunch date that he'd capitulated and the two soon eloped.

Despite the questionable start, the marriage had been going fairly well thus far. They had initially been quite happy, enjoying their time together. If Victoria had become a bit distant and cold as time had passed, Daniel had chalked it up to the advancing pregnancy.

Now, seven months after the night of the date, Daniel's eyes were being opened to the possibility—the certainty—that he'd been used all along. The R-rated movie, the dinner, the seduction, maybe even the fact that he'd suddenly become unwell—all of it had been leading up to cornering him and forcing him to marry Victoria because the real father of her child could not. Daniel brought his attention back to the present and noticed that Professor Hargreaves was still standing on the terrace with his younger counterpart blocking his only exit... unless, of course, he could vault the six-foot wall that surrounded their private back yard. Victoria was in the kitchen making herself a cup of tea. And he was standing in the doorway while his life crumbled around him.

He turned to face his wife. "You used me."

Professor Hargreaves was sputtering again.

"Daniel, you don't understand." Victoria noticed that her husband was starting to take deep, measured breaths. She hadn't seen it often in the even-tempered man she lived with, but she knew he was becoming angry. She figured it was best if she made a quick exit, so before he could open his mouth again, she said, "I'm going to give you a few hours to compose yourself." She headed towards the front door, grabbing Professor Hargreaves' keys as she made her exit. There was no argument, no discussion, no goodbye.

The next time Daniel had seen his wife, she had been lying lifeless on a slab in the morgue and he was identifying her body.

⋘

Bringing himself back to the present, Daniel shook his head in disgust. Just when he'd started to feel like it was time for him to start seeking the Lord again, all the same questions he had asked during the lowest point of his life were resurfacing with a vengeance.

Yet at the same time, he knew that something had to change. He had been living a life that was too uncomfortable, too distant, too disconnected, for too long. In the past couple of weeks since his aunt's accident, he had begun to feel like it was time for him to rejoin the land of the living while he was still *in* the land of the living. He knew firsthand that life was too fragile to waste, and yet in many ways, that was exactly what he had done since losing his wife. Sure, he had progressed in his career in leaps and bounds, but the truth was, it was as if he had buried a big part of his own personality—the characteristics that truly made him Daniel Donahue—at that cemetery where Victoria had been laid to rest. Gone were his ready smile, his trusting nature and his hope for the future. They had been replaced with a permanent frown, an unwillingness to let anyone get close to him and a conscious decision to live each day without thinking too much about any future other than his professional one.

He was more confused than ever. He needed to talk to someone who could help him sort out his thoughts and make a decision about how to live his life going forward. He had already wasted way too much time. He decided he would call his old friend Robert Marsden in the morning. He wouldn't waste another day. He couldn't afford to.

ଔ

The next morning, Hope was sitting at the kitchen table when Daniel drove in from Lake Butler some minutes before six o'clock. She was so engrossed in the book she was reading that she didn't even look up when he came through the mud room and into the kitchen.

Daniel had not expected anyone to be awake at that hour. He hadn't slept a wink, so at four o'clock he'd decided to stop waiting until daylight and come straight to the place he considered his home. He'd been surprised to see the kitchen lights on when he'd driven to the garage, but he figured Aunt Ruby had started her devotions early. He stopped short when he saw that it was Hope who was sitting at the kitchen table.

Her distraction gave him the opportunity to observe her, so he did. She was sitting about twelve feet away, with her right side to the kitchen.

He imagined that she would never have been sitting there in that particular outfit if she had expected him to come in. She generally dressed fairly modestly, but this morning, she was wearing a sleeveless sleep shirt that ended mid-thigh. Its neckline was not particularly revealing, but it gave an indication of the swell of her breasts, perhaps made fuller by the fact that she was pregnant. Her long legs were stretched out in front of her and crossed at the ankles. He noticed that both her feet and her toenails were bare. She was chewing on her bottom lip with great determination.

For the first time in years, Daniel felt the now unfamiliar stirring of attraction. The recognition jolted him so much that questions immediately assailed his mind. *Why this woman? Why now, under these circumstances?* His greeting came out a bit more forcefully than intended.

"Good morning!" He leaned against the refrigerator.

She looked like she might jump right out of her skin. "Daniel!" She sat up and looked like she might get up, but she remained seated. "I didn't hear you come in."

Daniel could see the indecision in her face, and he imagined she couldn't figure out whether she should make a run for the stairs or stay put. He decided to have a little fun at her expense. After the night he'd had, he could use a little light-hearted distraction. Instead of going up to his room as he had first intended to do, he sat across from her at the kitchen table.

She sat back, looking a little defeated.

"What are you reading there?" he asked.

"*Chronicle of a Death Foretold*. García Márquez."

"How is it?" He could see she had almost finished the relatively thin volume.

"I haven't quite finished, but it is excellent."

"Interesting," he responded. "I've never heard of it."

"According to the blurb on the back cover, García Márquez covered an event as a reporter and then wrote a novel based on what happened."

"Maybe I should read it when you're done."

"No problem." She looked at the number of pages remaining. "I'll probably be done before Aunt Ruby gets up anyway."

He got to his feet, and he almost smiled when he saw the look in her eyes. It was clear that she was hoping he would leave the room so she could flee upstairs. Instead, he headed towards the percolator and began to make the coffee. Like Aunt Ruby, he preferred an extra dark roast. His aunt was of the opinion that his decision to add sugar and cream adulterated the unique flavor, but he didn't care. He hated the bitter taste of black coffee. He prepared his cup while the coffee brewed, choosing an extra large mug better suited for soup instead of his usual travel mug and putting in sugar and flavored creamer; Irish cream—his favorite.

Hope turned to look through the window behind her at the quiet house next door.

"I was so sorry to hear about Jasmine and Ryan's loss," she said.

"Me, too. I can't imagine what they're going through." He leaned against the kitchen counter, folded his arms and crossed his ankles as he waited for the percolator to work its magic. "Although, I suppose I can, on some level."

She looked at him with raised eyebrows but didn't ask any questions. Daniel briefly considered sharing his experience with her, but decided against it. He wasn't ready to share it with anyone who didn't already know the whole truth.

If she was disappointed that he didn't share his thoughts, she didn't give any indication, so he said, "So I know women love to talk," he began, "what has my beloved aunt been telling you about me?"

"What do you mean?" She stretched out her legs again, crossing them at the ankles in a move he would later learn was habitual. She probably didn't realize that the motion drew attention to her perfect legs. Daniel, definitely a 'leg man,' couldn't help but notice; however, he tried to channel his thoughts in another direction. He looked away from her legs and into her eyes. He'd forgotten the question.

"Hmm?" he asked absently, just as the coffee maker beeped.

She repeated herself, "What do you mean about Aunt Ruby and what she's said about you?"

"Well, I can't imagine what you two talk about all day. The topic of her favorite nephew must come up from time to time." He poured the aromatic brew into his mug and returned to the table.

"Well, I don't get the impression Aunt Ruby likes to spend a lot of time discussing other people, even her favorite nephew, no matter how very *modest* he is." The sarcasm dripped from her voice, but she smiled and it was clear that she meant no harm. "Although when she does talk about you, she makes it clear that she's very proud of you and your accomplishments." She frowned.

Daniel noticed. "But...?"

"But...?" she repeated in a questioning matter.

"You frowned. As if you weren't finished talking. As if you had something more to say."

"But..., well, she seems to be worried about your relationship with God. She hasn't said so in as many words, but it's something I've kind of picked up along the way."

"You're very intuitive, I suppose." He sipped the hot liquid. When she didn't respond, he continued. "Did your intuition pick up why she's concerned about my spiritual life?"

"No, actually. She really doesn't talk about your personal life. I think she respects people's privacy."

"She does. That's why she has so many visitors; people know that she means them well. She keeps their secrets and gives great advice. And when she says she's going to pray for you, she actually does." He smiled, "I'm so glad she's my aunt."

"She really is a blessing," Hope agreed. "I literally don't know where I would be today without her."

They both fell silent.

"I suppose it's a good thing for you that she didn't listen to my sage advice to put you out," he looked over her shoulder and through the window.

"The best thing."

He sipped the drink again and suddenly got up. "I can see Ryan out in the yard. I'm going to go talk to him," he smiled knowingly at her, "so you can run upstairs like you've been wanting to do ever since I got here." He chuckled as she blushed prettily and he headed out the back door.

"Tell him they're in our thoughts and prayers, please," Hope called after him.

CB

As she watched him leave, Hope allowed herself to wonder—albeit briefly—why he wasn't married. He was, from what she knew of him, fairly successful in both his teaching and his writing. According to his aunt, he had accomplished much in his profession, based on his age, which Hope put at mid- to late-thirties.

She supposed he was attractive enough—actually, if she was fully honest with herself, she had to admit that he was quite attractive, especially when he smiled. She hadn't even noticed his dimples before. His hair had started graying at the temples, and she wondered if it was a family trait or stress-related. He didn't look old enough for gray hair.

While aspects of his personality left a lot to be desired—he had been very rude to her when they just met, and although his disposition had improved slightly, he still wasn't very warm to her sometimes—she figured it was due to the peculiar circumstances in which they had met. Besides, his aunt was such a lovely woman and his best friends such a welcoming couple that there had to be some merits to his character! So why was he alone?

She briefly wondered whether or not he could be gay, but quickly dismissed the thought because it made her uncomfortable. She wondered if he might be divorced or separated, but she preferred to think he wasn't. She couldn't put her finger on what it was about the very thought of him having been married that made her uneasy.

She didn't want to ask Aunt Ruby or Jasmine because she didn't want either of them to know she was thinking about him—although obviously she was. The fact of the matter was, she was immensely curious about his life and she didn't want to even try to identify why.

ᴄ꙰

Daniel, cup in hand, hopped over the low hedge separating the two backyards, ignoring the opening amidst the shrubbery, and approached his friend, who was standing under a wide tree, talking quietly on his cell phone. Daniel stopped a respectful distance away in order to give Ryan some privacy. Ryan waved him in the direction of the patio at the back of the house, so Daniel went to sit in the porch swing. He absent-mindedly pushed it back and forth.

The phone call continued for some ten minutes, and there were times Daniel saw Ryan wiping away his tears.

Daniel could relate. His loss may have been of a completely different nature, but he, too, had suffered the death of a child, as well as the death of all the hopes and dreams one pours into that child before he or she is ever born. As he sat waiting, he found himself doing something he rarely allowed himself to do: he reflected on Victoria's pregnancy before that last day.

He remembered the feelings of pride and expectancy that he had experienced. He'd felt as if he had accomplished something tremendous. The circumstances may not have been ideal, but he believed only God could create a life, so he was grateful for the huge blessing. He'd had an excellent relationship with his own father, and he couldn't wait to pass on the lessons learned to his own children. Victoria's pregnancy was taking him one step closer to that dream. He couldn't wait.

Every day, as soon as he got home, he would find his wife and place his hand on her growing abdomen. He lived for those times when he could feel the baby move under his touch. He had taken a photograph that showed a clear imprint of a little foot against Victoria's skin. He had placed the photograph, along with the various ultrasound images, in a journal he hadn't opened in years. Maybe it was time to look at it again. There was no use in distancing himself from the pleasant experiences he had shared with Victoria and the son she would have had, had he not made the startling discovery that day. Perhaps the time had come to re-open the door to the past.

When Ryan ended his phone call, he walked to the patio and sat beside Daniel in the porch swing. Neither of them said a word. They just sat there swinging back and forth, each lost in his own sadness.

After a while, Ryan said, "That was Robert Marsden on the phone. I was letting him know what's happening. She's going into the hospital to be induced in a little while."

Daniel said, "I know."

"I can't do a thing to help her. I wish I could trade places with her. I'd do it in an instant."

"I know."

"I don't even know how to help her through this."

"Ask her."

"I have. She doesn't know, either."

"It's too soon. Ask her again tomorrow." Daniel sighed.

"I will." It was Ryan's turn to sigh.

They sat swinging.

"Daniel, when was the last time you prayed?"

"I prayed for you last night."

"Before that."

"I've been praying every couple of days for the past week or so."

"Good. I'm glad you remember how," Ryan stared off into the distance. "Will you pray for me?"

"I already am."

"No. I mean right now. Will you pray for me? Will you pray *with* me?"

Daniel was hesitant. He couldn't remember the last time he had prayed out loud for someone. Yes, he could. He had prayed over Victoria and the baby before going to work that last morning. The prayer had gone on so long that he'd been late and had run out the door, forgetting his cell phone as he did. He thought about saying no, but he couldn't. This man was his best friend; he had seen him through the worst experiences of his life, and he needed him. "Sure, Ryan, no problem."

He stood beside his friend and placed one hand on Ryan's shoulder and the other he lifted high with the palm upward, as if he were waiting for something to be placed into it. He stuttered over his words in the beginning, "Father, we know that You are El Shaddai, the all-sufficient God...." There was an awkward pause as he tried to think of what he should say next. "We come to You not because of who we are, but because of who *You* are...." Another pause. "We stand not in our righteousness because our righteousness is as filthy rags, but in Your righteousness because You are Jehovah Tsidkenu, the Lord our righteousness." He took a deep breath. This was harder than he had anticipated.

"We know that You are Jehovah Rapha, the Lord our healer, and we come to You for the kind of healing that only You can provide. We... we ask for Your healing power to flow over Jasmine's body. Step in, take full control and help her to have an uneventful delivery. Give her Your peace that passes all understanding."

Suddenly, it was as if a glass ceiling between God and himself had shattered, and the words started to flow from his spirit like he had never taken a sabbatical from praying.

"And now, Lord, I stand in the gap for my friend and brother, Ryan. He kneels before You a broken man. Not only is he losing his first child, but he feels as if he is losing control. Remind him that You are the one in full control, and that You are aware of everything that concerns him and his family. Nothing that happens to him surprises You, and for Your children, everything that happens is either God-sent or God-used. Let him know that Your will shall never take him where Your infinite grace cannot keep him.

"Help him to be wise and patient at this time, to be the husband Jasmine needs him to be, and the man of God You created him to be. I pray all this in Jesus' name, amen."

They both remained silent at the end of the prayer. Daniel retrieved his mug from the low table by the swing and walked away to stare out into the fenced backyard. He didn't want Ryan to see the tears streaming down his face. After a few minutes, he composed himself and wiped his face with a handkerchief he kept in his back pocket. The prayer had been a turning point for him.

He knew he hadn't prayed out loud for anyone in a long time, but he hadn't even realized that he had just about forgotten how until he opened his mouth and the words just didn't flow like they used to. There had been a time when Daniel had been considered a prayer warrior in the church, but he had gotten so focused on himself and his own challenges that he had completely forgotten that it is a gift to be an intercessor and to stand in the gap for others. He remembered that sometimes people are so overwhelmed with their personal circumstances, and so close to them, that they cannot even compose themselves to talk with their Creator. He had forgotten that intercessory prayer was a privilege of the highest order. He would strive never to forget again. The invisible barrier that had been separating him from God—a barrier he hadn't even been truly aware of until it fell—was gone.

Ryan stood and stretched. At least ten minutes had passed since he had echoed Daniel's amen, but he finally said, "Thanks, man."

"No, man, thank *you*. Thanks for giving me permission to pray with you."

"No problem." Daniel suspected that Ryan understood exactly why he had said that. Ryan continued, "Hey, I'm gonna go help Jasmine and Momma Hyacinth get ready for the hospital. It's supposed to be all over by the afternoon. Will you come by?"

"Sure. I'll bring Aunt Ruby."

Neither of them mentioned Hope, although she and Jasmine had become fast friends. Daniel suspected she wouldn't want to go to the hospital anyway. She probably wouldn't want Jasmine to have such a stark reminder of what she was losing. She wouldn't want to make things any worse than they already were.

They said their goodbyes, and Daniel hopped over the hedge again. By the time he went back into the kitchen, Hope had put on a pair of jeans and a T-shirt and returned to the kitchen, where she had prepared grits and eggs and was eating with Aunt Ruby, whose eyes were swollen from the tears she had shed the night before.

Their breakfast that morning was solemn. Nobody said much. Neither Daniel nor Hope had to be invited to share in Aunt Ruby's devotion; they all needed to hear a Word from God that morning.

Aunt Ruby didn't use her devotional this time. She simply turned her Bible to Genesis and began to speak. She retold the story of Joseph for Hope's benefit, ending with the line, "What the devil had meant for evil, Joseph told his brothers, God had turned around for good."

Aunt Ruby didn't need to explain the relevance of the story she had recounted, but she shared her feelings regarding the situation at hand. She explained that she didn't know why Jasmine and Ryan were being asked to travel on this painful road. She didn't know if it had been ordained by God or if it was simply being allowed by Him. What she *did* know was that with God, even the worst situations can have a positive side if one is willing to seek it.

The story of Joseph had something of a familiar ring to it for Hope, and it gave her a lot of... *hope* for the future. Surely, God was able to turn every situation around for the benefit of all concerned. He had done it for Joseph. Hope wondered if he would do it for Jasmine and Ryan, too. Did she even dare approach Him and ask that He do the same for her? Hope had a lot to think about and, for the first time since meeting Aunt Ruby, she felt like she needed to start praying about something. As soon as Aunt Ruby finished praying, she excused herself from the kitchen and hopped towards the bedroom. "I need to talk to God. I don't really know what I'm going to say, but I have a lot to tell Him and a lot of questions to ask, and I've got to start somewhere."

CHAPTER SIXTEEN

Jasmine had been home from the hospital for three days. During that time, she had seen only Ryan, her mother, Reverend Marsden and Aunt Ruby. No one mentioned Hope to her, and she wasn't in a position to think about anyone but herself and Little Praise—James Lucas—for a while. They would be having a memorial service the following week, but she couldn't even think about that. Especially not that. There were times she genuinely felt like she wasn't going to make it, and there were other times when she allowed a little bit of hope to seep into her spirit.

For three days, everyone had been tiptoeing around her. She remained in her bedroom, refusing to go anywhere near the room that should have been the nursery. She kept the shades and curtains drawn. She felt dark inside, and she wanted her immediate surroundings to reflect what she was feeling. She didn't want to see the light, because she felt like the light of her life was gone.

Her mother tried to coax her to eat, but she had no appetite. The only thing she could be persuaded to have was a protein shake with lots of fruits and soy milk in the morning and soup at night. She was glad her mother was there, and she was glad Aunt Ruby was there. It helped to have someone to take care of her, and these two women were equal to the task.

ඥ

Aunt Ruby went into a period of prayer and fasting that had Hope concerned, but the older woman would not listen to reason. She explained that she was fasting from food in order to focus on more spiritual things. She tried to help Hope to understand that it wasn't that she thought God would be more likely to answer her prayers if she starved herself, but she needed to be reminded that as a woman of God, she was called to feast on the Word of the Lord, and not on food. Still, she was ailing, and so she did not do a complete fast; instead, she was on what was known as a Daniel Fast, which involved eating only fruit and vegetables. She wasn't even having coffee—which Hope understood was a huge sacrifice for her—nor was she watching television. Even the religious programming was off-limits for her. If she was awake, she was either in her room praying or reading her Bible, or she was next door offering a helping hand. Hope would help her to make the short trip through the opening in the hedge that separated their yard from Ryan and Jasmine's, but she never ventured inside the house itself. She didn't expect to ever be close to Jasmine again. If Jasmine never wanted to see her again, she couldn't blame her.

Still, she continued to pray for Jasmine's physical and emotional healing. It felt good to think about someone other than herself and her child, and now that she was doing that, she really understood how self-centered she had been for the past few weeks. She had been so caught up in what was happening to her that she had not even really thought about the challenges other people were facing. Now those challenges were on her doorstep, and she couldn't avoid thinking about them. As a result of Jasmine's loss, she was now reading her Bible and praying on a regular basis, and she felt like she was developing a hunger and thirst for righteousness and knowledge about the Lord and His ways. She was hopeful that Jasmine would be able to survive and to thrive despite the depths of despair in which she no doubt found herself at that point in time.

One afternoon, she was alone in Aunt Ruby's house watching television when she heard the front door open. It was Ryan, who had accompanied Aunt Ruby from next door. He looked at the television and then at Hope with an odd look on his face. Aunt Ruby did the same. Hope, confused, also looked at the television. She didn't understand why they were both looking at her the way they were. Aunt Ruby hobbled in with the crutches and thanked Ryan for walking her over, but he didn't leave. Instead, he came inside and they both sat down, Aunt Ruby positioned herself beside Hope and Ryan in the arm chair angled towards the television.

"What is it?" Hope looked at them with expectancy on her face.

Aunt Ruby smiled, "Hi, Hope. What are you watching?"

Hope looked at the television again. "An interview." Wasn't it obvious?

"I see," Aunt Ruby said slowly. "So who are they interviewing?"

"This young man just won a singing competition last night. He got the highest number of votes."

Ryan smiled, "Ah, I know those shows."

"Yeah. This is the first time they've had this particular show in Mexico, so he's the first winner."

"Oh," Aunt Ruby had a mysterious smile on her face, and it was mirrored by Ryan's.

Hope looked from one to the other with a puzzled expression, "Can someone please explain what's going on here? You two are looking at me like I've grown horns or something."

Ryan looked at Aunt Ruby and smiled, "Do you want to tell her, or should I?"

"Tell me what?" Hope was becoming exasperated.

"Well, that program is in Spanish, Hope. You understand Spanish."

"What?" She looked at the television again and this time she focused on the actual words, rather than the meaning being conveyed, and noticed for the first time that they really *were* in Spanish. She was amazed. She was bilingual and she didn't even know it. What else did she not know about herself?

ଔ

Daniel was sitting in his office a few days after Jasmine returned home from the hospital when his cell phone rang. Seeing his best friend's picture on the screen of the phone, he whispered a quick prayer for wisdom before answering. He had spoken to Ryan more often on the phone over the past few days than he had since he had clawed his way out of his own tragedy.

"Hello?"

"Hey, Daniel." Ryan's voice was low.

"Hey, Ryan." Daniel knew that more often than not, these phone calls were about listening to Ryan breathe, rather than doing anything else.

"It's been three days since the birth."

"Yeah, man. I know."

"Jazz... she's beat down, man."

"I can only imagine."

"Her breast milk came in today."

"Breast milk?" Daniel was confused. "But I thought...." His voice tapered off as he failed to find the words he needed.

"Yeah. Dr. Elaina told us to expect it, because it's a woman's natural response to childbirth, but I didn't expect...."

"Yeah?"

"I didn't expect it to break her, man." Daniel heard the other man take a deep breath before going on, "I mean, she's full of milk and there's no baby to feed, you know? She's got everything she needs to sustain a baby's life right there inside of her body, and there's no baby. And if that wasn't bad enough, she says it hurts a lot."

"Aw, man."

"And she's my wife, and I love her more than life, and there's absolutely nothing I can do to help her, Danny. All I can do is hand her the painkillers and some water, and she doesn't even want that."

"Yeah, I know she's not a pill-popper," Daniel murmured.

"I mean, if I could take her place, I would. This is just so hard. And do you know what the worst thing is, Danny?" He continued before Daniel could answer, "It's that she didn't even *want* kids, you know? She didn't even want them."

"So why...?"

"She was doing it for me, man. She did this for me."

"She must really love you. A woman doesn't make those kinds of decisions lightly."

"She does. And I think that's why the pregnancy hit her so hard at first. We didn't even get a chance to really become man and wife before we were going to become Mom and Dad, you know? And she was doing it just for me, because she knows how much being a father means to me.

"A couple of months ago, when she was still sick all the time and she couldn't eat and she was losing weight instead of gaining weight, we were in the car, and she told me that this was *my* baby. She said to me, 'Now that I know what it's like being pregnant, there is no way I'm going through this again unless I fall in love with our baby as much as I've fallen in love with you.'"

Daniel felt a strange tugging at his heart... a yearning he couldn't even put into words as he listened to his best friend's love story.

Ryan went on, "And she wasn't even upset or anything, man. She was just stating a fact, like, 'This one is yours, and if we ever have other kids, they'll be mine, because I'll know they're worth it.' And now this."

"That's rough."

"And I feel like it's my fault, Danny. Like, if I didn't want kids, we would have taken steps not to get pregnant, and she would never have fallen in love with the baby, and she wouldn't be hurting so much right now. And I can't even help her. I can't take her pain away and make it better, and that's all I want to do."

"Because you're a man, Ryan, and that's what we do. I get you." Daniel rocked back in his chair.

"I mean, we did everything right, Ryan. We weren't completely innocent, you know? We had our pasts; we weren't angels before we got saved, but once we did, we put our pasts behind us. Once we became a couple, we saved ourselves till that wedding night. We did what we were supposed to do. And then when she got pregnant, we gave the baby to God and said, 'This child is Yours, Father; have Your way.' But this? This is not what we were expecting!

"And I gotta ask, man. Where are the rewards for doing it right? Where's the joy a new baby is supposed to bring? Where's the fulfillment? Where's the happiness promised to the father of many children in Psalm 127? Where's the opportunity to raise my child in the way he should go? To teach him to serve the Lord and to respect his elders? Where are the promises of new life now?"

Daniel's eyes filled with tears as he listened. He prayed for the right words to say, but nothing came to his mind. He had cried on

Ryan's shoulder when he needed to, and now Daniel allowed him to do the same.

"I've prayed so much these last days and nights, Danny. It seems that it's all I can do. I'm the high priest of the household, and I've asked the Lord to give me exactly the right words to say—the words that will uplift her spirit and take her out of the depression that I know is going to get much worse before it gets any better, but I don't think anything I'm saying is getting in through her ears, much less into her spirit."

There was a long silence.

"You know what I'm praying for, Ryan? I'm praying for peace that passes all understanding. I'm praying for God to show up in this situation and take a hold of it. I'm praying that you two will come out stronger than before. I'm praying for God to *be* God in this."

It was a long time before Ryan responded. "You know, Danny, I have a lot of questions I've been asking, but I still know certain things to be true: God is good. His plan is good. I may not see it now, but every time I've gone through something in the past, He has been able to teach me something that eventually helps me to help others. That's why I'm so into the youth ministry in the church. I've overcome so many challenges with God's help that I want to show them that they can do the same. And because He has always made a way for me in the past, I am just gonna trust Him to make a way for me and Jazz this time, too. I'm just gonna give the whole thing to Him and say, yet again, 'Lord, have Your way.' And I'm gonna trust Him while we're riding out this storm. I'm gonna hold fast to Him, and I just know He's going to get us through this."

As they ended the call, Daniel found himself envying his best friend for his enduring faith.

CHAPTER SEVENTEEN

The morning of James Lucas Phillips' memorial service dawned sunny and bright, which was the exact opposite of the way any of those who would attend the ten o'clock service was feeling.

In Aunt Ruby's household, everyone moped around, keeping to themselves and stewing in their own juices.

Aunt Ruby was glad Ryan and Jasmine would have the chance to have a service and experience some level of closure.

Hope was in two minds about even going to the service. She wanted to go to show her support for her friends, but she was afraid her burgeoning abdomen would only cause Jasmine more pain. She hadn't seen Jasmine since before the loss. It wasn't that she hadn't tried, but every time she called and spoke to Ryan, Aunt Ruby or Jasmine's mother, she'd been told that Jasmine wasn't up to having visitors. She understood. She probably wouldn't want to have visitors, either, especially a pregnant woman.

On top of that, she didn't necessarily want to be confronted with the mortality of the unborn child she was finally beginning to accept and love, either.

Still, Aunt Ruby had encouraged her to go to the service. She had agreed, but was determined to stay out of the way and away from Jasmine if at all possible.

ॲ

Daniel was trying not to get sucked into an abyss of bitter and sometimes overwhelming memories. The child Victoria was carrying may not have been his, but he hadn't found out until that last morning, so he had truly suffered when both Victoria and her son had died so suddenly.

As he got ready for James Lucas' memorial service, he couldn't help but remember getting ready to lay his wife and her baby to rest.

ॐ

Everyone rallied around him during the difficult time. His own mother was still alive, and she mourned the loss of her daughter-in-law and the grandchild she was anticipating getting to know. Aunt Ruby, too, was devastated.

They hadn't been particularly enamored with Victoria, but they had tried to embrace her because of her status in Daniel's life, and they were all looking forward to his first child.

All of Daniel and Victoria's friends, family and associates turned out to mourn with him and offer their support.

If anyone had wondered why he'd seemed so detached and aloof during the service, no one said a word to him. After all, the man had just lost his young wife and their unborn child. No one really expected him to participate in the service. And if he had disappeared from the repast that was being held in a building on the same premises as the cemetery, well, that was probably his way of dealing with the grief.

Only his mother and aunt knew that he had gone for a drive with Ryan. Only Ryan had known the truth at that time, and only he could understand that Professor Hargreaves' presence during the service had been bad enough, but his decision to turn up at the repast with his wife caused something to shift inside of Daniel. Where he had been overwhelmed with grief before, now he was seething with anger at the nerve of the other man who knew what had triggered off the chain of events that had led to Victoria's death in the first place.

Daniel, with Ryan by his side, had been receiving guests when Professor Hargreaves came into the room. His eyes turned to ice and his face to stone, drawing Ryan's attention. Daniel's hands curled into tight fists and his breath quickened. Thankfully, Ryan quickly grabbed Daniel by the elbow and pulled him away without attracting anyone's attention.

Ryan took Daniel far away from the cemetery. They drove for miles and miles without saying a word. On a deserted section of a St. Augustine beach, Ryan stood aside and watched as Daniel walked out to the edge of the water and stood staring out at the choppy ocean. He loosened his tie and, his shoulders drooping, he began to shake as he wept in a way he'd never wept before.

Daniel wept for the loss of a child he'd been looking forward to. He wept for the loss of the woman he'd expected to spend the rest of his life with. He'd cried for them several times since that terrible knock on the door, but this was different. These tears were cathartic. This time, he was weeping for the loss of his innocence and naiveté regarding human beings and their flawed nature. He was weeping for the loss of his trust in much of humanity. He was weeping for the loss of his blind faith in a God who was allowing him to experience such a tremendous loss, one that was even more than the double blow others saw. He knelt on the shore and cried his heart out, and when he was done, he was a changed man.

CЗ

As Daniel looked in the mirror to check the knot in his tie, he shook his head in an effort to bring himself back to the present. Now was not the time to drown in his bitter memories. Now was the time to be a tower of strength to Ryan, who had done no less for him when he had needed it. He squared his shoulders and looked himself in the eye before donning his jacket and heading to the door of his bedroom at Aunt Ruby's house.

As he opened the door, he came face to face with Hope, who was at the top of the stairs, about to descend. They had shared an almost silent breakfast that morning, each absorbed in thoughts about the beautiful baby boy who was about to be honored—thoughts that no one wanted to discuss at the breakfast table. They had hardly noticed one another as they moved their eggs around on their plates and stared into their mugs.

Daniel stopped short when he saw her. She was gorgeous, her long legs encased in black pants and her slightly rounded tummy difficult not to notice in the bright orange top with its lacy cap sleeves and V neck. She had complied with Jasmine and Ryan's request for their family and friends to wear bright, cheery colors. Her makeup was limited to a tinted lip gloss and mascara. She had somehow tamed her naturally wild curls and swept them away from her face, bringing attention to her rosy cheeks. He stared at her hair and briefly wondered if the curls would be as soft to his touch as they appeared.

He snapped his mind back to attention. *What am I thinking?* Again, he wondered what it was about *this* woman, under *these* circumstances, that had awakened his hormones again. He could not deny that he was physically attracted to her. He couldn't understand it, had been avoiding even thinking about it. Of all the women he came into contact with on a daily basis, he was drawn to a pregnant woman. Would wonders never cease?

He had to physically restrain himself from reaching out to her on the landing. As he pulled his eyes away from the rest of her and finally made eye contact, he noticed a slight raising of her eyebrows, as if she had noticed his appraisal of her and was amused and perhaps slightly confused. Beyond that, he could see that her eyes were red and slightly swollen, as if she had been crying earlier. He cleared his throat and used his hand to indicate that she should allow him to precede her down the stairs. It *was* the gentlemanly thing to do, after all.

ᘓ

Hope had to admit to herself that she felt undeniably drawn to Daniel. He was quite handsome in his dark blue blazer, crisp white shirt and khaki pants, and she fought the instinctive desire to compliment him. For a fleeting moment, she wondered what it would be like to walk into the church on the arm of this appealing gentleman. She imagined she might stride a little more confidently, smile a little more, and maybe even feel a little bit like the luckiest woman in the world. She swallowed the attraction she was beginning to feel, quieted the questions she was beginning to ask herself, and gave him a weak smile. She would have to have a strongly worded talk with herself later about the direction her mind had started taking.

She followed him down the stairs, and they both accompanied Aunt Ruby, whose bright yellow suit belied the somber mood she was in, to Daniel's SUV.

CR

The service was understandably brief, but it was filled with scripture. In front of the pulpit was a large floral arrangement featuring bright yellow lilies and roses. Beside it stood a large photo frame bearing a photograph of Ryan kissing Jasmine's baby bump as she giggled and caressed his head. It was a candid shot, taken a few weeks earlier by Daniel's camera phone, but it had captured more than words could say. James Lucas had been loved and wanted, and he would never be forgotten.

The order of service cards were classic and elegant, made of baby blue cardstock paper on which various Bible references were printed in embossed navy ink. A silver butterfly perched on a silver flower to the right of James Lucas' name. On the back, close to the bottom of the card, was a lovely thank you note from Ryan and Jasmine.

Jasmine stared at the cards and wondered whose idea they had been. She knew that her husband had asked her lots of questions about what she wanted the service to be like, but she couldn't remember if she had ever given him an answer. Either way, the cards were a beautiful keepsake. Perhaps one day she would be strong enough to read all the words. Several people rose to speak during the service, but Jasmine didn't hear much. She remained composed, sitting stoically between her husband and her mother, but nothing really registered for her except for the sense of grief and loss that had overtaken her.

CR

The situation was not the same for most of the people in attendance. The sermon from Reverend Marsden was a profound one that centered on Romans 14:7-8, which he paraphrased, "For we don't live only for ourselves, and we don't die only for ourselves. If we live, we live for God, and if we die, we die for God. Therefore, whether we live or die, we are God's."

The minister shared his belief that each person is created to do the sovereign will of God and that free will sometimes interrupts God's will. In the case of James Lucas, he explained, he had prayed for answers about the loss, and his answer had always come in the form of that scripture. He was convinced that James Lucas, whose sojourn on earth had been so brief and of such a private nature, had lived for the Lord and that even in his death, he had died for the Lord. In other words, he elaborated, James Lucas' purpose could be fulfilled despite—and perhaps even *because of*—his death.

Hardly anyone who heard the minister's words remained unmoved, but Jasmine, though she sat right in front of Reverend Marsden, didn't really hear any of them. The truth was, she wasn't ready to hear them.

໐ჳ

At the end of the service, there was a brief repast in the church's fellowship hall, and Ryan and Hyacinth greeted everyone. Jasmine sat with Aunt Ruby to one side. From her position across the room, Hope could see her friend greeting those who came with kind words, but her smile never really reached her eyes.

Hope had helped Sister Claire to serve the light refreshments that had been prepared, but outside of that, she had remained in the background as much as she could. She was happy that her friend seemed to be holding up so well, and she really wanted to go over and give her a hug, but not wanting to rock any proverbial boats, she remained content just sitting close to the exit and watching from a distance.

She had been aware of Daniel throughout the service and the reception afterwards, but she had lost track of him and Ryan and was surprised when he suddenly appeared close to her with two cups of punch. "Hey," he greeted her.

She jumped. "Hi!"

"Sorry to frighten you."

"That's okay. I guess I kind of drifted off."

"Where, exactly?" Daniel handed her a cup, which she accepted with a weak smile, and pulled up a chair.

"To the same place I usually go. I wonder where I'm from, who I am and if anyone is out there looking for me... for us."

"Hmm," Daniel sipped his punch.

"It would be nice if I could have that all figured out before the baby comes," she sighed.

"I'm sure."

"I was also thinking about Jasmine."

"That's hard *not* to do, on a day like this."

"I simply cannot imagine what she's going through. I mean, it's got to be the roughest thing she's ever experienced."

"To say the least," Daniel took another sip. His own mind seemed far away.

"And I have to ask, can she ever get over this? Does anyone ever fully recover from such a loss?"

"Some people do."

"I guess I've heard that before, but until and unless we've done it ourselves, we can never know for sure, can we? I mean, people might *say* they've recovered, but have they? I just don't know."

Daniel shifted uncomfortably in his chair. "I'd say people do recover. They may never 'get over it,' as you put it, but they do learn to live with loss."

"But only someone who has survived such a deep loss can really say that, you know? And you're just guessing." Hope's mind was full of concern for Jasmine.

"Am I?" came Daniel's cryptic response, and then he stood abruptly and walked away without saying another word. Hope was at a loss as to what had just happened. All she knew was that this was the second time she had inadvertently said something that had resulted in an abrupt end to a conversation with Daniel that had seemed to be going okay, at least to her. She pinched the bridge of her nose and shook her head in disbelief. Without intending to, she had managed to offend Daniel twice in the last two weeks. Her life was a mess and now she was disrupting everyone else's.

CHAPTER EIGHTEEN

Jasmine had regressed to her childhood habit of chewing on the back of pens. As she sat in her darkened bedroom with the flashlight app on her cell phone shedding light on the blank page of her journal, she made a meal of the pen before beginning to write.

May 7

These past few days have pretty much passed in a blur. I've been in my bedroom, mostly, curtains drawn, lights dim. Darkness outside, darkness inside.

James Lucas' service was today. I don't remember much about it. I was there in body, not so much in soul. My spirit, mind and emotions were mostly absent. I didn't break down, though I'd certainly expected to. It was more than surreal.

Only a handful of people came to the service, but only a handful of people knew we were expecting. It was the first time I've seen Hope since the loss. I didn't talk to her, but I didn't talk to anyone, really. I remember smiling at some people and saying some words, but I didn't really <u>communicate</u> with anyone.

Robert Marsden did the sermon, and Sister Claire led the service. She sang a beautiful solo, but I don't remember the song.

I looked at her and remembered how she laid hands on my tummy and told me this baby was going to reach people for the Lord without having to say a word. Where's that prophecy now? So many hopes and dreams died with him. Did God's Word die with him, too? Doesn't the Bible say that God's Word doesn't ever go back to Him void? How could my son be an exception? Or was it that what she had said had come from her and not from God? I guess I'll never know for sure.

And yet, as time passes (when it passes, because sometimes I feel like life is at a standstill), there are times when I feel like I will climb out of this pit one day, maybe even soon, but most of the time I just want to lie here in this dark room, and sleep my grief away. I haven't seen a doctor; I haven't been taking any medication, but I think there are moments when I understand why people become anti-depressant junkies. I'd give anything not to feel this way all the time.

J.

ଓ

The night after the memorial service found Jasmine shaking with rage as she sat on the bathroom floor. She struggled to find the words that would capture how upset she was in that very moment.

May 8

I have never been this ANGRY in my LIFE. The NERVE of that man! I swear he must be out of his mind. Asking me out to dinner? On a DATE? The day after we buried our son? What must he be THINKING? Maybe he doesn't think AT ALL. I'm so mad I can't even see straight. Men are just such INSENSITIVE JER—

May 8

LOL. I just read my entry from a couple of hours ago. I was so mad. I totally misinterpreted what that sweet man was trying to do. He came into the bathroom while I was writing and sat down on the floor beside me with his Bible in his hand. I was thinking, "Really? Your Bible?" but I was so mad I couldn't even say anything.

He sat there and he told me the story of David and Bathsheba, but not the part about him seeing her bathing and getting her pregnant and all that. Instead, he told me about their first child together. The baby was born weak and sickly, and the whole time that he was sick, David fasted and prayed for his healing. But he died anyway. And instead of wallowing in grief, David got up and washed his face and went to the table to eat, much to everyone's amazement.

At first, I was like, "How insensitive can this man get?" But then Ryan explained that going out to dinner just a day after burying James Lucas wouldn't have been a way of forgetting about him. It was just his way of trying to change the scenery and get me out of the house. When I calmed down a little, I could see his point. He was trying to help me feel better.

As if that wasn't enough, he said that living a fulfilling life—instead of a mournful one—would honor James Lucas. He even suggested doing things to memorialize him, like planting a tree or donating a scholarship in his name. What great ideas!

But he didn't stop there.

He went on to talk to me about the Shepherd's Psalm, and he focused on the fourth verse, where it says, "Yea, though I walk through the valley of the shadow of death...." And he said something that only a man involved in the construction trade could conceptualize. He said to me, "Jazz, the Word says we should walk through *the valley. Don't put up a tent there. Don't start drawing a plan. Don't put down a foundation and build a permanent structure there. Baby, we have to walk* through *it. If we don't, we'll never get to the other side."*

I guess I didn't respond too well, and I let him leave the bathroom before I really thought about what he had said.

It hit me like a ton of bricks.

I was all ready to take up residence in the valley of the shadow of James Lucas' death. Now I know that is not what God—or James Lucas—would want for me. He was here for such a short time, but he was no accident, and it's up to me and everyone else who loved him to make his time here count for something.

So right now, I'm more hopeful than I've been for a while. I'm still sad. I still miss my boy. I miss his kicks and his twists and turns. I grieve over the son I expected to have, but I also know that with God's help, Ryan and I will be able to leave this dark valley some day. Maybe even soon.

J.

May 11

Mother's Day ... I was thinking about going to church today, but now I'm not so sure....

J.

CƷ

The Sunday after the service—Mother's Day—Daniel, who had sequestered himself in the office all weekend since returning on Friday, emerged to take Aunt Ruby to church. Hope was ready to go, too.

The memorial service had had a profound impact on her. Whereas she had found all of the scriptures enlightening and thought-provoking, she was particularly convicted by Romans 14:7-8.

She had been living with Aunt Ruby long enough, and had had enough candid conversations with her to believe without a shadow of a doubt that God existed and that He had sent His son to die for the sins of the world; however, she had not felt any kind of urge to claim Jesus as her own personal savior and Lord the way Aunt Ruby, Jasmine and Ryan so clearly had. Still, she was interested in learning about Jesus and His impact on the world, and she expected that a day would eventually come—maybe even soon—when she would want to become a Christian. She just didn't feel a yearning to do so just yet.

Even so, the scripture had connected with something deep on the inside of her. She wondered if it would be acceptable, or even advisable for her to dedicate her child to the Lord under her present circumstances. After all, the child had been created by the Lord and was the Lord's. Still, she didn't know if she could willingly and wholeheartedly commit the baby to God and say, "Have Your sovereign way with him or her." Isn't that what Jasmine and Ryan had done? Look where that had gotten them.

She was so confused, and she felt like the best thing to do was to meditate on God's Word. With so much to think about, she was happy for the opportunity to go to church and hear what the preacher had to say.

It had only been a few days since James Lucas' memorial service, and on top of that, it was Mother's Day, so Hope was surprised to see Jasmine in attendance at the church service that day. Not only was she there, but she was on the stage singing during the praise and worship session! Hope was confused. Aunt Ruby, on the other hand, was obviously delighted. Hope noticed that when Aunt Ruby and Jasmine made eye contact, they both waved happily. Jasmine also smiled and waved at Hope, which gave Hope a warm feeling inside. She was beyond relieved. It seemed her friend was back.

Hope found it hard to keep her eyes and mind off Jasmine and on the actual praise and worship session. Jasmine seemed transformed. She raised her arms and looked towards the heavens while singing, giving the impression that, as far as she was concerned, there was no one there but her and God. Hope found it hard to reconcile this person with the one who had seemed so far away during the service days earlier.

Jasmine was Hope's entire sermon that day. Hope didn't spend a lot of time focused on what the minister said after the praise and worship period was over. Jasmine had joined Ryan in the pew to the front and right-hand side of the sanctuary, and Hope could no longer see her clearly, but she could hardly focus her mind anywhere else. What had caused such a remarkable turnaround in such a short period of time? How could such abject sorrow have been changed into such profound joy? She needed to know. Whatever it was, she wouldn't mind having a little bit of it for herself.

❦

As had been the case only days earlier, Jasmine may have been in the church sanctuary physically, but she felt like her spirit was in another realm. She felt as if she needed to release her praise or it would cause her to explode. The curious thing was that God was being very silent that day. She could usually tell when He was soaking up the praises during praise and worship. She would feel chills. Her body would be filled with goose bumps, and her scalp would literally tingle. Nothing like that was going on. She couldn't even tell whether or not He was listening, but that didn't matter to her. No. Her spirit had been dormant for a long time, and it was crying out for the opportunity to worship the Lord for who He was and praise Him for all He'd done.

Of course, there were times when she was forced to question *all He'd done*, but He had already been so good to her; He had already done so much for her; He had already blessed her in so many ways, that even when she couldn't see what He was doing or why He was allowing certain things to happen... even when He was more silent than He'd ever been, deep down inside, her spirit already knew that He was a good God who was good all the time, regardless of the prevailing circumstances.

Although she was heartbroken, her spirit—now that she had allowed it to re-surface from that dark place she had been hiding it for so many days—could still praise God because He was always worthy to be praised.

She knew from her own experiences and those of others that God's thoughts and ways were higher than her own. She understood now that she needed to live out the praise and worship she had been giving to the Lord for years. She had been singing about His goodness and His grace when they were evident, but now she knew she needed to continue to praise and worship Him even when He was withdrawn from her. After all, didn't the Word of God say that if she kept quiet the very stones would cry out in praise?

She had come to the revelation that there comes a time when one has to put one's emotions aside and rely on the things that one knows *for sure*. Her *feelings* told her God was punishing her for her early ambivalence towards the pregnancy, but her mind *knew* that God was a loving God who wanted to bless her. She didn't know if He had orchestrated the pregnancy loss or if He had allowed it, but either way, she could not deny His goodness for another day.

Nor could she deny how alone she felt. Every day, she battled feelings of guilt over her initial resistance to being pregnant, her refusal to take prenatal vitamins, her hesitancy in telling anyone— even her own mother—that she was pregnant, for fear that they would accuse her of having already been pregnant when she and Ryan had married. She questioned every cup of coffee, every rare sip of soda, every painkiller consumed before she'd even learned of the pregnancy. Every meal she had missed afterwards and every time she and her new husband had been intimate had become suspect. Every day she asked herself, *Am I to blame? Was it my fault? Was there something I did? Something I didn't do? Something I could have done differently?* And every day the answer was the same: silence.

So she had changed her strategy and had started to question God, "Did You do this, Lord? Why did You allow this to happen to us? We are Your children! We thought we were the very apple of Your eye? Why did You allow me to become pregnant if You knew the baby wouldn't survive? What will become of the prophecy that he would change lives for You without having to say a word? Are You listening, Lord? Do you even care? DO YOU EVEN CARE?"

And every day she would listen for His answer, and every day she heard nothing at all. Until one night when her husband joined her on the bathroom floor and poured out words of wisdom that could only have come from the Holy Spirit Himself. His words had so moved her that she had decided to rejoin the church's praise and worship team for their usual energetic session that Sunday. Afterwards, she figured she would remain in a virtual cocoon for the remainder of the service. She sat beside her gentle giant with her eyes closed and gently rocked from side to side as she gripped his huge hand. Through her reverie, she heard something flutter to the ground. She bent to retrieve it, and saw that it was the Order of Service card from the memorial service. All she had been able to do during the service was take note of the way it looked.

As the service continued around her and mothers were celebrated and made to feel special, Jasmine read every single scripture mentioned. She didn't remember hearing any of it on the actual day, but whoever had put the program together had thoughtfully included them for future reference. Reading them gave her something to do other than focus on the fact that she had thought she would have been celebrating her first Mother's Day in a totally different way.

She sat there repeating each of the scriptures—Psalm 61, Psalm 139, Jeremiah 1:5 and Romans 14:7-8—to herself and meditating on them. She knew it wouldn't be enough for her to read them and think about them; she would also have to say them out loud. She had always interpreted Romans 10:17—a reminder that faith comes by hearing the Word of God—to mean that one's spirit needed to actually *hear* the Word of God in order to really have it sink in. She almost couldn't wait to go home to start speaking them into her spirit.

But what really resonated in her spirit was a poem printed on the blue card. She didn't know who had written the poem or whose idea it was to include it, but the author had clearly lived through exactly what she was going through:

"Butterfly"
In honor of our beloved son

Deep down inside me,
The seed of life new;
Nestled 'neath my heartbeat,
Created by love true.

Awaited, prayed for;
Beloved from the start;
Anticipated, blessed,
Owner of a family's heart.

But there came a sad time
He was hid from our sight,
Wrapped within a cocoon,
Protected from all light.

And we mourned the loss,
We so missed him,
His promise, our plans —
All was grim.

We searched for love,
Couldn't find it,
As in his stark absence
Each of our hearts was split.

And then he emerged, triumphant,
In the midst of our despair,
And showed glimpses of God's glory,

And erased our every fear.

For once wrapped up, once hidden,
Now he soars free, so high —
Beautiful, magnificent!
Our airborne butterfly.

She struggled not to burst into tears as she read the first few stanzas of the poem, each a true reflection of her feelings, but when she got to the last two, she read them over and over and over again because, as she acknowledged, she just wasn't 'there'—at that place of hope from which the author had written—just yet.

As she meditated on the words, she turned them this way and that inside her mind. She read them forward and backward and forward again, deconstructing each word to get at the real meaning beneath it.

There in the sanctuary, she found herself with her eyes closed, envisioning a butterfly breaking free of its cocoon. In her mind's eye, the large butterfly that emerged was various shades of blue with a silvery hue to its wings. She imagined James Lucas' laughing spirit, wrapped inside the butterfly's body, circling the sanctuary a few times before alighting on her nose and giving her a little tickle. In her vision, it then flew out through the window to join dozens of other colorful butterflies among the flowers outside As Jasmine pictured the beautiful fleet fluttering across the pale blue sky, a single tear trickled down each cheek. "Take flight, James Lucas. Mommy will always, *always* love you."

When she opened her eyes, she finally began to feel as if someday—maybe not today or tomorrow or even next month—the time might come when she would feel genuine joy in her life again. For the past few days, she had been wondering if any good could ever come of such a profound loss, and now she was finally feeling something akin to peace blooming inside her chest. It was an assurance that God was there, in that place, in that situation, walking with her and Ryan and all the others. She prayed that the feeling of peace would remain and even increase in the days and years to come, and she decided to do what she could to dig herself out of the hole of depression in which she had found herself.

CHAPTER NINETEEN

It had been a long time since Daniel had gone for a bike ride. He used the stationary bike in his town house, but it wasn't the same as this—the wheels of his old bicycle in contact with the concrete, the afternoon sun beating down on his bare back and sweat running down his chest. Instead of cold walls, he was surrounded by life and movement.

As he pedaled he liked to let his mind wander in any direction it chose. These days, his mind had developed the most disturbing habit of choosing to wander towards Hope. Daniel was more than a little annoyed with himself. Even though he hadn't said much to her since the memorial service, he just couldn't get her out of his mind. Usually, as soon as her face popped into his head, he would banish it to the farthest recesses of his mind. Usually, it would pop right back up again. It was terribly infuriating.

There was so much that made him uncomfortable with the fact that he was attracted to someone after all these years. He actually hadn't minded that his so-called love life had given up the ghost eight years earlier. He hardly remembered what it was like to date. It had been so long. He had gone out a couple of times in the first few years, but then he had given up. He just wasn't interested in that life.

Now that he looked back, he knew he could do without the uncertainty—the *anxiety* of putting himself out there—getting his hopes up, only to have them dashed by the other person's indecisiveness or lack of interest. He had never liked the almost inevitable façade everyone constructed for the first few dates—and he had been no exception during his dating days. He despised the pressure he had always felt to put his best foot forward and impress his date, only to have her disappointed when she learned that he was more comfortable in jeans and sneakers eating burgers than in three-piece suits nibbling on pretentious hors-d'oeuvres, or the first time his unbelievable stubbornness reared its head. He was a homebody who enjoyed the occasional movie or trip to the amusement park. For years, he just couldn't be bothered.

And now this woman—this *pregnant amnesiac*, of all people—had upset everything.

She exasperated him. She had an inquisitive mind, which was perhaps the most attractive thing about her, but that same mind had forgotten who she was and her marital or relationship status. She had a great figure, but it was growing with pregnancy. She had a generous spirit, but she didn't know God. She should have been the last woman on Earth to resurrect those kinds of feelings in a widower with his history. Yet there she was.

He needed to get her out of his thoughts. Today.

He rode about three miles in one direction before turning around and heading back to the Victorian. As he neared his aunt's house, he saw that Ryan was just turning into his driveway. Panting, he waited by the drive as the muddy truck rolled to a stop. Ryan stepped out and the two greeted each other.

"Hey," Daniel's breath came in short spurts; he'd over-exerted himself a bit, "how's it going?" It had been a couple of days since they'd spoken.

"Good, all things considered," Ryan reached into the passenger seat and pulled out an armful of blueprints.

"How's Jazz?" Daniel stepped off the bike, lowered the stand and started doing some stretching exercises as he spoke. He knew he'd never forgive himself if he woke up with super sore muscles the next day.

"You know, she's doing much better than I'd expected. She's gone to church for a meeting with the praise and worship team." Ryan reached in with the other arm and pulled out more plans.

"So you're a free man for... how many hours?" Daniel grinned.

"A few. Got something on your mind?" Back into the cab the blueprints went.

"Why don't we go shoot some pool at that place near the library?"

"Isn't it a bit early for pool?"

"Naw, man. They open for lunch. And this way we get to shoot a few rounds and leave before the happy hour crowd gets there and starts getting loud."

"No problem. My car or yours?"

Daniel looked pointedly at the dozens of plans on the front seat of Ryan's truck, and Ryan immediately withdrew the suggestion, "I take that back. I'll walk over with you and wait while you take a quick shower. You *are* going to shower?" At his friend's grin, Ryan continued, "I can chat with Aunt Ruby while I wait."

"I don't think she's awake at this hour, and Hope is more than likely gone for a walk or something. I didn't see either of them when I got in from Lake Butler an hour and a half ago."

Ryan leaned against the truck as Daniel finished his warm-down exercises. "How's that working out? You still skeptical about Hope? Still think she's trying to scam Aunt Ruby?"

"No, not really." Daniel did his last few stretches before taking some sips from his water bottle.

"I find that hard to believe. A stranger—a pregnant one who claims she has no idea who she is or where she's from, at that—is living alone with your aunt, and you—Mr. I-Trust-Nobody—are *okay* with that?" Daniel knew it would be a long time before his best friend forgot how suspicious he had been about Jasmine when they'd just started dating. It was a good thing that, knowing what they both did, Ryan didn't hold it against him.

"I don't know about being *okay* with it," Daniel kicked the bike stand away and began pushing the cycle towards the opening in the low hedge between the two yards, "but let's just say she passed my little test."

Ryan came to a stop close to him so they were both standing on either side of the bicycle just inside Ryan and Jasmine's yard.

Daniel quickly told his friend about hiding the cameras in his office and enticing Hope there to look at books, ending with, "She had no idea the cameras were there, but all she did was check out my bookshelf and choose books."

"You. Did. *What*?" Hope's anger was controlled, but Daniel could see that there was rage bubbling just below the surface. She had happened to step outside of the open garage door a few feet on the other side of the fence. Inside the garage, she had been perfectly placed to hear every word Daniel had said.

"Excuse me?" Daniel raised his eyebrows.

"You did *what*?" Her pitch had become higher, her voice slightly raised. She was wearing an old straw hat and was carrying a trowel and a small plant of some kind in her gloved hands.

Daniel pushed the bicycle through the opening and strode past her, intending to put it back in its place on the garage wall. Ryan stayed where he was in his own yard.

"Don't you walk away from me!" Her voice was becoming fairly loud now.

"What right do you have to ask me anything?" Daniel wanted to know, "Anything you may or may not have heard was a private conversation between two friends. You were eavesdropping."

"I certainly was *not* eavesdropping, *Professor*." She raised her hands to show the garden implements and potted plant. "I was gathering gardening supplies in the garage. In fact, I've been out here for a while, and I just went inside," she indicated a hole in the ground close to the hedge. "If you had waited another minute to have your very public 'private conversation,' you would have seen me coming out. Anything I heard was said out in the open. And don't believe you can sidestep the issue. You secretly recorded me!"

"So what if I did? I was within my rights to use security cameras in my own office in my home."

"Security cameras? Where else are there security cameras? Do you have some in the Lilac Room of *your home*—the room where I undress? Or perhaps in the hallway bathroom of *your home*, where I take a bath? Are there bugs on my cell phone and the phones in *your home*? Yet you have the audacity to accuse me of doing something wrong by what you define as eavesdropping? What moral authority do you have to accuse me of anything?" She dropped the plant and placed a gloved hand on her hip. "*How dare you?*"

"Pardon me?" If Daniel weren't so upset, he might burst out laughing at the self-righteous indignation in her tone—she who had just been caught eavesdropping on a private conversation.

"I said, 'How *dare* you?' I don't know who you think you are, Professor Donahue, but I am a human being and as such I have rights, one of which is the right to privacy."

"For someone with no memory, you seem very aware of your so-called rights. How does that work, exactly?"

"Because, Professor, as your undercover surveillance would have proven, *I read!* Do you think I haven't spent hours researching my situation, trying to figure out what to do and where to go from here? Do you think I'm just sitting back, enjoying my life and waiting to see what will happen? No! I've been trying to figure out how everything works!" Her voice had taken on a shrill effect. Daniel noticed Aunt Ruby's head appear in the kitchen window overlooking the driveway and yard, a quizzical expression on her face.

"I suggest you lower your voice," Daniel said.

"And why would I take *suggestions* from you? You act like you're all high and mighty, looking down your nose at me and putting me down with your snide and inflammatory remarks. You look at me like I'm the scum of the earth because I'm carrying a child and I don't know who or where the father is. You figure if we were married or in some kind of long-term relationship, he would be searching for me, but since he's not, then with or without amnesia, I must not even know who he is.

"You spend so much time judging me and evaluating every word I say, trying to catch me in some kind of lie. I guess I should be grateful that you recorded me without my knowledge. At least it means you finally know for sure that I'm not some kind of criminal trying to steal anything from anyone. You walk around here like you're better than me because you know exactly who you are and where you're from and I don't. I may not know my background, but I know where I am today. And at least I appreciate the people I know. I listen. I pay attention. Can you say the same for yourself? You act like my being here is a bother, but I add value. I contribute something. I *mean* something. Which is more than I can say for you!

"Did you know your aunt is concerned that she's not healing quickly enough? Did you even notice that the cast should have come off a while ago, but she's still wearing it? Did you know she's been to the doctor, and he's not satisfied with her progress even though they can't figure out why the healing isn't happening as expected? Did you know she's been having heart palpitations and shortness of breath? Did you know she's worried sick that you're not taking care of yourself when you're working, that you spend so much time writing that you probably don't even eat? Did you know she prays for you more than she prays for herself? Do you even *care*?

"What can you say for yourself?" She didn't allow him to answer before she moved on, "You're nothing but a lonely man with no one to love you but Aunt Ruby."

She moved to stand directly in front of Daniel, who had parked the bicycle on the driveway, and stood with both arms on her hips. If she knew that she was only drawing attention to her pleasing figure, expanding waistline and all, she would have dropped her arms immediately. Although distracted by the fire in her eyes and the rapid rise and fall of her full chest, Daniel succeeded in bringing his attention back to her words. By letting her say all she had on her mind, he figured he was giving her all the proverbial rope she needed to hang herself, as his mother used to say. Besides, he really hadn't known any of those things she was saying about his aunt.

"Your life revolves around who you are in the world of academics and the work you do, to the point that you can't understand how someone like me—who simply cannot be defined by material things and professional accomplishments—can even get up and face the day. No wonder you have no one but your aunt; you're nothing but a self-righteous voyeur who gets his kicks watching secret videos of unsuspecting women!"

Daniel had to try hard not to focus on how attractive Hope was even though she was upset. She was almost glowing, and with her lips slightly parted like that, he had to stop himself from planting a kiss on her mouth and shutting her up... for a while.... And she had no idea how wrong she was about most of the things she had been saying thus far. He shook his head slightly to bring his thoughts back to the matter at hand. "You know absolutely nothing about me or my life. You know even less about what is or is not important to me. It sounds to me like you're projecting your own insecurities about your background and about the father of your unborn child and where he's been all this time onto me. You're doing an excellent job of putting words in my mouth. As if I have the time or interest to put so much thought into your situation," he lied. "After all, according to you, I spend all my time with my nose buried in a laptop, no? You know, if you have questions about me or any aspect of my *private* life, you should ask, instead of indulging in what you're actually doing—speculating, at best, and, at worst, making things up in some desperate, misguided attempt to divert attention to yourself."

"Daniel! Hope!" Neither of them had noticed Aunt Ruby coming through the garage door on her crutches. "What in blazes is going on out here?!" It was as close as she had ever come to swearing.

"Ask him!" Hope shouted at the same time Daniel yelled, "Ask her!"

"You two are acting like children, and I will not have it. Daniel, although this is as much as your home as it is mine, Hope is my guest. You will *not* speak to her in such a manner. She is a young lady and a mother-to-be, and as long as she lives here, you will treat her with the respect that is due to her, regardless of the circumstances by which she came to be here." Ryan, who had been watching from his yard, moved to stand close to Aunt Ruby but said nothing.

Before either Daniel or Hope could react, she turned towards Hope and continued, "And as for you, Hope, there can be no doubt that Daniel was wrong when he tried to set you up—" she looked at Daniel, "—which you did." She turned back toward Hope, "Regardless, he is my nephew and any reasonable human being would understand his concern."

As Hope opened her mouth to comment, Aunt Ruby spoke again, effectively cutting her off, "In spite of the circumstances, as long as you, Hope, are living under my roof, I will expect both of you to treat one another with mutual respect. And that is all I have to say on this matter." She turned with more agility than one might expect for a seventy-three-year-old on crutches, but then turned again and said, "Now apologize to each other."

"Excuse me?!" They chorused.

"You heard me. Apologize." Everyone got the impression that if it weren't for the crutches she would have folded her arms, just as Daniel and Hope had done.

They both glared at each other, each determined to remain silent.

"I'm old. I have only a few good years left in me. Don't force me to waste them waiting on you *grown adults* to say I'm sorry to each other." The words were barely out of her mouth before she started to slump forward. Ryan was just in time to catch her before she fell to the ground.

He gently laid her on the grass and checked her vital signs before looking up at Daniel, "Call 9-1-1!"

ଔ

The doctor at the Alistair Bay Medical Center was quick to examine Aunt Ruby and explain that she appeared to have simply blacked out. Several scans showed that her blood pressure, though slightly elevated, was not in the danger zone, and she had had neither a stroke nor a cardiac episode. She had merely fainted due to over-exertion.

As Hope and Daniel waited for Aunt Ruby to be ready to go home, they sat quietly on opposite sides of the waiting area. Hope could not believe the things she had said to Daniel. She knew that she had vocalized much more than she should have. She had said things without thinking them through, and she had embarrassed herself and her gracious host. She knew she could—and would—apologize to Aunt Ruby, but she had no idea how she could even begin to bridge the gulf that had already existed between her and Daniel and that had now widened considerably. She didn't think she wanted to, but it was important to make Aunt Ruby happy. Besides, she needed to at least *try* to exhibit some humility, right?

ଔ

Daniel sat staring at the screen of his smartphone, but he wasn't really seeing the ebook he was pretending to read. He was only looking at the phone because it allowed him to avoid looking at Hope, who was sitting diagonally opposite to him.

Aunt Ruby's episode may have been little more than a false alarm, but it was doing a great job of reminding Daniel of how short life really was and that he needed to cherish the woman who had helped to raise him even more than he already did. He could not get the argument out of his mind, and was appalled at his behavior.

Now that he was trying to look at the situation objectively, he was ashamed. He kept his eyes off Hope as she stood and stretched before walking away to the window overlooking the parking lot below.

What had possessed him to try to set her up as he had done? What had he been thinking? He had known all along that he was wrong, but had tried to rationalize his actions by telling himself that it was necessary to do what he had done in order to keep Aunt Ruby safe. His act may or may not have been legal—he didn't even know, really, had never even thought about it—but it bordered on immoral, and he knew he would have to apologize to Hope at some point. But how?

"I hope you're happy." He was talking to himself, and it was only when he heard his voice that he realized that the words had actually come out of his mouth.

"Huh?" She half-turned so that she could look at him.

Unwilling to let her know his words had been self-directed, he said, "You wanted me to know that my aunt wasn't in the best of health. Now I know. I hope you're happy." His tone was colder than he knew it should have been, and he would argue with himself over his word choice later.

She opened her mouth to speak, and he fully expected her response to be sharp and quick, but she closed her lips again without saying anything. Instead, she turned back towards the window and put her hands into the pockets of her jeans.

When she did speak, it was to say, "Aunt Ruby is the closest thing I have to family right now. She means the world to me. Now if you'll excuse me, I'm going to get myself a cup of tea."

Her body language spoke volumes as she walked away. He had never seen her look as defeated as she did in that moment, and he was ashamed of himself. Again.

This woman had a peculiar way of getting under his skin as no one else ever had. A moment ago, he had thought about getting up and giving her the hug she seemed to desperately need, but he knew she wouldn't have been receptive. For a fleeting moment, he had felt like he was supposed to protect her, to insulate her from anything the cruel world would throw at her. Where had this sense of responsibility come from?

Then there was the attraction. Even when they had been arguing earlier, he couldn't help but notice how appealing she was. Everything she did had some kind of effect on him, and now he wondered if he was losing his rational mind. He needed to do a lot of thinking. There were some things he needed to figure out. And soon.

CHAPTER TWENTY

A few days later, Jasmine found herself with Aunt Ruby and her mother discussing something that had nothing to do with her loss. It was the first time that had happened in weeks. They were on the patio of Jasmine and Ryan's house chatting over slices of Hyacinth's famous orange cake when Hyacinth saw Hope through the kitchen window of the house next door. She seemed to be wiping the countertops.

"Aunt Ruby, how are things working out with Hope these days?" Jasmine was so in-tune to her mother's voice that even after so many years away from her island home, she didn't even hear the Jamaican accent with which Hyacinth spoke.

Aunt Ruby smiled. "Well, things were a bit awkward after I came back from the medical center, but she apologized for her role in what happened, and we're okay. Things are working out pretty well. I can admit to you—but never to my nephew—that I hadn't exactly thought everything through when I invited her to come and stay with me, but I'm pleased. She's respectful and generous and very intelligent. She has a way of knowing what I need before I do, and she never seems to be put out if I need her help to do anything at all. I wonder if she might be a nurse or caregiver.

"Besides taking care of me, she does a great job with the house, too. It's always spic and span; the laundry is always done; she cooks; she runs the dishwasher; she even irons my church clothes better than I've ever done. The only thing I have to do is wake up. I've gotten so used to having her around that I don't know what I'm going to do when she leaves."

"Which will be…?" Hyacinth took a sip of her tea.

"I'm not sure. Nobody is. A lovely young lady like her… you'd think somebody would be searching high and low for her, but she has been in constant touch with the police and nothing has changed. It's as if she appeared out of thin air. I don't know how she keeps everything together. If I were in her shoes I would have had a breakdown by now."

Jasmine piped in, her voice quiet, "The situation can't be good for the pregnancy."

Aunt Ruby covered her hand with hers and gave it a little squeeze that made Jasmine smile inside. "No, but all things considered, things are working out pretty well for her and the baby."

Hyacinth nodded in agreement. "You are so right, Aunt Ruby," she used the term although Ruby was only a few years older than she was. "She really could not have ended up in a better place. I mean, she has food, shelter, a gracious home, a stable environment. I don't know what her relationship with the Lord was like a few months ago, but He has to be real for her now. I hope she knows that."

"I think she's coming into a realization of who He is and who she is in His sight."

"Aunt Ruby, have you ever wondered if the Lord orchestrated this whole series of events so that you could usher her into His presence? Into a right relationship with Him?" Hyacinth asked.

"I do think about that sometimes, and I really do hope she comes to know Him as her savior and Lord before that child is born."

"So what are you going to do when the baby comes?" Jasmine was curious. It hadn't been that long since she had lost James Lucas, and it hurt to even think about being around Hope when she became a mother.

"I don't know. We're still a few months away. The good thing is that she's been getting a deposit on her prepaid card every two weeks, just like her social worker said, and she's hardly spent any of it at all, so she's not destitute. She even offered to pay her way while she's here, but I explained that she's saving me more money than she costs. I hate to think what I would have been paying for someone else to stay with me all this time."

"So she can afford to buy the essentials." Hyacinth looked in the direction of her daughter, and Jasmine could tell what was going to come out of her mouth. Her spirit fell, and she could feel unbidden tears coming, but before she could say anything, Aunt Ruby spoke.

"Don't even think about it, Hyacinth. I know those wheels in your mind are turning, but Jasmine will be using those things you all bought for her *own* child. I have no doubt in my mind or spirit about that. God is going to give her double for her trouble. You'll be rocking your own grandbaby in your arms before you know it."

Jasmine smiled, but she wasn't so sure. She didn't know if she could ever go through another pregnancy, always knowing that the possibility of another tragedy lay just around the corner. She struggled to change the subject. "So, Aunt Ruby, are Hope and Daniel getting along any better now?"

Aunt Ruby sighed, "Yes, perhaps a little better than I would like."

Jasmine's eyebrows shot up as if they had a life of their own. "What do you mean, Aunt Ruby?"

"Well, I don't have to tell you, Jasmine, that what I'm about to say shouldn't leave this table, but I think Daniel might be getting a little too close to her."

"Really?" Jasmine asked. "How so?"

"Maybe I'm seeing things that aren't there, but these days I find that I don't have to be refereeing as much as before. Up until a few days ago, they were having actual conversations instead of heated discussions or arguments. Before the service," she looked in Jasmine's direction and continued, "they'd talk about books she's reading or his writing, sometimes it would be something that happened in the news.... But then they had words after the memorial service, followed by the argument in the yard." She sighed. "I guess it's just the worst possible timing for some things."

Hyacinth piped in, "In what respect, Auntie?"

Aunt Ruby stared over Hyacinth's shoulder for so long that Jasmine turned to see if someone was standing there before Aunt Ruby spoke. "Well, it seems like something is reawakening in that boy—something that died a long time ago. When Victoria and the baby died, he kind of dug himself into a hole and isolated himself from the world, and now.... Well, it's like he is finally coming around. I see the way he looks at Hope, and I can understand why. She's gorgeous on the outside, but she's also respectful, generous and quite intelligent. Daniel is pretty smart—even if I *am* a little biased—but when they spar, she matches him wit for wit and thought for thought. I've seen her ask him questions about his work that disarm him, that make him think about things he never considered before. I can see the respect he has for her mind stamped across his face. She could quite possibly be the perfect woman for him."

Again, Jasmine felt her eyebrows arching. She hadn't noticed a thing, but then she hadn't been spending any time around Hope recently.

Aunt Ruby went on, "And I can see that he's struggling with his feelings, because she's pregnant. And I see him looking at her when she's not aware. He looks at her belly all the time, and with a kind of longing. It breaks my heart. He would have been such a good father, and she's so caring that I know she'll be an excellent mommy."

Jasmine swallowed hard.

"Just like you, Jasmine." Aunt Ruby continued. "You'll be great at it when the time is right."

The younger woman nodded but made an effort to redirect the conversation away from herself, "So what do you think will happen?"

"I genuinely don't know. I don't even know what to pray for, to be honest with you. As much as I would love to see Daniel fall in love again and come back to life, there's no hope in these circumstances. I can only pray that the Lord's will be done and that He will orchestrate the best possible outcome for all concerned, including Hope's family and the father of her child."

Jasmine was amazed. She had been so caught up in her grief that she had missed the development. She wondered if her husband knew, but she had promised Aunt Ruby she wouldn't say anything, and she wouldn't. It would be interesting to see how all this unfolded.

CHAPTER TWENTY-ONE

Hope was amazed that with everything that she was going through, with everything on her mind on a daily basis, she still found time to think about Daniel and the unwarranted things she had said to him. She knew the time would come when she would need to apologize, but she certainly wasn't looking forward to it. She was also trying to practice forgiveness, though Daniel had not asked for it. For now, though, any time he popped into her mind—which was often, even if she didn't want to admit it to herself, let alone anyone else—she would tamp down those thoughts and try to distract herself.

She knew there was some detail about him to which she was not privy—some important background information that perhaps explained his behavior and attitude—but she couldn't figure out what it was and she was determined never to ask.

Several days after their confrontation, Daniel was not the *last* thing on Hope's mind, but she certainly had a lot of other things to think about, a lot of things she was trying not to worry about.

It had been more than two months since she had woken up in that hospital bed, and though she kept in touch with Detective Warren and Miss LaHaye, as well as the case worker in St. Augustine, the soon-to-retire Mrs. McKay, there was still no indication that anyone anywhere in the country was looking for her. No one had contacted the hospital; no one had contacted the police, and although dozens of missing person reports matching her description had been filed, none of the photographs looked anything like her.

She had to wonder, where was her family? Where were her parents? Her siblings? The father of her child? How could she simply disappear off the face of the earth for weeks and weeks without anyone noticing she was gone? Here she was, essentially living off the kindness of strangers with no indication that she would ever go home... wherever home was.

And then there was the baby to think about. She was now more than halfway through her pregnancy and was about to have an ultrasound to make sure the baby was developing well. She could see and feel that she was gaining weight, but she wanted to make sure everything was okay. Of course, Jasmine had accompanied her to her clinic visit before, but she didn't expect her friend to do that again. Certainly, that would have been too much to ask someone dealing with a recent pregnancy loss. With Aunt Ruby still wearing the cast, she had decided to go alone.

She walked to the bus stop a block away from Aunt Ruby's and caught the bus to Main Street. After signing in at the clinic, she walked over to the shopping center close by and browsed the shelves at the bookstore. She had to literally restrain herself from purchasing dozens of books, but she chose a lovely book of daily affirmations as a gift for Aunt Ruby, and allowed the clerk to persuade her to buy herself an inexpensive tablet that could serve as an e-book reader. The clerk walked her through setting up an email address—not that she had anyone to send her a message—and showed her how to download books. He even showed her how to find a wide selection of free e-books that would guarantee her hours and hours of reading time.

She went into an accessory store and chose a large tote for herself. She only had the small black bag Miss LaHaye had chosen for her, and it wasn't large enough to fit the tablet she was sure she would be taking everywhere so she could read.

Eventually, she walked to the nearby café on the outside of the shopping center and sat at one of the tables reading a book she'd borrowed from Aunt Ruby's collection. She was drinking water poured from a ridiculously large bottle, purchased from the café, in her attempt to prepare herself for the ultrasound, which required her to drink plenty of fluids first. She was quite early for the clinic, because it was her first time taking the bus, and she hadn't known if the bus would run on schedule, so she had a lot of time to kill.

She opened George Orwell's *Animal Farm* and quickly became engrossed in the entertaining story. As she sat there giggling about the antics of the animals, she was unaware that she was being observed.

C3

Daniel had stepped out of a men's clothing store close to the exit of the shopping center just as Hope was heading outside. As soon as he'd seen her, he had stopped in his tracks, torn between ignoring her and finding out what she was doing in town by herself on a Thursday afternoon. While he tried to make up her mind, she had walked to the café, made an order, and opened her book. He knew Aunt Ruby would probably be napping, so he wasn't too concerned about her being alone at home.

Although he had made an effort to visit every weekend, he and Hope hadn't said more than a few words to each other since Aunt Ruby's fainting episode.

In the moment that he decided to pretend he hadn't seen Hope and head instead for the Victorian, he heard the musical ringtone of a cell phone. As he observed from a safe distance away, Hope answered it, a broad smile gracing her face. He was close enough to hear her side of the conversation, and he tried to justify why he was about to eavesdrop on her when he had been so vocal in his judgment when he had caught her doing the same thing.

"Hi, how are you? It's been a long time." She waited for a response. "Yes, this is a good time; perfect, actually. No, it's okay. I'm alone." She paused, "I'm doing well. And you?" She nodded as if the person could see her. "I'm so glad to hear that. I've been concerned. Where am I? I'm at the clinic." Daniel frowned as she went on, "No, I'm not busy later. I'd love to. Your house? Sure, I could stop by before I go back to Aunt Ruby's." Daniel was intrigued. Here was the evidence he'd been waiting for. This didn't sound like a woman who didn't know who she was. This didn't sound like a woman with no friends except his aunt and her neighbors. And whoever she was talking to was probably nearby. Something was definitely up. And this time, he was going to find out exactly what it was.

Without waiting for her to hang up, he moved with purpose as he went to stand behind the chair across from her. He noticed that her eyes widened when she saw him, but she didn't seem overly concerned. She continued her conversation as he sat down without waiting to be invited.

"Okay, I'll see you then. I look forward to it." She smiled again and disconnected the call, turning her attention to her 'guest.'

"Daniel, fancy meeting you here. Do have a seat," Her tone was laced with sarcasm and the smile had evaporated from her face, leaving a blank slate.

He clasped his hands together on the table in front of him. "Hot date tonight?" He got straight to the point.

She raised her eyebrows. "Somehow I didn't think you were the kind of man to *eavesdrop* on someone's *private conversation*." She took a sip of water.

"The kind of man I am is not the issue here. This is a public place. It's not like I'm holding a drinking glass to your bedroom door at night, listening while you talk on the phone."

"Or looking for potting soil in the garage, perhaps?" He knew she was baiting him, but he did not respond. Instead, he waited for her to continue, "Anyway, you'd have to listen very hard outside my door. I don't speak to anyone on the phone at night."

"Be that as it may, I distinctly heard you making a date for later."

"You heard what you wanted to hear. I don't have a 'date,' as you put it." Her tone told him she was not amused by his line of argument.

"Then that makes two lies you've told in the last five minutes."

"Indeed? What two lies would that be?" She took another sip.

"Is it that you've been telling so many you can't keep track?" he asked, without really expecting an answer. He pressed on, "I heard you tell your... date... that you're at a clinic, which you clearly are not. And you just told me you don't have a date, when I just heard you say you'd meet him at his place before heading back to my aunt's."

He could barely hide his disgust. Now that he'd actually caught her in a lie, he was a lot more disappointed than relieved. After all, as it related to his aunt, he was finally becoming comfortable having Hope around. As for himself, well, he chose to disregard the other emotion that was vying for his attention—a green-tinted emotion he didn't want to name.

She took another drink of water and sighed, "You're right, I lied."

He smiled as he leaned back in his chair and clasped his hands on the table. She was going to come clean. Finally. He tried to ignore the racing of his heart in anticipation of whatever she was about to admit to. Would she concede that this whole thing had been a set-up all along? Was she meeting with the father of her child? Was she from somewhere close to Alistair Bay? Had she and her accomplice targeted Aunt Ruby in particular? He tried not to think about how the admission to come would impact him personally. After all, he couldn't deny that although the mystery surrounding Hope was frustrating, it had also added some interest to his usually mundane life. He fought the urge to sigh.

"I'm not at the clinic, obviously, but I just came from the clinic, and I'll be heading back there in another forty-five minutes to see the doctor. I have an ultrasound today. I didn't think it was necessary to tell my—my date, was it you said?—that I'm sitting here drinking water. I lied. I confess. I'm going to burn in hell, huh?" The smug look on her face suggested that she knew exactly in which direction his thoughts had headed.

He twiddled his thumbs, waiting for her to continue.

"Maybe I should call *my date* and come clean. In fact, I think it would be a good idea if you spoke to *my date* yourself. Then you can ask all the questions you want." She slid the phone across the table to him. "If you press the green button you can dial the last number in the call log." Surprised, he took up the decidedly 'un-Smart' instrument and did as she'd instructed. Curiosity had definitely gotten the better of him. He put the phone to his ear without bothering to look at the screen. The call connected almost immediately.

"Hello?" The male voice was very familiar.

"Hello?" He frowned.

"Yeah. Hi, Daniel, how's it going?"

"Ryan?" Daniel wrinkled his brow. What was going on here? Did Hope have a date with *Ryan*? "Yeah, what's up? You around?"

"Umm… yeah." He looked at Hope, who suddenly seemed to be engrossed in her book. "Were you just talking to Hope?" Could she really have been making plans with his best friend? His very *married* best friend?

"Me? Naw, man. Must have been Jazz. She's right here. Hold on."

Daniel heard Ryan say his name and then Jasmine came on the line, "Hi, Daniel! Are you in town?" She sounded better than she had in weeks, and he could literally hear the smile in her voice.

"I'm in town."

"You are? Well, could you do me a favor? Could you swing by and check on Hope? She's over at the medical center. I think she may have taken the bus there, so she could probably use a ride home. She's going to come see me later. We haven't talked since… well, you know. I was just going to ask Ryan if we could take a drive to go pick her up. You being there would save us the trouble."

"Yeah. Okay. No problem. I can do that." He felt an apology coming on.

"Thanks, and see you later, Daniel."

"And you, Jasmine."

He looked up from the phone's screen, where he could now see that the last call that had come in had been from Ryan and Jasmine's home phone. In fact, there were only a few numbers in the call log that was showing on the screen. It appeared Hope only spoke with his aunt, their neighbors, and three people listed as Det. Warren, Mrs. McKay and Miss LaHaye. There were also a couple of calls to the Alistair Bay Medical Center.

He was too embarrassed to say anything for a while and was glad Hope was making quite the production of pretending to read. He wondered if he could force the words he needed to say out of his mouth. He took the coward's way out, "So, *Animal Farm*, huh?" He placed the phone in front of her.

Hope placed her forefinger between the pages to mark her spot and looked into Daniel's eyes. Her face was devoid of expression and he couldn't anticipate what she was about to say.

"Daniel, do you dislike and distrust everyone? Or is it just me?"

He finally released the sigh he had been holding in, "I don't dislike you, Hope." He wished he did. It would certainly make his life a little less complicated at the moment.

She pressed on, "You seem to be walking around with this giant chip on your shoulder, and I can't help but wonder about it. I mean, I can understand not trusting *me*; in your shoes, I probably wouldn't trust me, either, but I'm curious about how you respond to everyone else." She set the book down. "Not everybody out there is trying to take advantage of other people, you know. Not everyone is dishonest and looking for the next person to swindle. I may not know who I used to be, but I know for sure the person I am today isn't like that." She drank some more water. "I just want to find out who I am and where I belong. And don't think I haven't tried, but Google can only help if you know where to start, and I can only use the Internet next door. So, of course, my search has been stalled with everything that's happening with Jasmine and Ryan."

Daniel wasn't sure what to say, but he was spared having to answer right away by a waitress who came and asked if he would like anything. After perusing the menu, he told the waitress, "I'll have a large Irish cream-flavored coffee and a couple of lemon drop cupcakes." He looked at Hope, "Would you like something to eat? You did mention that you have quite a long wait ahead of you."

Hope considered the menu card that was on the table and asked for a vanilla bean cupcake with chocolate ganache. "Separate tabs, please," she instructed the waitress.

"You don't have to do that; it's my treat."

"That's okay. I wouldn't want you to think I'm trying to take advantage of you or anything."

"*Touché.* I don't mind buying you a cupcake."

"I'd rather you didn't," she responded matter-of-factly.

Daniel frowned. That stung, but he couldn't blame her. "I'm sorry if I've been suspicious of you, Hope. You, yourself, have admitted that your... situation would raise red flags in anyone's mind. Outside of that, though, you've given me little reason to doubt you. You've been nothing but good and kind to my aunt, and believe it or not, most of the time I'm really glad you're there. I worry about her less, knowing she's not alone in the house, and you've been doing a great job taking care of her and the house and the cooking and everything. Thank you." His words came out quickly, as if he wanted to say them before he changed his mind and took them back.

Hope blushed and stared into her water, "You're welcome, but I should be the one saying thanks. I genuinely don't know what would have become of me if it wasn't for Aunt Ruby."

"I guess it was orchestrated that way for both of you." He glanced toward her belly but quickly looked away. "You and Aunt Ruby, I mean."

"I guess." The waitress set their orders on the table.

"And as it relates to how I feel about people, generally, well, let's just say I've been hurt by someone very close to me—someone who was only using me—and it's taking a while to get over it." He sipped his coffee and smiled despite his somber mood. He rarely consumed alcohol, so he never had a real Irish coffee laced with whisky, but he loved the taste of the Irish cream syrup in his brew. His lemon drop cupcakes were excellent, as well. He had a sweet tooth the size of Texas. He cut off another bite and chewed it thoughtfully.

"Perhaps you should try learning to live with it instead of getting over it?" Hope suggested.

Daniel recognized his own words from the day of James Lucas' memorial service and smiled wistfully, "I suppose. But suffice it to say, it has caused me to have a somewhat skewed view of humanity."

Hope spoke thoughtfully, "I get it, I really do, but look how it's affecting the 'humanity' around you. While it's not wise to trust everyone, I think it's equally unwise to trust *absolutely no one*. It's bound to take a toll eventually, both on you and the ones you are close to. Look what happened to Aunt Ruby. I mean, I know the doctor said she just fainted, but we can't ignore the fact that she's never fainted before, so we have to take at least some responsibility for that. Your aunt has been generous enough to extend her hospitality to me until we know who I am and where I'm going to end up. That means that you and I will be spending some amount of time together, at least for the foreseeable future. Can we call another truce? Bury the hatchet again and maybe keep it buried this time? Forgive the past, try to forget it and move forward?"

"Don't you think that's a bit hypocritical?"

"Why do you say that?"

Daniel thought for a while before explaining, "We both said some things that were perhaps inappropriate, no doubt about that, but I wonder if you've completely changed your mind about your perception of me. Because if not, then what's the point? Do you still think I'm too consumed by my work to focus on the more important things in life, like Aunt Ruby?"

"Do you still think I'm trying to scam your aunt?" she countered without answering his question.

"Well, no."

She took a deep breath before saying, "Look, some of what I said was downright disrespectful, and for that, I apologize."

"*Some* of what you said?" Up went his eyebrows.

"Yes. I meant some of what I said, and it wasn't all disrespectful."

"Fair enough. I also apologize for *some* of what I said. *Some* things were inappropriate and I should have known—and acted— better."

She almost smiled, and he could see that she had physically relaxed a little. "Fair enough," she echoed his words and stuck out her hand. "I guess we can move on, then." Oh, how he wished he could.

She leaned back in the chair and smiled. He hadn't noticed how rigidly she had been sitting before. He gazed at her smile, sorry he hadn't seen it more often.

"So, you spoke about having a skewed view of humanity, and if someone really hurt you, I can understand that. Care to share?"

His answer was curt, "Nope."

She smiled as if that was exactly the answer she had been expecting. Without missing a beat, she asked, "And what about God?" as she tasted her first bite of the chocolate-covered cupcake.

He watched her reaction and hid a smile. She closed her eyes as the pastry hit her taste buds, and chewed as if she was trying to prolong the experience. Pure rapture was stenciled across her countenance. It made him want to taste the cupcake himself. It made him wonder if she would taste like chocolate if he just leaned across the table and.... Not for the first time, he wished their circumstances were different. He wouldn't mind removing that spot of chocolate from her lower lip for her. She wasn't even aware of it.

He absentmindedly brushed something away from his knee as he reluctantly tore his gaze away from the ecstatic look on her face and forced himself to remember what she had asked. Before he could respond, his eyes widened suddenly as he felt something pierce the skin of his left thigh through his khakis. He almost shouted out loud at the sudden pain, but grimaced instead. There was another sharp pain. And another.

જી

Hope was waiting on Daniel to respond when he suddenly looked as if he had seen a ghost. His expression became panicked and the blood drained from his face. Hope dropped her fork and asked, "Daniel? Are you okay?"

He was pointing to his throat in alarm, but he didn't seem to be choking. His breathing was shallow; in fact, he was wheezing as if he was having an asthma attack. Hope quickly moved toward him and was just in time to grab his upper arms and prevent him from slipping off the chair as he slumped over. "Daniel!"

Some kind of instinct kicked in as she gently slid him down to the floor and laid him on his back, checking his airway as she knelt beside him. She could see that his tongue was swollen. She noted that his breathing continued to be shallow and quick and his face had taken on a pallor. He appeared to be having an allergic reaction—a serious one—to something.

She waved at a waiter who was just stepping out of the café's main entrance. "This man seems to be in anaphylactic shock. Run over to the medical center and tell them he needs epinephrine right now!" The waiter stood there as if he hadn't understood a word. "Hurry! Tell them to bring epi-neph-rine *now!*" she urged him, breaking down the word so he would remember it, "We're talking life and death here!"

As the young man's ears, brain and feet finally connected and he took off running, she scanned the surroundings. From her vantage point on the ground, she noticed a small nest attached to the underside of the table. Daniel had been stung by some kind of insect.

"Daniel, are you allergic to bees? Or wasps, maybe?"

He tried to shake his head, his eyes wide.

She maintained eye contact and remained calm, instinctively understanding that panicking would cause him to become even more frantic. "I think you've been stung by something. You're going to be fine. The doctor will be here any moment now." She spoke in a soothing tone and stroked his hand.

He looked terrified, but she continued to encourage him until he slipped out of consciousness.

Although it was only a couple of minutes, it seemed like forever before Hope finally saw the waiter running back to the café, accompanied by a young woman dressed in green surgical scrubs and sneakers, carrying a medical bag. Two men with a stretcher between them brought up the rear. The doctor parted the small crowd that had gathered and made a quick assessment of the situation, taking note of Daniel's loss of consciousness, wheezing, swollen tongue, ashen appearance and clammy skin. He had developed huge hives in the three or four minutes since he had started to act strangely. The doctor retrieved a huge needle from her bag and jabbed it into Daniel's outer thigh. After a short while, his frantic breathing slowed a bit and his chest stopped heaving. The doctor told Hope that she was going to have the aides put him on the stretcher and take him just across the street to the medical center for proper attention.

Hope paid both bills at the café and got to the medical center in record time. There, Daniel had already regained consciousness and was being administered oxygen. He was hooked up to a blood pressure monitor and an IV tube had been inserted into the back of his hand. Thankfully, he didn't need to be intubated since the swelling of his tongue was not too severe. He'd received the epinephrine in good time. He was responsive and was able to tell them that he was not allergic to bees but couldn't remember being stung by wasps before.

Hope hovered in the background, paying keen attention to what was going on. All of this felt somehow familiar to her, but she didn't have the time to process the fact that she might be remembering something. There would be time to think about that later. She completely forgot about her ultrasound, and it was only when the clinic called her cell phone that she remembered. She told them she was in the emergency area and asked if she could reschedule.

While Daniel rested, Dr. Wills explained that although the case didn't warrant transferring him to hospital in St. Augustine, she was going to keep him under observation at the medical center for a few hours to ensure that he didn't have a relapse. She wanted him close to medical attention in case he needed another dose of medicine. Hope called Jasmine, who promised to bring Aunt Ruby, then waited by the side of his bed in a curtained area of the emergency floor as he slept.

At first, she just watched him, taking in his features and noting that she thought him more handsome now than when she'd first met him. Just as she was chastising herself for her train of thought, he opened his eyes and caught her staring at him, then his lips crooked in a contented smile, and he fell asleep again.

Embarrassed, she decided to try and lose herself in her book. Somehow the antics of the animals weren't as entertaining as they had seemed earlier. Her attention kept straying back to Daniel. She knew he wasn't aware of what she was doing, so she took his hand and prayed out loud that he would be okay. She had never prayed aloud for anyone else, and even though she knew he couldn't hear, she struggled with finding the right words as she asked God for his recovery to be swift and complete.

Again, he opened his eyes unexpectedly, and when she tried to drop his hand, he curled his fingers around hers and went back to sleep. Although his grasp wasn't particularly tight, Hope did nothing to remove her hand from his.

She sat there staring at their entwined fingers for a couple of minutes and, for once, allowed her mind to stray in a direction she would usually try to avoid. For just a few minutes, she wondered what it would be like if Daniel were hers and she were his. She imagined knowing exactly who she was—Hope Donahue, Daniel's wife and the mother of his unborn child. She pictured him with his hands on her tummy and his lips on hers. As she sat close to the bed, she let her mind drift away to a place of safety and security, a place where she never had to doubt what the future held for her... a place where no matter what came her way, she would know that the two of them would be able to face it together.

She instinctively knew that Daniel could make a woman feel safe and taken care of, although she would be perfectly capable of taking care of herself. In the world she was busy imagining, she had a great job that allowed her a lot of time to devote to her husband and her child. They would leave the baby with Aunt Ruby during the days and each would go their separate ways. Maybe they would meet for lunch once or twice a week. After work, they would take the baby to the park or for a walk. They would sit with Aunt Ruby for a home-cooked meal, and when the baby went to sleep—for the whole night, of course—she would curl up in Daniel's arms on the sofa, and they would discuss their day or watch something hilarious on TV.

The Daniel she was dreaming of was caring and compassionate. He listened when she had a concern and, without trying to solve every single problem she had, he would offer suggestions and she would take them into consideration. He would be honest with her, and she with him, and although challenges would come, they would take them on together.

Their life together would be just awesome.

She was so lost in her daydream that she didn't notice that the object of her fantasy had opened his eyes and was staring intently at her. When she finally noticed and made eye contact with him, she read so much in his eyes that she froze, forgetting to withdraw her fingers from his. As he gently pulled her towards him, she couldn't find the strength to resist, although her brain knew she should. It was as if every single cell in her body was standing at attention, as if she had been waiting for this very moment from the first time she had seen Daniel come through the mud room of Aunt Ruby's house so many weeks earlier.

CB

Daniel pulled Hope towards him as if it were the most natural thing on earth. He successfully ignored the warning signals going off in his brain as he looked at her full, pink lips and anticipated how they would feel against his. He purposely shut down the knowledge part of his brain—the part that told him that this was somebody else's woman and that what he was doing was wrong. Instead, he chose to follow his feelings. It had been so long since he had touched the hand of someone other than Aunt Ruby, so long since he had kissed a woman, and all he wanted was—for one brief moment—to forget the past, ignore the future regrets that were sure to come, and live only for the present.

Brushing her lips with his was like coming home for Daniel.

Her lips were just as soft as he had anticipated. He closed his eyes and sighed, eager to deepen the contact but unwilling to push. When it ended—which was all too soon for his liking—he knew his life would never be the same again. It was as if he could hear the sound of the carefully constructed wall around his heart crumbling.

It was Hope who pulled back first. Daniel opened his eyes to find her staring at him like a deer in the headlights. She sat back, seemingly dazed. Daniel could anticipate the words of chastisement that would erupt when she caught her breath. Instead, she leaned back in the chair and said nothing; she only gazed at him with her eyes moist and full of questions she would not ask, questions he could not answer. Before either of them could speak, the curtain was pulled back to reveal Aunt Ruby, Ryan and Jasmine.

At the unexpected intrusion, Hope quickly pulled her hand from his, and although he instinctively wanted to protest and hold on to it, he knew that she was not his to hold. As she broke the physical contact, his body and soul missed her immediately.

CB

As Hope dropped Daniel's fingers, she was painfully aware that with the kiss, there had been a shift in the atmosphere. Her mind was full of regret at what had happened, because she knew that somewhere out there was the father of her child, and that she owed him her loyalty because—even though he hadn't found her yet—a part of her was convinced that he was searching high and low for her. Even so, she had enjoyed the kiss, and although she could have pulled back at any time, she had not ignored the magnetic pull towards Daniel because the truth was... she really hadn't wanted to. She had wanted to have just that one taste of what it would have been like if her daydream were actually her reality. Now, however, her mind was being assailed with judgment directed at her, and it was taking everything she had inside of her not to fall apart.

Although she was reluctant to leave Daniel's side, there was still time for her to go to the clinic and have the ultrasound done, with Aunt Ruby in attendance.

ଓ

They both looked at the screen in amazement as the doctor showed them an arm here, a leg there. They could even identify fingers. Tears moistened Hope's eyes as she looked at her child. She could still hardly believe she was pregnant, but as she saw the baby's small movements on-screen, she knew that she would protect that tiny little being with her life, if necessary. She was officially in love.

She could hear Aunt Ruby whispering a prayer over the baby, and she was grateful.

"Everything seems to be progressing well, Hope. The baby seems to be doing fine, though he or she is a little bit on the big side for this stage of the pregnancy. There's nothing to indicate any health challenges, though, so that's a relief." Dr. Elaina was quick to continue with a disclaimer, "Of course, there are some things that don't show up on scans, but we won't dwell on those. There's no reason we should borrow from tomorrow's trouble, right? Tomorrow might have no trouble at all, and then we would have wasted our worry for nothing." She smiled.

Hope wanted to ask if Jasmine hadn't been told the same thing at this stage of pregnancy, but she wasn't sure she wanted to hear the doctor's answer. She felt a sense of paranoia rising within her, but took a few calming breaths and tried to think about all the babies in the world who were born healthy and strong. She hoped hers would be among them, but her heart ached for Jasmine once more.

"Do you want to know the baby's sex?" Dr. Elaina interrupted Hope's reverie.

She hadn't thought of that. "No, I think I'd rather be surprised."

"No problem. I'm going to write it down and put it in a sealed envelope in case you change your mind. I'll give it to Aunt Ruby; she'll keep it safe for you," she looked at Aunt Ruby and added in a stern voice, "and she *won't* peek."

Aunt Ruby chuckled and agreed.

Later, all four of them crowded around Daniel's bed for a couple of hours until Dr. Wills told them he seemed to be doing fine and that he was free to go. Hope listened intently as the doctor gave him a prescription for a pre-filled self-injector and gave them all instructions on when, where and how to use it. She explained that he needed to make an appointment with his own doctor as soon as possible. Ryan drove him home in his SUV, and Jasmine drove Aunt Ruby and Hope in theirs. It had been a long and eventful day.

Later that night, Hope made the herculean effort to *not* think about the kiss. Instead, she finally took the time to reflect on the fact that she had finally had some kind of memory... if one could call a case of instinct kicking in 'a memory.' It wasn't much, but it was something, and it gave her a glimmer of hope that perhaps her memory wasn't as far away as it had seemed for the past few weeks.

She couldn't quite put her finger on it, but she knew she had been in a similar situation before. She had known exactly what to do, and the acronym ABCDE had come to her mind as she was moving towards Daniel. She had known that she should check his airway, breathing, circulation, disability and exposure, but since the doctor had come so quickly, she had only needed to do the first three.

Now she had even more questions. Was she a nurse? A doctor? An EMT? And if she was, wouldn't someone she worked with have noticed she wasn't at work by now? Was she between jobs? Had she been fired? She simply had no idea.

CHAPTER TWENTY-TWO

Just over two weeks after his allergic reaction had landed him on a gurney at the medical center, Daniel found himself on a plane headed to the Caribbean. He had been offered the opportunity to conduct research with a team from a Jamaican university and had jumped at the chance. He would miss the Fourth of July celebrations, but it was now or never. While he was excited about the work he would get to do, more than anything else, he knew he needed to put as many miles as possible between Hope and himself. And he couldn't do it quickly enough.

Despite his best efforts, since what he now thought of as 'The Incident' —not to be confused with the earlier one he had labeled 'The Confrontation'—he was more drawn to Hope than ever.

He had tried to forget the way she had taken command during 'The Incident,' but he couldn't, especially because he knew that she may have saved his life.

And then there was the kiss to consider. But he was making a supreme effort not to consider it. They had succeeded in avoiding each other since The Incident, although he had taken the time to buy her a simple thank you card (at Aunt Ruby's suggestion) acknowledging what she had done for him. Rather than handing it to her, he had slipped it under her door early one Monday morning and then had hightailed it out of the house and back to his townhouse.

Instead of staying and dealing with the emotions that were surging inside of him, he had taken the coward's way out. He was running away—as far as he could get on relatively short notice.

At first he couldn't imagine what it was about this woman in this particular complicated situation that had drawn his attention and, frankly, reawakened his dormant hormones. Sure, she was physically attractive—anyone could see that—but his interest in her went much deeper than that. And yes, she was smart, causing him to question long-held beliefs and attitudes even about his own academic work. But that wasn't it, either. There was just something about her.

Maybe it was the attentive way she took care of Aunt Ruby. Or the support she had given Jasmine when she was finally able to interact with her after the loss. Perhaps it was in the way that she had humbled herself and apologized for the things she had said to him during 'The Confrontation'—well, *some* of the things she'd said. And he had to admit that she hadn't been totally wrong in her assessment of him. Even though he felt justified in the stance he had taken in guarding his heart, truth be told, some of what she said had really hit home with him.

He really *had* been too self-involved lately to pay Aunt Ruby enough attention, and he was willing to concede—to himself, at least—that the fact that she wasn't alone in the house had made him spend even less time with her. He could hardly even believe he agreed with Hope, but he did.

He couldn't help but compare Hope to Victoria. Where Victoria had been clingy and needy, he was sure Hope would maintain her independence. He could see it in her desire to pay her way at Aunt Ruby's, even if she wasn't allowed to. She wouldn't need a man to provide things for her, and she wouldn't want a man to live beyond his means in order to make her happy. No, he was convinced that in other circumstances, her happiness would be her own, and any man she chose would only add to a life that was already full.

Although he didn't know the background of her pregnancy, he was pretty sure that the woman Hope had become in front of his own eyes would never use a man as a scapegoat to cover her own failures. She would stand up and take responsibility and deal with whatever consequences may come.

Perhaps he was only idealizing her because he knew he couldn't have her. And maybe if Victoria had taken the time to defend herself, he would understand—at least on some level—what had prompted her to make the decisions she had made. But Victoria was gone, and all he had left were questions about what his life would be like if he could take Hope as his own. He sighed. He would never, ever know.

As he stared through the window, he didn't really see the clouds just outside. He was too busy trying to figure out exactly how he was going to get around his growing feelings. He had the perfect excuse for staying away today and for some weeks to come, but he would have to return to his aunt's home some time. He sighed. Maybe by then Hope's memory would have returned or she would have been identified by some other means. Maybe by the time he returned, she would have walked out of his life and gone back to her own. He frowned. He was surprised at how unhappy the thought made him.

He had been so comfortable with his life, but that was before Hope had appeared. That was before she'd stood up to him in Aunt Ruby's yard. And it was before she had saved his life at the café in town. Now he was going to have to find a way to make his life comfortable again, whether he had to deal with her when he got back to Alistair Bay or not. He would have to figure out a way of getting her out of his head. That would not be as easy to do as putting physical distance between them. Still, he was determined not to think about her or her very kissable lips while he was away. He chided himself immediately, *Whoa, Danny! Those are exactly the kinds of thoughts you need to get under control. And quickly!*

Based on past experience, he figured the only way to get her out of his thoughts was to put something else in. "Lord, help me find a way." He didn't even know he had said the prayer out loud until the woman beside him asked him if he had said something to her. He'd prayed before he'd even noticed that he was doing it. Ever since the day Ryan had asked him to pray for him, he'd found himself talking to God more and more often—at first it had started happening once every day or so, and then it began to take place throughout the day. He'd forgotten how easy it was to keep in constant contact with the Almighty.

He leaned back and started twiddling his thumbs on the tray table in front of him. He reflected on the days when he'd just gotten saved, and it was as if all he could do was think about God and pray. Back then, he'd spent every spare moment devouring the Word of God. First, he'd read the book of John, and then Acts of the Apostles, followed by Romans. When he felt like he had a good understanding of who God was and how he was expected to live as a Christian, he had gone to Genesis and had read every chapter of every book, even the censuses captured in the book of Numbers. It had been as if he'd been thirsty, and only the scripture could satisfy him. He hadn't been interested in finding himself a girlfriend—or more than one, as he'd liked to do as a younger teen; he had had no social life of which to speak, and even his parents had encouraged him to put down his Bible sometimes and go out with his friends.

His appetite for the things of God had been voracious, and every week he'd been in church on Sunday, at the prayer meeting on Tuesday, at Bible study on Wednesday, and again at Friday Fun and Fellowship with the other young members. Now that he looked back, he was pretty sure he could have repeated scripture in his sleep.

And then life had gotten in the way.

He'd had to work to help pay his way through his first two years of college, and even with a scholarship that covered his tuition for his junior and senior years, he had started tutoring his classmates at their request. The work schedule tended to clash with most of his weekday meetings at church, but he was still there every Sunday.

After graduating, he'd started to teach, but just when he'd started his graduate work, he'd met Victoria and had become quite wrapped up with her. His spiritual life had taken a beating, especially when they had married. He had still gone to church most Sundays, but she didn't like to go with him. She had blamed her traditional upbringing for her dislike of what she termed his "loud and chaotic" modern, non-denominational church, but when he had offered to take her to one she liked, she'd found countless excuses not to go, at least until she had been placed on bed rest. Now he wondered if she'd been pricked by her conscience and so preferred not to hear why all the lies she'd been perpetuating were detestable to the God she had only pretended to fear.

When she had died, he had felt himself becoming more and more distant from God. He had always been taught—and had come to believe—that God was a good God who had a good plan for his life. So he had made a mistake one night and had fallen into sin. Hadn't he done the right thing by marrying Victoria? Even before their marriage, he had repented and sought the Lord through prayer and fasting, trying to put it behind him. And he thought he had. Yet look what had happened.

He had never been able to completely shake the feeling that God had been punishing him. Where had His mercy and grace been? Why had God allowed Victoria to deceive him in such a manner? Why had He allowed him to believe he was going to be a father, only to have his hopes and plans dashed so cruelly—and twice in the same day, at that?

So he had turned away from God. He still believed in Him, but he was no longer convinced that God was an always-benevolent being who was perpetually forgiving, merciful, gracious and kind. His experience had taught him that that wasn't necessarily the case. At least, not for him.

Yet he looked at his friend Ryan, and he had to wonder if there wasn't some kind of benefit to trusting in God wholeheartedly. Like Daniel, Ryan had suffered a heartbreaking loss, but he hadn't turned away from God. He had, instead, turned *toward* Him for support and had discovered a level of peace Daniel found himself craving. For the most part, Ryan had remained calm and collected although it was evident that he was distressed, and even though he had done his share of crying.

Ryan hadn't shouted at God or accused Him of being unfair. He hadn't lost faith; instead, his faith seemed to have increased. When Daniel had asked him what was allowing him to handle the loss so well, Ryan's response had been simple, "God is good, Daniel. He's good. There is good in this loss, even though we can't see it, and God can still use everything that concerns me and Jasmine. He hasn't forgotten about us. He hasn't abandoned us. No, His Word says in Job thirty-nine that He knows when the mountain goat gives birth, so I know He is with us even if He feels far from us right now. I just hope He will allow me to understand, at some point, why He chose this route, if this is His doing. But the truth is, Daniel, that having faith is believing without understanding. I'm exercising my faith."

Until Ryan had said that, it had never occurred to Daniel that any good could have come out of the loss of Victoria and the baby so many years before. He had never considered that God might be able—no, *was* able, without a doubt—to turn the situation around and use it for good. He had been so angry at God that he hadn't taken everything He had already done for him into consideration. A sovereign God could orchestrate a good outcome even after the death of someone who had turned far away from Him, as Victoria had. Only time would tell, however, what that outcome could be.

Daniel could feel his countenance changing when he thought of Victoria and how she had caused his life to change. It was always better not to tread down that historical path. He always ended up upset. It was better to think about positive things. Didn't positivity always trump negativity? Wasn't that what his mother had always told him?

Suddenly, it was as if a light had come on in his brain. He would have jumped to his feet if it weren't for the 'Fasten seatbelt' sign above his head. That was it! That's what he would begin to fill his thoughts with! He would go back to his Christian roots and think positive things, as his mom and Aunt Ruby had always advised him to do. He stared at his hands and thought about Philippians 4:8 and what it instructed Christians to do—think about things that were positive. Specifically, he would try to keep his mind on those things that were excellent and praiseworthy—things that were true, noble, right, pure, lovely and admirable. He would try not to think thoughts that led to bitterness—thoughts about his late wife or Professor Hargreaves, for example.

Daniel turned on his tablet, ensured that airplane mode was selected, and swiped until he came to the Bible that he'd downloaded when he had bought the gadget. He hadn't used the app much—okay, he hadn't used it *at all*—but as he sat there in seat 4C, he was glad he had it.

He found the fifth chapter of Galatians and started to read Paul's advice to put away thoughts that eventually became sinful actions. Daniel was a conservative person by nature, so many of the characteristics Paul mentioned didn't describe him, but he knew in his logical mind that thoughts of his late wife and her married lover led him, more often than not, into fits of rage. He detested the pair of them—'hate' was too demure a word for the emotion he felt—and he knew that those thoughts were the product of his carnal—not his godly—nature. He knew that if he banished the thoughts and the images they tended to conjure up in his mind, he would be better off, since he would no doubt think fewer hateful and disturbing things.

He took a deep breath and smiled. Yes, he would change his approach to his very thoughts, and by doing so, not only would he be inviting more positivity into his life—and who didn't need that?—but he was also confident he'd succeed in getting Hope off his mind. He couldn't wait.

CHAPTER TWENTY-THREE

Jasmine Phillips's fear of public speaking was unparalleled. The very thought of it was enough to set a few families of butterflies free in her stomach and would eventually cause her to flee to the bathroom. She'd almost missed her own wedding because she was literally sick to her stomach at the thought of having to recite her vows in public, even though on that occasion, the only 'public' present consisted of her closest family and friends.

If she ever succeeded in making it to a microphone, she would get the chills and begin to stutter as soon as she took a breath to speak. She would ramble on and on and repeat herself, never ceasing to pray that the earth would open up and swallow her, if that was what it took for the torture to end. She had tried many tricks, like imagining the audience in their underwear. Nothing had ever worked. There had been moments in her life that she had honestly felt that it would have been better to die than to open her mouth and speak. She rationalized her feelings on the matter by telling herself that to be absent from the body was to be present with the Lord, which was far better than standing in front of a crowd!

It had gotten to the point where anyone who knew her well was fully aware that if they needed Jasmine to open her mouth in front of even a small crowd, the best approach to take was to call on her suddenly... like at the very moment she was required to speak. That way, not only would she have no opportunity to refuse, but she would also probably be finished before she got the chance to get nervous. Many people who knew her well found it strange that she could be so comfortable singing in front of hundreds of people, but she explained that singing was her gift and her ministry, and it was the part of her she was most comfortable sharing with anyone and everyone. When she sang, she was doing it onto the Lord, and Him alone. His opinion was the only one that mattered.

So it was not overly strange that it was after leading praise and worship the first morning of the church's annual three-day women's conference that Jasmine noticed her name printed in the program.

It was an event that saw hundreds of Christian women from all over the country flooding the small town, and she was scheduled to speak after the welcome. According to the booklet in her hand, her talk was to be a twenty-minute testimony entitled 'Even this, Lord.' Other members of the church would also be testifying about what God had done in their lives, but Sister Claire had wisely put Jasmine first. She only had a few minutes to prepare.

While Sister Claire welcomed the ladies and gave them an idea of what was expected that day, Jasmine found herself completely oblivious to what was going on around her. She felt dizzy, as if she might faint, and looked around wildly for the nearest exit. She identified the hallway to the restrooms and tried to compose herself as she went, clutching her program and pocket book tightly.

Hope, who was sitting in an aisle seat on the other side of the sanctuary, noticed Jasmine's departure. Seeing the wild look of fear in her eyes, she quickly—well, as quickly as her seven months-pregnant frame would allow her—got up and followed her friend. She found Jasmine splashing her face with water at the bathroom sink.

"You okay?" Hope asked, her eyes showing her concern.

"N-n-no. I'm so not okay right now!" Jasmine responded, her eyes wide as she regarded Hope.

"What's wrong?" Hope moved to her side and put her hand on Jasmine's elbow.

"I've g-g-got t-t-to sp-sp-speak!"

"Didn't you know?"

"No! I'd never have agreed to it!"

"Oh. I'm sorry you're so frightened. I saw your name on the program, but I figured you knew." Hope's voice was calm.

"Th-th-there's hundreds of people out there!" A toilet flushed in the background.

"I know, Jasmine."

"Th-th-there's only one of me!" Jasmine's voice was almost hysterical, so much so that the young woman who had just exited one of the stalls looked as if she was contemplating leaving without washing her hands. She eventually decided to give them a quick rinse under cold water before making a run for it.

Hope remained collected. She leaned her hip against the counter and looked at her friend, "I know. There's only one of you, but that means you're the only one who knows what's going on inside your head, in your *spirit*, that needs to come out. You have a message to share, and you're the only one who can do it."

"I do? I am?"

"Yes. You have a story, Jasmine. There are people out there who need to hear it, and they need to hear it today."

"But doesn't the Bible say, somewhere, that if I don't answer my calling, the Lord will send another messenger?"

"Probably, but where does that leave you? Maybe you need to share it as much as they need to hear it. Are you sure you'll get another chance?"

"What could I possibly have to share with these people, Hope? They're strangers! Hundreds and hundreds of strangers!"

"I know, sweetie, but Sister Claire wouldn't have done this if she didn't have a real good reason."

"I can't do this, Hope," Jasmine closed her eyes against the tears that threatened to overflow.

"Yes, you can." Hope's tone was measured.

"I'll die out there. I'm not strong enough for this."

Hope moved to stand in front of her friend, both hands taking Jasmine's. "No, you *won't* die, and yes, you *are* strong enough. You're the strongest woman I know. Jasmine, I look at what you've gone through. It's so fresh, you know? It's so new and so real, and yet you still have a smile on your face—well, maybe not *now*, but usually.... I want to know how you've managed to do that. My situation is so much less intense, and I can't even smile, yet you do. I want to be like you, Jasmine; I really do." She smiled, "Besides, isn't your favorite scripture the one that says that in all things God works for a good outcome for you?"

"Yes, Romans 8:28." While she was grateful for Hope's words, she didn't even have the time to process them in that moment.

"Then maybe He can work this out for your good, too."

"Y-y-yes, when you put it that way, I'm sure He can."

"Good, now wash your face and come on. Sister Claire is closing her welcome." Hope waited till Jasmine washed her face again, whispered a quick prayer for strength and wisdom, and composed herself. They both wore minimal makeup, so repair wasn't an issue.

"Will you stand up there with me?"

"I will, if and when you need me to."

"I do. I will."

"Okay, sweetie. I'll be there." Hope gave Jasmine's hand a gentle tug and they walked slowly back to the sanctuary.

Inside, Jasmine tried not to notice how many women were in the room. Instead, she kept her eyes trained on the pastor's wife, who was already introducing her.

"This next sister is a dynamic woman of God, a worship leader, a prayer warrior. Her singing is anointed, as you no doubt heard earlier. She loves the Lord, and she loves her husband of less than a year. She has a story to share with you all. I just know lives are going to be changed and history is going to be made in someone's life here today." She beckoned towards Jasmine, who was now standing on the steps to the right of the stage, clutching Hope's hand.

"Now before she comes, I must make this very public apology. Jasmine, I'm sorry for calling on you suddenly. I knew you would have said no, but I do believe the Holy Spirit was prompting me to put you up here. Be still and know that He is God. He will be the one exalted here today, in spite of your nerves, and remember that He can work *even this* out for your good." Jasmine nodded in acknowledgement of Sister Claire's gesture, but was too worked up to smile. She planned to have a strongly worded discussion with the first lady of the church when all this was over… if she survived.

Sister Claire held her hand out towards Jasmine. "Ladies, Jasmine Phillips has tremendous stage fright, so let's show her some love!"

The church itself did not have a large membership, but they had recently begun streaming their Sunday morning services live on the Internet, and would be broadcasting sections of the women's conference as delayed installments. Jasmine tried not to notice the cameras.

She was sure that nothing would come out when she opened her mouth, so she was surprised when she heard herself through the speakers. "Good morning, ladies." The voice was shaky, but it was hers.

There was a chorus of greetings from the audience. A few who were members of the church shouted their own greetings, like, "You can do it, Jasmine!"

"Um, I should explain that Sister Claire knows that I'm terrified of speaking in public, so I understand her reasons for calling on me very suddenly. I'd never have been standing here otherwise," she took a deep breath and continued, "but a wise woman reminded me backstage while I was hyperventilating—" there were a few chuckles from the audience "—about my life verse. The scripture I cling to during the good and bad times in my life is Romans 8:28. The various versions and translations say different things, but I like to tell myself that as long as I love Him and am walking in His will for my life, no matter what happens to or around me, God is working out the details for my good." There were murmurs of agreement from the audience.

"So I had to remind myself that everything—and I do mean *everything*—is working out for my good. Even this." As she subconsciously voiced the topic of her speech, she felt as if an electric shock had started running through her body. It was the same feeling she had when she was leading a praise and worship session and she felt like she was all alone with God, communing with Him in a private sanctuary. Suddenly, she knew what she wanted to share. "But I have to admit that there have been times when I've forgotten that He can— and *does*—work everything to my benefit," she gulped in some fresh air and plodded on, "even losing my firstborn son, my only child."

There was a collective gasp from the audience members, many of whom knew Jasmine personally but had never known she was pregnant.

"My husband Ryan and I got married less than a year ago, and we became pregnant within the first month. Although we wanted kids, it was unbelievable that I was already expecting, and I was in major denial. I just wanted to wake up and have it all be a dream. It didn't help that I was so sick all the time, either. You know that pregnancy glow other women seem to get? I didn't have that. My glow was a shade of green. I was sick *all day, every day.*

"I began to resent the pregnancy, and I resented my husband for being so happy about it." The audience was transfixed.

"All along, very few people knew. I wasn't showing, and I was so sick I even stopped coming to church. I kind of disappeared off the scene for a while. I missed church. I missed the praise and worship sessions. I missed the fellowship, but the truth was, I simply couldn't trust my body to behave in public. It was a rough time for me and for my poor husband.

"And then it happened—the turnaround. At some point around the fifth month, I began to feel—well, not *better*, necessarily, but at least I wasn't so sick anymore. My mother came to visit from Jamaica, and we did all the shopping—for the baby's room, maternity clothes that I was just starting to need, and clothes for the baby. My appetite was returning, and I was finally able to eat something other than won ton soup. My husband was getting his bride back, and I felt like I was coming alive, finally beginning to enjoy my pregnancy."

"And then one day Little Praise—that was the nickname Sister Claire gave him—just didn't move. I went to the doctor, but it was already too late. We had lost our honeymoon baby."

Jasmine had to clench her teeth for a while to avoid crying when she braved a glimpse at the enraptured audience and noticed that several women had tears streaming down their faces.

She took a deep breath and quickly prayed for strength to continue. She was strengthened by the feel of Hope's hand making small circles on her lower back. She needed the support more than ever.

"Ladies, this has been, hands-down, the toughest period of my life. Little Praise, whom we named James Lucas, was due on the same day as our Fall Festival. Everywhere I turn, there are stark reminders of that date. When I was pregnant, that date gave me something to look forward to, something to hold on to. It reminded me that though the pregnancy was proving difficult, there was an end in sight and I could keep my eye on the prize.

"When we lost him, however, that date became a reminder of everything I had lost, including hope. It's still tough to see the constant reminder, but I can tell you, ladies, that I have recovered my hope. The first couple of weeks were rough. Losing Little Praise was... indescribable.

"At first, we were surrounded by family, but life goes on and people had to go back to their own lives. Even Ryan, who had been given compassionate leave from his job, had to go back to work. Many days, my mother and my neighbor, Aunt Ruby, were my only companions," she smiled at the elderly woman. Mama Hyacinth had already gone back to Jamaica.

"My friend, Hope, who's staying with Aunt Ruby, wanted to come visit, too, but... well, to be honest, I wasn't ready to spend a lot of time with a pregnant woman." She looked over her shoulder at Hope and gave her an apologetic smile. Hope's lips may have been smiling, but there was a hint of sadness in her eyes. Jasmine didn't have time to think about that now; maybe they could talk about it later.

"After a while, I started to feel like everyone was moving on except me. And then, all kinds of things started happening at once. Every one of them was part of the process of giving me back my hope. There was one night in particular when I felt so low, and everybody was busy with their own lives. My husband was working late; my mother was asleep; Aunt Ruby had gone home. I called my best friend and got her voice mail.

"That night, I paced the floor. My spirit was angry within me; it felt agitated. Do you know what that's like?" Every head nodded and a few hands waved. "I tried praying, reading, listening to music, watching television, but nothing helped.

"When I read my nightly devotional, God's Word hit me right in my spirit. It spoke about going through a tough time and feeling abandoned; looking around and seeing no one standing with you. I knew it was a Word in due season for me. It went on to say that those were the times we needed to look to God. Those were the situations that brought us back to the throne of grace. They reminded us that God should be our first resort, not the last. We should seek Him *first*, confide in Him *first*, look to Him *first*." A few audience members stood in agreement, but Jasmine barely noticed them.

"Ladies, I was overcome with remorse. I had been looking to man to support me when the Word says that it is God who heals the broken-hearted and binds up their wounds. My husband couldn't do that for me. My friends couldn't do that. Even my pastor couldn't. That was a role only God could—and *should*—have played in my life at that time, but I hadn't invited Him to.

"I lay on the floor of the nursery that night and wept. I poured out all my grief and heartache before the Lord. There was no holding back. I let it all out. All my pain, all the broken dreams, all my questions, all my feelings of guilt over the reservations I'd had about becoming a mother, and about not taking my vitamins. All my remorse over praying that the sickness would end. I lay everything at God's feet that night on the floor.

"And then I waited to hear from God. I waited for hours for Him to speak a restoring Word into my spirit. But He didn't. I lay there till I fell asleep on the floor, hugging one of James Lucas' blankets. That was the night before the memorial service. I felt like I needed God more than ever, and He was more silent than He had ever been."

Jasmine could see that several women in the audience could relate. Out of the corner of her eye, she noticed a middle-aged woman in a black and white hound's tooth jacket and a red flare skirt quickly move from her seat near the middle of the room, up the aisle and out through the main entrance to the sanctuary. She was followed closely by a younger woman who had been sitting beside her. Jasmine took a few deep breaths. Hope placed her open palm against the small of Jasmine's back, and she was reminded that she wasn't alone.

She took another deep breath and pressed on, "As you can imagine, the service passed in a blur. I was there physically, and that was about it.

"The next day, my husband... my poor, poor husband," she smiled, "came in and invited me out to dinner. Ladies, you can imagine my reaction! I was not amused! I chewed him out in no uncertain terms. And in his typical 'Ryan' way, he remained so calm that even his composure bothered me. He just stood there and listened, and he didn't say a word. And then he went for his Bible and came into the bathroom—where I'd run in order to be alone—and there on the floor, he told me the story of David and Bathsheba and their firstborn son." She then related the story Ryan had shared with her. When she recounted as best as she could his plea for her to walk through the valley instead of dwelling there, it was as if the place had caught on fire.

Jasmine didn't think half of the crowd had even heard the last thing she had said. They were too busy jumping to their feet, shouting, "Amen!" and "Hallelujah!" clapping their hands and stomping their beaded sandals, platforms and stilettos, as if this was a Word in due season for many of them. Jasmine noticed something red move close to the entrance and saw that the woman in the red skirt and her friend had come back into the sanctuary and were standing close to the door, as if prepared to make a quick getaway if necessary. She knew her words had struck a chord and that she could have stopped right there and that would have been enough, but now that she had started speaking, she knew she had more to share.

She waited until the crowd calmed down a bit. "Ladies, I don't have to tell you how deeply his words affected me; I can see they've affected you, too. Even though it wasn't what I wanted to hear at the time, even though I didn't think I was ready to move forward, I knew that message was straight from the Lord. I had been waiting for a Word from Him; it came in the form of a soft-spoken giant of a man. He uses different ways and means of delivering His message.

"Ryan didn't wait for me to respond. As quietly as he'd come in, he closed the door and left me alone with the weight of God's words.

"And then there was also Romans 8:28 to consider. If I really believe it, then I have to accept that God will fix it so that all things will work together for my good."

There were shouts of agreement from the audience.

"Ladies, the Word does not say 'some things', or even 'most things' can be worked out for my good. Nor does it say, 'all things except this one thing.' It says 'all things!'" Almost all the women were now on their feet. Some were praying, others were jumping. Jasmine noticed that the woman in the red skirt had fallen to her knees and that her friend was comforting her. One of the middle-aged deacons moved towards them, so Jasmine focused on the crowd again. She couldn't believe she was still talking, and without palpitating, at that.

"I couldn't claim that promise for every other circumstance in my life and not claim it for this one. Wasn't my God able to work this out for my good, too? Did His omnipotence, His *Godness*—if you will—take leave because I was suffering? Had His love become diluted because we lost James Lucas?"

"No!" came the response from the crowd.

There was such a commotion that Jasmine wasn't sure she would be able to make her last point. She had to wait until the noise died down, which was just as well, because she soon found herself comforting Hope, who, like many others, had broken down and was weeping behind her. Jasmine could only hug her friend as the tears flowed.

"No. He didn't withdraw His promise at the time we needed it most. Do you know why?"

The crowd was in full participation mode now. Some pleaded, "Tell us!" while others responded, "Why?"

Jasmine moved from behind the lectern she had been glued to and stepped closer to the edge of the stage. She knew that, for some member of the congregation, what she was about to tell them would break down walls and open a floodgate of understanding, if only she could find the right words. She paused to whisper a silent prayer.

"Beloved, it's because God. Is. Faithful." She paused to let that sink into their very spirits. Among the now-familiar shouts of agreement, she sensed that some of the women were holding their breaths in anticipation. "And don't forget this: He is able to work through anything. *Even this.*

"In the third month of my pregnancy, Sister Claire had prophesied that the child I was carrying would change people's lives without saying a word. She declared that people who never met him would be drawn closer to the Lord just by hearing about him." She sighed, "That prophecy was one of the things that really got to me when he died. What had happened to it?" Jasmine looked sheepishly at Sister Claire, who was standing just off-stage, before admitting, "I began to doubt that she had really heard from God. After all, doesn't the Bible say that God's Word will never return to Him void? Doesn't it say it must do what He purposed for it to do? How could my son reach people for Christ if he was gone?"

She lowered her voice. "God is able to do more than we can imagine. He doesn't operate under the same limitations as we do. His ways and thoughts are higher than ours and He exists beyond the limits we set on ourselves and on Him. If you hear—*really hear*—only one thing this morning, let it be this: the God we serve is not limited by something so inconsequential in the grand scheme of things as our breath."

The crowd hushed.

Suddenly, a loud wail could be heard from the back of the room. All eyes zoomed in on the woman in the red skirt as she knelt on the floor. Her companion and the deacon appeared to be at a loss. And then just as suddenly as the shrieking had begun, it stopped. As she covered her face with her hands, everyone in the sanctuary could hear her repeat, "Thank You, Lord. Thank You, Lord."

She seemed to be in a world of her own. She lifted her hands high as she rocked back and forth and repeated the phrase more and more loudly. And then as she continued to thank the Lord for whatever breakthrough she was clearly experiencing, other ladies began to repeat her words, too. The simple phrase spread like wildfire, until almost all the voices were raised in a chorus of thanksgiving to the One who could use any circumstance—even this one—to achieve His greater purpose.

Jasmine was overwhelmed at what was unfolding before her eyes. She began to sob as the tears overflowed unchecked. It was as if the message that had settled inside of her was resonating in the spirit of every woman in the room. Tears sprang to her eyes when she realized that, in that very moment, the prophecy she had just mentioned was being fulfilled as surely as she was standing there.

CHAPTER TWENTY-FOUR

The video of Jasmine's testimony went viral in the Christian world in a matter of days. Jasmine was being recognized wherever she went, to the point that some days she just preferred to stay home. She had known that everyone in Alistair Bay would learn her story, but she was getting emails and text messages from people all over the country and as far as Jamaica, where she had been born and lived before moving to the USA for college. Everyone had learned of the loss of James Lucas, and thankfully, almost all the messages were positive and uplifting, although a few accused her of having been pregnant when she got married or of having had abortions earlier in her life. Scores of emails had come in to the church's inbox with women, and even a few men, pouring out the details of their own losses and the impact Jasmine's story had had on their lives. It was very encouraging.

Jasmine sat in the office that she and Ryan shared in their home and read and re-read the latest email that the church secretary had forwarded to her. It was from the woman in the red skirt, who now identified herself as Reverend Dr. Philomena Ayers, who had traveled all the way from Detroit to attend the conference and had experienced her breakthrough during Jasmine's testimony.

Dear Jasmine,

I looked for you after you spoke at the women's conference, but you disappeared. I just wanted to tell you thanks for sharing your story with us. I am the first lady of a fairly large church, and although I came to Alistair Bay with an open heart, I did not truly think that God would have been able to heal my twenty-year-old heartbreak.

You see, my husband and I had a perfect daughter during our third year of marriage. Noemi was with me at the conference, and I give thanks for her every day, but after having her, I struggled for years to have another child. We experienced nine heartbreaking losses before I had another pregnancy that lasted beyond ten weeks. And when our son was born, he was perfect. But he was stillborn.

There was no medical reason found, and though twenty years have passed, I still ask God why, but I believe I was inspired to come to Alistair Bay so I could learn that there is purpose in the pain, that God really is not limited by our breath. What a profound lesson! When you said that, your words touched a part of me that no scripture, no sermon, no prayer, no book on grief has ever reached. They gave me hope that the lives of my babies were not in vain.

I have taken that message and I have decided to run with it here in Detroit. I have been meditating on it. I have been repeating it to myself because I know that if I do, there will come a time when I know that I know that I know deep down in my spirit that God has a good plan for my life and that His plan can come to fruition even with all our losses. I have already shared it with a group of battered woman I am counseling, and they have been touched, too. I thank you for using your story to reach me and others, and I just know that many of us will see God using our negative and sad experiences for good, if not for us, then for others. May God bless and keep you and your husband.

Sincerely yours,
Philomena Ayers

Jasmine wiped away the tears that had formed, whispered a prayer for the woman and so many others who had written to her, and then put pen to paper.

July 19
God is truly amazing. I mean, I've heard that phrase all my life, memorized the song before I even became a Christian, and it's really only now in the midst of this situation that I can truly relate, truly begin to grasp the meaning of the words.
GOD is truly amazing.
God IS truly amazing.
God is TRULY amazing.
God is truly AMAZING.

So many ways to write it, to think it, to say it out loud, and all of them mean something different. All of them capture only one element of the truth. My God is amazing.

As Orchid so often says, "God BIG!" And she is so right. He is big and He is wide and He is wonderful and.... I mean, I don't even have the words to say what is happening on the inside of me.

Losing James Lucas was horrendous. It was an experience I would never wish on my worst enemy—not even Lydia Lewis from the third grade who threw that hideous croaking lizard on me in primary school. I almost stripped down to my undies right there in Mrs. Weller's class, trying to get it off me. And then I got punished for disrupting the class. Sigh. I am terrified of geckos to this very day.

(Note to self: pray about forgiving Lydia Lewis.)

I would never wish the loss of a child on anyone, but the Lord had me go through it, and I am still going through it today.

I am a changed woman.

Ever since I gave my testimony, I feel like I am one step closer to God, to understanding Him. I feel like He revealed Himself to me on that stage, and I know I will never truly be the same. And then for Him to use my breakthrough and my experience to reach so many people? God is so good!

The church has had so many emails, phone calls and letters in the days since they released the video. So many people have been touched, so many lives have been changed for the better, so many women say they have started to heal, all because God used little old me and my experience for His glory. Hallelujah! I can't contain the praise sometimes. It's like I just want to dance and sing and jump around.

I mean, it still hurts not having James Lucas with me. He shouldn't even have been born yet, but that little boy is serving his purpose just as much as if he was still with us. Maybe even more so, but I guess I'll never know on this side of Heaven.

He has drawn so many people closer to God. When I think about Hope... when they gave the altar call that day, she and so many others surrendered their lives to the Lord. It was my privilege and my honor to stand with her as Aunt Ruby led her in the sinner's prayer. Whatever happens from here on out, she is saved and sanctified, living in the light of the Lord. James Lucas didn't even have to say a word. God used him anyway.

Thank You, Lord. Thank You for using me and my testimony. Thank You for the strength You've given me. Thank You for giving me the right platform at the right time. Thank You, thank You, thank You. I praise Your holy name.

J.

Chapter Twenty-Five

Daniel may have missed one of his favorite holidays in the USA, but he had been told by his best friend that he hadn't missed much—only the usual barbecued and Jamaican jerk chicken, potato salad, grilled corn, vegetable kebabs, baked beans and more. He had salivated on the phone, but other than that, he had been having a great time in Jamaica and was oblivious to their celebrations of Independence Day in his home town. He hadn't spoken to anyone but Ryan and Aunt Ruby, and they seemed to be excited about some video of Jasmine that had been making the rounds on the Internet, but Daniel didn't pay much attention. Jazz was a phenomenal praise and worship leader and he figured some record producer would scoop her up eventually. He didn't see the big deal if someone had recorded her singing. At least, he thought that's what Ryan had said.

The staff of the university department that was hosting him was warm and welcoming, and he had even been invited to dinner and drinks at several homes. He spent his days in the library or on accompanied tours, and his evenings in the company of his new friends and colleagues.

He had even surprised himself early in the second week of his visit by accepting a dinner invitation from one of the tutors there.

Karyn Lue was a pretty, confident, twenty-six-year-old tutor of Caribbean Civilization. She was finishing up her dissertation and expected to have her Ph.D. within a year. With facial features that left no doubt as to her Chinese heritage, she didn't look like many people's idea of the stereotypical Caribbean woman. As Daniel had come to learn, however, she was Jamaican through and through. She wore her jet-black hair quite short, and it was always immaculately styled. Her wide array of five-inch platform heels added to her five feet five inches of height. She was a beauty.

She had taken Daniel for dinner at a vegetarian courtyard restaurant in Half Way Tree, a few miles from the university. They had chatted for hours as they consumed red beans stewed in coconut milk and served with Basmati rice and a steamed Spinach-like vegetable known as callaloo. It came with fresh avocadoes and ripe plantain baked with ginger and cinnamon on the side, and was accompanied by chilled coconut water served straight from the coconut. The tasty meal was topped off with locally-made Blue Mountain coffee ice cream. Although not a vegetarian himself, Daniel was in foodie heaven. He wished he could take some of the ice cream back home with him. The one Aunt Ruby had from time to time, which he had always considered excellent, had absolutely nothing on this.

He and Karyn had finished early and had gone to listen to a live band that played jazz and reggae music before she dropped him back at the university housing he was staying in close to the campus.

After that first outing, they met for lunch at a tiny café on the university campus a few times. She even invited him to her tiny church with is rustic wooden walls and polished wooden pews. It was a new experience of worshipping the same God in a totally different culture. Here, there were no multimedia projectors or even traditional hymn books, although Karyn was quick to explain that many larger churches used those. Instead, they received photocopied song sheets at the beginning of the service and returned them at the end. While most used printed Bibles, Daniel noticed that many of the members used e-readers and tablets instead, just as he was doing, and it seemed just about everybody had a smartphone. He was immediately comfortable, and everyone was so focused on God—and a few on their text messages and social media pages—that they paid scant attention to those around them.

Karyn was smart, witty and well-read. She had studied in Jamaica but had travelled widely throughout the Caribbean doing research for her dissertation. She was proving to be an incredible source of information, and she would definitely deserve at least a mention in the front matter of his book.

Daniel enjoyed her company immensely. It didn't hurt that she seemed to be a bit awestruck every time she looked at him. After his experiences over the past several years, and especially because of the direction his thoughts had been taking for the past month or two, he wasn't doing much to discourage her, either.

Although he was feeling a bit guilty about the whole thing, he continued to soak up the attention. The truth was that it was nice to have someone look at him as if he was the most brilliant, most attractive person she had ever met. It was nice not to argue with someone because they felt you could say or do no wrong. Under different circumstances, he could actually imagine this relationship heading somewhere. Instead, he just couldn't return Karyn's feelings, because he couldn't get a certain kiss with a certain pregnant someone out of his head.

He found it difficult to believe how badly his heart had betrayed him. He had had enough time and distance to know that he was in love with Hope. He knew he didn't have a chance with her, and he figured he must have imagined that once or twice he had caught her staring at him with attraction and maybe even a hint of longing. But it was all too complicated, and no matter how many different scenarios he played out in his mind, none of them had a happy ending for him. He hadn't spoken to her, had barely even asked about her for weeks, yet in all that time, she had never been too far from his thoughts.

ᘓ

Sunday morning dawned bright and sunny. Hope woke earlier than usual. The baby had been very active the night before, and she wondered if he or she was turning in preparation for delivery, which was expected to take place in the next ten weeks or so. She stretched and looked around the Lilac Room—the only home she could remember other than the hospital. She had put off making any kind of plans for the baby for as long as she could, but the fact of the matter was that she didn't feel any closer to remembering who she was than the day she had first awakened, and this baby was not going to wait much longer to make his or her appearance. She needed to go out and make some purchases. And she needed to do it sooner rather than later.

She looked around the room as the early morning sunlight streamed through the window. She hoped Aunt Ruby wouldn't mind if she moved some things around. She would need to make a little space for a bassinet and... maybe... eventually... a crib. She needed somewhere to keep the baby's clothes. Come to think of it, she needed to buy clothes for the baby! She had a lot to think about, and in so little time, too!

She stood in front of the closet for a long time, but the truth was that her selection was fairly minimal. She had not spent a lot of money buying maternity clothes; in fact, she had saved a lot over the months she had been living with Aunt Ruby and had a nice little nest egg laid aside. Thanks to Aunt Ruby's generosity and the free medical clinic, her expenses were practically non-existent, and she had hardly touched anything. She knew that someday, once her family was found, she was expected to return the funds to the private donor if it was at all possible, as Miss LaHaye had mentioned. She wanted to have most of those funds available when the time came. After all, she had no idea if her family had the financial resources to pay it all back.

She *would* need to spend some money to make her child comfortable. She made a mental note of all the things she would need. She would have to talk to Aunt Ruby to make sure. There would be diapers, diaper rash ointment, clothes, and bedding, but she wasn't sure what else she would have to buy. There was so much to think about.

But not today. Today, she would not focus too much on the future or on the past. Just for today, she wanted to spend a little time in thanksgiving. Today, she would go with Aunt Ruby to church. It was time to give the Lord His due. They would celebrate the health of Hope's pregnancy; they would celebrate the great work that the Lord had done through Jasmine's testimony. Most of all, though, they would celebrate the fact that Hope had now claimed Jesus as her savior and that she could truly say she had a personal relationship with Him.

Today would be a day of gratitude. It might not be the actual national holiday, but she was going to be making a special effort to take a mental vacation from all her cares and worries, just for today, and focus instead on thanking her Creator for all He had already done for her. Yes, today was going to be a special day.

CHAPTER TWENTY-SIX

If ever there were a day Jasmine was looking forward to church, today was that day. Jasmine could sense excitement in the air, so real she could almost reach out her hand and touch it. She expected the Holy Spirit to move today, and she couldn't wait to see how the move would manifest.

She wasn't disappointed. The service was on fire. The praise and worship session was so anointed that Reverend Marsden abandoned the sermon he had planned and allowed the adulation to continue unhindered. Jasmine and the worship team moved as the Spirit led them, and without it having been planned that way, the entire service became one of thanksgiving and praise.

℅

During the service, Hope felt as if she was all alone with the God she was just getting to know. She had spent a lot of time reading her Bible and meditating on several scriptures, and as difficult as it was most of the time, she was trying to emulate Paul and be content regardless of her circumstances. She had made up her mind to let God move in her situation. Like Jasmine, she was beginning to believe that God could — and would — work her situation out for her good.

As she stood with her hands raised and her mind set on her Creator, she reflected on her promise — made a few days before at the conference — that she would serve Him even when she didn't understand Him. That she would dedicate herself to Him for the rest of her life. That she would place not only her future, but her very past into His hands and trust Him to use them for His glory. Tears streamed down her face as a feeling of peace invaded her and she felt completely calm and secure in His presence.

She had no idea of the storm that was just beyond the horizon.

CB

After the service, Hope and Aunt Ruby remained in their seats, chatting as they waited on Jasmine and Ryan to take them home. The usual crush of people headed toward the door, hoping to get a good table at brunch in one of the town's restaurants, but as she spoke to Aunt Ruby, Hope noticed a lone body moving against the crowd, a rebel salmon swimming upstream.

Something unlocked in her brain the moment she locked eyes with the man who was coming purposefully towards her. Important scenes from her entire lifetime returned all at once, and it was truly as if a levy had broken inside her head.

She remembered falling and hitting her forehead on the apartment steps as a five-year-old, sharing her ice cream with her best friend at ten, arguing with her next-door neighbor at twelve, and having her heart broken by Jonathan Farris at sixteen. She remembered moving into her college dorm room at eighteen, and not knowing what to do later that year when her roommate suffered from anaphylaxis after eating a banana nut muffin. She remembered the phone call when she was twenty—her mother crying into the phone and telling her to come home when her father had died in an accident at work. She remembered that it was only a year later that her mother went to be with him, having been diagnosed with metastatic ovarian cancer at fifty-five. She remembered praying every night for those fighting for freedom halfway across the world.

She remembered everything, including things she would rather forget.

Hope opened her mouth to speak, but before she could utter the name that was coming to her lips, she felt an intense and almost unbearable pain rip through her lower abdomen. She cried out and gripped the man's hand with both of hers as he reached her and knelt beside her, speaking her forgotten name, "*Maya!*"

Everything happened so quickly after that, and Hope hardly had the time to breathe, much less to explain anything to anyone. As Jasmine and Ryan appeared, she cried out that there was something wrong with the baby. Ryan immediately moved into action.

"Hospital?" he asked, and Hope admired the economy of his words.

"Ambulance!" She responded. Instinctively, she knew she needed medical attention... *now.*

As Jasmine dialed 9-1-1 and Aunt Ruby and the small crowd of church members who had gathered prayed, Ryan asked, "Do you recognize this man?"

Hope nodded frantically as another pain gripped her. What was wrong with the baby? It was ten weeks before her due date!

"Is he from your past?"

Her movements were rather like a bobble-head's.

"Do you want him around?"

She nodded again, biting her lip until she tasted blood. The pain was too intense for speaking, though there had never been so much to say. She continued to squeeze the man's hand as if her life depended on it. She was holding on to him as though she may never let him go. Never again.

Aunt Ruby approached the pair and placed her hands on Hope's extended abdomen as she prayed out loud for the health of both mother and child. The other members of the church who remained behind joined in, and soon it was almost too loud for Hope to bear. Where was the ambulance?

The sirens were heard in a matter of minutes, and Hope was quickly ushered into the vehicle. She still refused to let go of the stranger's hand, leaving him no choice but to leave his rental car in the parking lot at the church. He spoke encouraging words into Hope's ear and prayed quietly.

In the ambulance with its sirens and flashing lights, Hope was experiencing much more than just the physical pain of whatever was happening to her baby. Every wail of the siren took her back to a time she had once hoped to forget—and actually *had,* as it turned out. She was transported in her mind to another time in another place—another country, actually, and she finally began to understand why the Lord in His wisdom had allowed her to lose her memory for so many months. The tears that were flowing from her eyes were an outward sign of both the physical pain and the emotional anguish she was experiencing. And still, she couldn't speak because it was hard for her to take a breath. All she could do was clutch the hand in hers and try to deal with everything that was going through her head. It was all she could do not to fall apart.

ᗚ

As the plane touched down on the tarmac, Daniel reflected on his trip. He had spent a very productive few weeks in Jamaica, but he was glad to be coming home. In addition to all the professional work he'd done, he had spent a lot of time in prayer and reflection, and he knew what he needed to do. He had to tell Hope how he felt and let the proverbial chips fall where they may.

The situation could not be more complicated, and he didn't for one minute expect her to return his feelings, nor did he harbor even the tiniest bit of hope that there could be anything but a sad ending to this chapter of his life story. But he knew he needed to humble himself and be honest with God, with others and with himself. Nothing else would do.

And now the day was finally here. He hadn't told anyone he was coming home, but he planned to talk to Hope after dinner. He would confess his feelings then, and then he would drive to his town house and hide out for a week. Or maybe a year. He still had a couple of weeks before he needed to be back at work. He would simply immerse himself in his research and writing until he felt brave enough to surface. She would have had the baby by then.

The baby.

The baby was another reason he needed to stay away. While he had not expressed much interest in the pregnancy, he was acutely aware of the fact that there was a baby on the way. How he had wanted to place his hands on Hope's protruding abdomen and feel the kicks. How he had wanted to press his ear close and listen to what was happening within. Countless times he had wanted to put his mouth close and tell the child secrets they alone would share. And he could not deny that he had found himself fantasizing more than once about rubbing Hope's belly with olive oil or cocoa butter to prevent stretch marks.

From the moment she had first accused him of being too busy for a family, he realized that he *did* want a family. And more and more since then, he had found himself wanting her to be a big part of that family.

The situation was hopeless, and although he had always learned that while there is life there is hope, he didn't think it applied in this situation; his rational mind knew there wouldn't necessarily be *Hope*, but his heart wasn't ready to let go.

He also knew that even though the Lord heard the prayers of the righteous, he would never pray for the Lord to give him another man's woman. And clearly, she had been just that... until at least about seven months ago and maybe even today.

He was still in a pensive mood when the plane pulled up to the gate and he turned his cell phone on. He listened to his voicemail while the flight was being cleared, and his heart fell when he heard the tremor in his aunt's voice, "Daniel, could you give us a call on Ryan's phone? We could sure use some prayer here. Hope's been taken to the hospital in an ambulance, and it seems she recognized a stranger who came to church today. She's hanging on to him for dear life in the ambulance, and we're on our way to the hospital in St. Augustine. We're not sure what's happening, but we'll talk to you later. Please be praying. Please."

It would appear, for all intents and purposes, that the man he had just been thinking about—the father of Hope's child—had resurfaced on the very day he was planning to reveal his feelings to her.

That was beside the point, however; an hour ago when the voice mail had been sent, she had been on her way to the hospital in St. Augustine. It would take him forty-five minutes to get there. He wished he had left his car at the airport instead of asking Ryan to drop him off when he was leaving. Now he would have to take extra time to rent a car. Whatever he needed to do, he was going to do it in order to get to the hospital as quickly as possible. He had an hour to prepare himself for whatever would unfold when he got to the hospital and came face-to-face with his worst nightmare.

୧

Daniel did not even think to call Aunt Ruby or anyone else on his way to the hospital. He was too busy driving above the speed limit and praying he wouldn't be pulled over. He wasn't sure why he felt he should be racing towards Hope when it was clear he wasn't needed; he wasn't sure why his first instinct was to protect her from any discomfort or pain, but he was moving as fast as he could... within reason. On his way, he had a long talk with the Lord, asking Him to give him the peace to be content in the circumstances at hand. He had a lot to say to this man—Hope's husband? Fiancé? Boyfriend?—about where he had been the last few months and why he was only now coming to claim her. He would try his best to leave out any reference to himself being in love with the woman. He was trying not to hope that the man could be an ex. After all, hadn't Aunt Ruby said Hope was hanging on to him for dear life? He guessed her memory was back and everyone would finally learn everything they had been curious about since she had stumbled into their lives.

When he got to the hospital, he didn't even know what name to ask for. Hope had always gone by just the one name, and he didn't know what name she would be registered in. Fortunately for him, they had had only one pregnant woman arriving in an ambulance that day, so he was soon able to find her room. He made a mental note to call the hospital the next day and talk to them about security.

He knocked at the door and heard an unfamiliar bass voice respond, "Come in." His heart stopped for a second, then moved into overdrive as the door creaked open. He had expected to find Aunt Ruby, Ryan and Jasmine there to act as buffers, but the only people in the room were a tall, dark-skinned man and Hope, lying in the bed and holding a tiny blanket-wrapped bundle. She was staring at it with a look of joy and wonder on her face.

"Daniel! Come in, come in and meet my little blessing." He was surprised that she actually looked pleased to see him. Despite the circumstances, he could not contain his smile. She was fine, and by the looks of things, the baby was fine, too. That had to be some kind of miracle.

"Hi," he nodded a greeting to the man who was sitting in a chair right by Hope's side. He, too, was staring at the baby with a look of amazement. He looked away as he stood in order to shake Daniel's hand. Daniel felt a little of his testosterone evaporate into thin air when he realized the man was at least three inches taller than he was, and quite muscular. He had to be in the military... or maybe he was a bouncer or a professional wrestler. Whatever it was, Daniel had to have a quick, strongly-worded conversation in his own head about who he was in God's sight—a man of God, called to His purpose and created to do good works—in order not to feel like a dwarf beside the stranger.

The new mother barely looked in their direction as she performed a quick and—for Daniel, at least—too brief introduction, "Professor Daniel Donahue, Captain Isaiah Hendricks. Isaiah, this is Daniel. Isaiah has been serving in combat for several months. He just got back a week or two ago." As she turned to look at her precious bundle of joy again, it was clear that the whole world had effectively disappeared, at least as far as she was concerned.

For Daniel, his world was very real and he could almost hear it crashing down around his ears. The man was a veteran. He hadn't come looking for Hope because he had been fighting to defend the United States and its interests, or perhaps to restore democracy to some underprivileged nation. Wonderful. Just wonderful.

He didn't know what to say, and it appeared Captain Hendricks was also clueless, so instead of speaking, they both stood there awkwardly for a moment before the stranger pointed in the direction of the bed with his oversized hand and asked, "Would you like to see the baby?"

Hope surfaced from her reverie, "Of course, I forgot my manners. This is all just so... new." She sent another genuine smile in Daniel's direction, one that would have given him endless hope if only the circumstances were different. "Daniel, come see. I haven't even named her yet."

"Her?" Daniel smiled as he tiptoed toward the bed.

"Yes. A perfect baby girl. Born about two hours ago in the back of the ambulance. Six pounds, thirteen ounces and nineteen inches long. Perfectly developed, considering she's early. The doctors are thinking she must have been closer to full-term than they had thought. Either that, or all that praying Aunt Ruby did must have paid off." She smiled again, and Daniel briefly wondered if he had ever seen her smile so many times in such a short period of time.

"Speaking of Aunt Ruby, where is she, anyway?" he wondered out loud.

"They're gone to buy a few things. I was totally unprepared," she grinned down at her daughter.

As he lowered himself into the chair by the bed, Hope put the baby into his arms. He didn't even get the chance to tell her no. He had never actually held a newborn before, and this one immediately started squirming and making small mewing sounds. He handed her back to her mother and said in a quiet but anxious voice that betrayed his nerves, "Take her, quick! I don't want her to start crying."

"It's okay. Here, let me."

"I can't believe she's here." Even to his own ears, his voice was full of wonder and amazement.

"Me, either." They were both staring at her as if she were the most fascinating thing either of them had ever seen. She probably was.

"Congratulations. May God bless and keep her... and you," Daniel suddenly remembered the gentleman who was observing quietly from the other side of the room, "... and her father." He tipped his head towards Captain Hendricks.

"Her uncle," Hope gently corrected him without tearing her eyes away from her bundle of joy.

"Her... uncle?" Daniel looked at Hope with a hundred questions across his face, his heart in his mouth and plastered across his sleeve.

"Yes, my brother, Isaiah Hendricks."

"Your *brother*?" His tone was incredulous.

"Yes. My brother. What did you think?" Hope had questions of her own.

"I thought he was your husband... or fiancé... or something."

Isaiah grinned, "Innocent. I'm just her overprotective older brother who had to go defend human rights for a while, and, well, I lost track of her."

Daniel was not amused, "How do you lose track of your sister? Especially since you're so overprotective?" He had moved to stand in front of Isaiah, his chest rising and falling with a mixture of anger and apprehension. He didn't know this man, but he didn't appear to be the type who took accusations lightly.

Hope intervened, "Hey, Daniel, it's nothing to get worked up about. I was working overseas, myself, and, for several reasons, it was… difficult for me to contact him and let him know what was going on." Daniel thought he saw a shadow pass over her face, but the fleeting look of concern fled when she looked back to the baby, who had fallen asleep in her arms. She gently transferred her to the bassinet on her left.

"Anyway, I don't want to talk about any of that right now. I just want to enjoy some time with my little girl. And come up with a name. Although Aunt Ruby says she has a couple of suggestions," she smiled. "She's known the baby was a girl since we visited the clinic that day you were there, Daniel." She covered a yawn.

Isaiah went over and kissed her cheek. "Sis, I'm going to suggest that Professor Donahue and I give you some time to rest. We'll wait for Aunt Ruby and the others outside, and then I'll ask someone to take me to my car. There's still so much to figure out. But we'll let you sleep for a while, okay?"

"All right." She smiled and looked over at Daniel, who was standing close to the door, "Thanks for coming. I didn't even know you were back in the country."

"I wasn't. I just got back an hour ago." Daniel's response was a bit terse. Just when he thought he had figured everything out, there were more questions than answers. Again.

"Well, welcome home." Again, the smile was sincere. A flicker of hope threatened to rise in Daniel, but he tamped it down.

"I'll probably just take your brother to his car, so I'll see you later, okay?" He waved and ducked outside.

Isaiah stayed another minute before joining him in the hallway, his face more serious than it had been inside the room, "What's your problem, man?" he asked Daniel.

"I don't have a problem."

"Man, you have a problem. You almost barked at her in there. She just had a baby, dude."

"Did I? I'm sorry. I just... I thought we had all the answers now, but it seems we don't. Or do we?"

Isaiah gestured towards a couple of chairs close to the nurse's station. The two sat with a chair between them.

"I don't actually know all the answers, either. Everything just happened so fast. But I will tell you what I do know, because you seem to care for her, and... well... anyway... let me tell you." He leaned forward in the chair, placing his elbows on his thighs and clasping his hands. He sighed. "She's Maya Grace-Ann Hendricks, second and last child of our parents, now deceased. We're originally from Fairfield, Connecticut, but after our parents died, we both decided we had nothing tying us there. We bought a small house in a little town in our home state, but neither of us spends a lot of time there. I joined the Army and Maya became a teacher. She's taught English in several countries, like Japan, Germany and France. She moved to Cartagena, Colombia, around two years ago. She was teaching at a Catholic high school, though we're not Catholic ourselves. She lived in an apartment at a convent, but she wasn't a nun. She was pretty happy there.

"She started dating an American who worked in the same city. An interpreter. And then around eight months ago, the emails she would send me every now and then stopped altogether. I was deployed in the Middle East, and I didn't know what had happened to her. When I finally made contact with the school, they said she had resigned abruptly. That was the last time anybody heard anything from her, and that was almost five months ago."

"Which is when she had the accident in Miami," Daniel contributed.

"Right. Now, it wasn't very odd for me to not hear from my sister for two or three months, but after four months without a word, I was becoming concerned. I figured she may have gotten a new contract in another country, but usually she would have let me know. We don't have any family but each other, and nobody in Greertown— that's where our house is—had seen her. Her friends are all over the world, in the countries where she's lived, but she wasn't really close to anyone in Greertown. Nobody has heard from her in all this time. I wasn't able to get out of my deployment until last week. I went back home and started looking for her. I couldn't even file a missing person's report, because it wasn't strange for her to be away for prolonged periods of time. I was planning to hire a P.I. to help me track her down.

"And then just yesterday, someone sent me a video from a church conference in some place I'd never have looked, and there she was, standing with the woman who was speaking, whom I now know to be Jasmine. You can't imagine the relief I felt that she was alive and well. I came straight here. Not knowing where else to go, I decided to start my search at the church from the video."

"And she saw you and what? Her memory just came back, just like that?" Daniel was a bit skeptical.

"She saw me in the church this morning, and she clearly remembered me, but then she went into labor and everything progressed so quickly that we haven't even had the chance to talk yet. I don't even know for sure whose baby she had. I figure it must be Mr. Interpreter's but... well, Maya has never been that kind of girl. This is not the kind of behavior I've come to expect from her, if you know what I mean."

"I see," Daniel stood and placed his hands in his pockets. "I guess we'll just have to wait."

"Of course, I can't figure out... if she was pregnant with this guy's child, how come he hasn't been looking for her? How come he hasn't tried to contact me? And why did she leave Colombia so suddenly in the first place? I thought she really liked it there," Isaiah also stood.

It was perfect timing, because as Daniel stood there wondering what to do next, Aunt Ruby, Jasmine and Ryan stepped out of the elevator at the end of the hallway. They had a couple of bags with them, and Aunt Ruby was carrying a small bouquet of bright yellow lilies.

"Daniel!" Aunt Ruby beamed as she saw him. "No wonder I couldn't get through to you. Did you just fly in?"

"Yes, Aunt Ruby," He gave her a hug and turned to greet Jasmine and Ryan, as well, "I came back just in time for some of the drama."

"Now, Daniel, be nice," she warned him with a smile. "What time did your flight land?"

Daniel looked at his watch, "It came in at 11:50."

Ryan raised his eyebrows at him. "And you're already here?"

He shrugged. He wished he hadn't seen Isaiah raise his own eyebrows in his direction, but the soldier said nothing.

"Isaiah, I see you've met my nephew. Has he been drilling you?"

"Aunt Ruby!" Daniel was appalled.

"Not *too* much," Isaiah replied. "We've just been catching up. I just finished telling him the same thing I told you earlier. I am just so happy I got here before the baby came."

"Yes," Aunt Ruby was pensive, "not a moment too soon. God really does work in mysterious ways, doesn't He?"

Ryan piped in, "Is she asleep?" as Jasmine took the bags to the nurses' station.

"They probably both are by now," Isaiah confirmed.

At that moment one of the nurses went to take the things into the room and check on Hope and the baby. She came out about a minute later, smiling, and said, "It's been an eventful day for both of them. I would love for them to get some rest. Were you able to get all the things on that list I gave you?"

"Yes," Jasmine confirmed. "Most of them are in the car, and we have a few things at home." She didn't explain why.

"Well, perhaps you could launder them and bring them back for us. Newborn skin is so delicate, you know?" She took the bouquet from Aunt Ruby, "They're going to have to stay overnight, but the baby is doing very well, and so is her mother. I don't anticipate any real delays in their being released into your care. Is someone going to stay with them tonight?"

"Not for the night, no," Aunt Ruby replied, "but one or two of us might come back later. What time would be best?"

The middle-aged redhead had green eyes. A dusting of bright freckles across her nose and deep dimples made her look like she was smiling even when she wasn't. "Our visiting hours are fairly flexible, depending on each patient's situation, but six-thirty or seven might be a good time. If Mama is still sleeping, I'll have to wake her for her supper around then." The dimples deepened, and Daniel wondered if she had ever been upset in her life.

"Great. We'll be going, then," Jasmine smiled. Daniel suspected that Ryan would be tremendously proud of how well she was doing, under the circumstances.

In the parking lot, it was decided that Daniel would take Isaiah back to his car, and then the two of them would return Daniel's rental car to the company's St. Augustine outlet. Then they would both end up at Aunt Ruby's and take it from there. Ryan and Jazz would take Aunt Ruby home, where Jasmine would help her with the laundry.

Daniel was a little anxious about even a relatively short drive to the church with Hope's brother—it was going to take a while for everyone to start thinking of her as Maya—but the time passed quickly. The two discussed Isaiah's time in the Army, his deployment to the Middle East and Daniel's work.

Isaiah also shared that Hope was fully bilingual in Spanish and English and was also fairly comfortable speaking French, German and a little Japanese. She had a master's degree in Comparative Literatures and had been teaching English as a foreign language for almost ten years. No wonder she had had so much to say about the books she had been reading; she had probably read some of them before. At least now Daniel completely understood her affinity to Gabriel García Márquez, who had maintained a home in Cartagena although he had lived in Mexico most of the year. While there was still a huge mystery surrounding her pregnancy, many of the missing pieces were finally falling into place. And Daniel was finally allowing a little hope to burgeon in his heart; he allowed himself to wonder whether it might be possible that Hope... Maya... wasn't attached to the father of her child at all. Why would she have left Colombia if she was?

CHAPTER TWENTY-SEVEN

By Daniel's return the following weekend, the 'family' had settled into some kind of routine that involved several people coming by each day to 'ooh' and 'aah' at little Joy.

Isaiah was staying with Jasmine and Ryan for a couple of weeks until they figured out what Maya would do. She now knew what her options were, since she had regained all her memories—both the good and the not-so-good—but she had not made any major decisions. There was nothing really drawing her back to Connecticut. She had hardly ever spent more than a few weeks there at a time since her parents had died.

She knew her brother enjoyed his work with the Army and that his wanderlust would kick in soon. He only used Greertown as his home base, an address he could use on his luggage tags and to write when he was filling in forms, but he was built for the road. If Maya went back there, she would essentially be alone with Joy.

Aunt Ruby wanted them—Maya and Joy—to stay with her for the foreseeable future. She still needed some help around the house, and now that they were able to verify Maya's identity, she could look for a job teaching English language or literature at the local high school or in St. Augustine. Since she had her Master's degree, she might even consider applying to teach at the community college in St. Augustine. If she chose to stay with Aunt Ruby, she would have no need to find daycare for Joy until she became a toddler, when it might be difficult for the older woman to keep up with her. Maya had decisions to make, but at least this time she had options.

Of course, she had also remembered the circumstances of Joy's conception, and she was finally beginning to understand her amnesia, at least in part. She knew that Daniel would have to be told what had happened, because she had already told the others, but she didn't really want to open up to him. She didn't want to see the look on his face when he found out.

CB

Daniel's first stop when he returned home the first weekend after Joy's birth was next door. He hated surprises, and he wanted to have an idea of what to expect when he got home to Aunt Ruby's. He had been working hard on his book the last few days and hadn't even spoken to Ryan by phone. He had also been following Aunt Ruby's advice to give the new mother some space while she tried to work out a routine and get some sleep when Joy slept. Instead of pulling into Aunt Ruby's driveway, he turned into Ryan and Jasmine's.

Ryan wasn't home yet, but he sat with Jasmine for a while at the kitchen table. It was the first time they had been alone together since before the loss of James Lucas.

"How are you handling things, Jazz?" He ran his finger around the rim of the cup of Blue Mountain coffee she had prepared for him from the souvenir package he had brought them. "I mean, it can't be easy having a newborn baby kind of thrust upon you at this point in your life."

Jazz was pensive, but she smiled, "You know one thing I've learned about myself during this whole situation? It's that God must think I'm pretty darned strong." She took a sip of the dark brew she had missed drinking during her pregnancy. "I mean, why else would He allow us to lose our first child so early in our marriage? Why else would He allow that to happen just when Hope—*Maya*—was going to kind of pop up in our lives? Why would He have allowed these so-called coincidences if they would break me? Well, I don't think He would have. He could have orchestrated things differently, but He didn't, and I just have to trust that some good can come out of this experience, you know?"

"That can't be as easy as you make it sound," Daniel was thoughtful.

"It's not easy. It's a struggle every day. Every day, I wake up, and before I even have a conscious thought, I can sense that there is something missing, something wrong. And then I remember. James Lucas is gone. And every day I want to bury my head under the covers and stay there, but I can't. That wouldn't bring God any glory, nor would it honor James Lucas' memory. So every day I choose to get up and live with hope and expectation, you know? Every time I see Joy, I wonder how my son would have looked and what type of baby he would have been. But I can't dwell on that. Joy is, herself, a little miracle, after all it took for her to get here, after all God did to protect her."

Daniel was confused, "What do you mean?"

"You haven't heard?"

"I have no idea what you're talking about."

For a moment, Jazz considered sharing the details with him, but instead, she said, "You and Hope—*Maya*—need to have a long talk. You need to hear her story, and she needs to hear yours."

"Mine? Why would she need to hear my story?"

"Because you're in love with her, Daniel. You have been for some time now."

Daniel opened his mouth to contradict her, but Jasmine wouldn't allow him to.

"Don't bother denying it, Daniel. I've seen the way you look at her when you think no one's looking. I've seen the way you light up when she comes into a room, and you aren't even aware of it. You're in love with her, and I think she feels something for you, too. But you're both broken, and you both need to heal before you even think about pursuing anything. And in order for you to heal, you both need to learn to trust other people. Perhaps you could start with each other."

Jasmine stood. "Are you done?"

Daniel handed her his empty cup, "You're kicking me out?" He raised an eyebrow.

She smiled, "Yes, but for good reason. I spoke to Maya just before you got here, and now would be a good time for you to talk. Isaiah and Ryan are out at a construction site, Aunt Ruby and Joy are both napping, and Maya is reading. Now, shoo!" She literally pushed him out of the door.

He didn't bother to move his SUV just yet. Instead, Daniel walked over to the house and went through the front door, which was hardly ever locked in the daytime. He found the subject of his dreams and the object of his affections sitting at the kitchen table with tears streaming down her face.

"Hey, what's wrong? Why are you crying?" He went to sit in the chair beside Maya's and handed her his handkerchief.

She accepted it but didn't say anything. She just sniffed and cried some more. She stared in the direction of the baby monitor on the table, but he got the impression she wasn't even seeing it.

Daniel sat there silently, not sure what to do. After a couple of minutes of no sound except her sniffles, he asked, "Do you want me to go?" She shook her head and grabbed on to his hand as if she were drowning and he were a lifeline. This was perhaps the third or fourth time they had ever touched, and his heart began racing so much he was sure she could hear it from across the table.

"Stay."

It may have been the most beautiful word he had ever heard.

Even though she wanted him around, it looked like she wasn't ready to talk, so after a minute or two he decided he would be the one to break the silence, "Hope, I mean, *Maya*, did you know that I was married once?"

Her eyes opened wide, and she shook her head as she tried to withdraw her hands from his, but he held them firmly.

"Well, I was. Eight years ago. My wife, Victoria, died in a car accident during our first year of marriage. She was pregnant at the time."

She couldn't hide the shocked look that crossed her face. "Daniel, I'm so sorry. I had no idea." Suddenly, she remembered all the horrible things she had said to him about not wanting a family. Her eyes filled with water again, "Oh, no. And I said all those things…. I'm so sorry, Daniel, I don't know what to say."

"It's okay. You didn't know. Although, truth be told, I'm surprised no one told you. I figured you must have heard the 'poor Daniel, I don't know how he got over the death of his wife and unborn child' story. Only a few people know the baby wasn't mine," Maya gasped, but he pressed on.

"Anyway, to make a really, really long story really, really short, she was only using me. She was pregnant with another man's baby when we got married, and I had literally just found out about that when she and the baby died. She wasn't supposed to be driving, but she was running away."

He took a deep breath and continued, "So when you turned up, pregnant and suffering from amnesia, well, it was just a bit too convenient. Or so it appeared. I figured you were running away from something or someone, and you were just using Aunt Ruby, and, to an extent, *me*, to do it. I'm sorry if my experience caused me to treat you poorly. I was painting everyone with the same brush. I understand now that I should take everyone on his or her own merit and not judge. Please forgive me."

Across the kitchen table, Maya took a deep breath of her own. Since her memory had returned, she had no choice but to begin to deal with everything that had happened to her... and was *still* happening. She could no longer deny the growing feelings she had for the man sitting close to her at the kitchen table, but neither was she anxious to confess how she felt. There was too much at stake. She had Joy to think about now.

"The truth is, Daniel, in a way I *was* running away." She got up and went to the fridge for a glass of water. Daniel declined her offer to get him something to eat or drink, so she leaned against the counter by the fridge and kept speaking. "I had been working in Colombia for about a year. I enjoyed teaching, I was involved in the community as a volunteer, and I was an usher in the church. That's where I met an American man—at church. He was an interpreter. Like me, he spoke several languages, and we just hit it off. He pursued me for a couple of months before I went out with him. Initially, I wasn't interested in being in a relationship. I knew I would probably be leaving Colombia at the end of the school year, and I didn't want to start something and then have to leave in the middle of it. How ironic."

She took a long drink, "Eventually, he wore me down and we went out on a few dates. We got along really well, and I even wrote to my brother about him—something I rarely ever did. I don't think I ever mentioned his name. Anyway, one night after a movie date, his car developed mechanical problems, and since it was late and we were closer to his place than mine, we walked there." She took a deep breath to control her breathing, which had started to become erratic. "That's where he raped me."

Daniel jumped to his feet, "He did *what*?!"

"Shhh!" Maya placed a finger on her lips and pointed towards the ceiling above and then at the baby monitor on the table.

"He did what?" Daniel made an effort to speak at a more reasonable volume.

Maya remained at the counter. He approached her and leaned beside her on the countertop, careful not to touch her.

"He raped me. I was asleep in his bed—he was going to take the sofa, he said—but then I woke up, and he was...." The rest remained unspoken.

"He acted like it was no big deal; like it was consensual. He made me take a hot shower, and then he called me a cab and basically put me out. I went straight to the police, but the case was weak because it was his word against mine. We were in an established relationship; he hadn't beaten me up, and he had made me clean up so there was no real evidence. They didn't even do a physical exam. There was nothing I could do. I already knew I couldn't stay, but then I found out I was pregnant."

She stopped talking for a while. Daniel placed his hand over hers on the countertop and she drew from him the strength to continue. "Have you heard what happened when Jasmine spoke at the women's conference?"

"She spoke? I thought she only led the praise and worship session. Ryan mentioned a video that was making the rounds online, but I thought she was singing, not *speaking*." He had a look of amazement on his face. "Jasmine Phillips... speaking to the world... imagine that."

Hope gave him the briefest of reports about what had happened, after which she continued, "You know, one of the emails that Jasmine shared with me was from a rape victim who was pregnant with her attacker's child. She was so glad she had heard Jasmine's testimony, because she had been contemplating getting rid of it. Jasmine's message convicted her, and she decided she would keep the child and maybe give him up for adoption when he's born.

"At the time—and it's hard to believe this was only two weeks ago—I imagined myself in her position, and I just knew that if it were me, I would never be able to love a child who was the product of that kind of violence against me. I just knew that I would seriously consider abortion. There was no way I could take care of an unborn baby under those same circumstances, yet that's exactly what I was doing the whole time I had amnesia. If, at that point, you had told me I had to give up my baby to save my own life, it wouldn't even have been a choice for me. I would have given everything—including my life—to protect her. And that was before I ever saw her beautiful face.

"You know, the psychiatrist in Miami said that sometimes amnesia is our brain's way of protecting itself from something it can't handle. I think that's what happened to me. I think if I hadn't had that accident, that whole experience... well, the truth is that one way or another, I don't think I would have Joy today."

"So you think making you forget everything was God's way of protecting you and Joy?" Daniel suggested.

"Yeah, without a doubt. I mean, I was already several weeks along when I resigned, and I had absolutely no feelings about the baby. When I took the home pregnancy test and it came up positive, I didn't go to the doctor. I didn't take my vitamins. I didn't change the way I ate, didn't give up my coffee habit—two huge, caffeine-packed servings every day and three on the weekends. She was just something I couldn't see or feel, so I could pretend she wasn't even there. When I allowed myself to think about her, all I wanted to do was not have the reminder of what had happened. I couldn't be a pregnant, unmarried teacher in a Catholic school without telling everyone what had happened, and I couldn't do that, so I quit.

"I had no plans beyond coming back to the States. I wasn't even sure where I was going to go, which is why I flew into Miami instead of New York. My brother wasn't around; no one was expecting me, and no one would miss me. I just wanted to be on American soil, so I chose the closest point. It's as if the Lord was orchestrating everything so I could meet Aunt Ruby and Jasmine and... you." She blushed and studied the floor.

Daniel raised his eyebrows. "And... me?"

"You know what I mean," she continued to memorize the details of the hardwood below.

"Do I?" His voice took on a flirtatious note, lightening the seriousness of the discussion.

She unconsciously bit her bottom lip, not noticing the way he was staring at her mouth as she spoke. "Yes, Daniel, you do. You have this way of... getting under my skin."

"I do?" he teased.

"Yes, you do, and you know it." She continued to avoid his gaze. "You have this... this *effect* on me. You make me think. You make me question the way I look at things, from the books I've been reading to my opinions about family and friendship. These last few weeks that you haven't been here... well, I missed you more than I can say. I tried to put you out of my mind, and sometimes I did, because there was so much to think about, but you kept making your way back in."

Daniel's heart leapt inside his chest as Hope's—*Maya's*—words mirrored his own feelings. "And I missed you," he confessed. "You have no idea how this whole situation has affected me. I looked at you, and it's like every time I saw you, you were more appealing to me. That whole time you and I were having that argument that day, I couldn't decide if I wanted to strangle you or kiss you senseless. I knew even then that you were perfect for me. You questioned me. You stood up to me. You challenged thoughts I'd held on to for years.

"But how could it be? I mean, you were carrying another man's child! And I looked at my history, the whole fiasco with Victoria, and I needed to run away from you... to try and get you out of my head. I even started seeing someone in Jamaica, because I needed to get you out of my thoughts." He tightened his grip on her hand when he felt her trying to withdraw. "But it didn't work. That's why I came back. I needed to tell you how I felt. I didn't even want to harbor any hope that you might feel something for me. I just needed to be one hundred percent honest with you. I needed to tell you that I thought I knew just what I wanted... until I met you.

"And then I came to the hospital, and there was this man, and he was holding your hand, and I just wanted to turn around and jump on another plane."

"I'm glad you didn't," she smiled. "Look, Daniel, I need you to understand that... well, the truth is, when I got to know you, it was clear that you were... how do I put this?" She gesticulated with her hands as she tried to find the words, "You were... you were everything I never knew I always wanted."

He grinned, the tension easing away from his face. He thought about kissing her then, but she held up her hand before he could move from his position beside her.

"But there's a *but*, Daniel."

He raised his eyebrows. Of course there was a *but*; he had one, too.

"So I'm attracted to you, and I really, really like you, *but* I have a lot going on inside my head, you know. Having Joy is... it's just wonderful, but I still have to come to terms with what happened to me."

"I agree. And I understand that I have some things I need to work out, too," he said, as he turned to face her at the counter, standing close and invading her personal space like he'd been wanting to do for weeks.

"It wouldn't be wise for me to jump into a relationship right now."

"Same here," he leaned towards her, his hand still holding hers.

"It would just be too complicated."

"I couldn't agree with you more." Despite his words, he leaned his head towards hers. Trying hard not to be aggressive, he delayed a moment to allow her to step away if she wanted to. Apparently, she didn't want to; instead, she let him capture her lips with his own in a long and gentle caress that held infinite promise.

Her lips were as soft and yielding as he remembered. Taking into account what she had just shared, he fought the urge to place his hands on her hips and pull her to him. Instead, he plunged his fingers into her unruly hair, pulling her closer. He wanted to be as close to her as he had ever been to anyone, but now was not the time, and this was not the place.

Afterwards, he reluctantly leaned back, looked deep into her eyes, and whispered, "I'll wait for you, Maya. I'll be right here when you're ready. I'll wait. As long as it takes."

A sense of peace invaded him when she whispered back, "I'll wait for you, too."

EPILOGUE

Eighteen months later

The day dawned bright and clear and the air in the church was abuzz with excitement. Joy was dressed to the nines in a frilly yellow and white dress, white socks and white patent leather shoes. From her vantage point on the porch at the main entrance of the church, her mother looked at her and marveled at Joy, who had recently developed the most infuriating habit of running everywhere without having the necessary balance to avoid accidents. Now and then she would fall over, and the hysterical tears would come in the same moment that the lips would protrude in a perfect pout. Then whoever was closest would pick her up and brush her off, and off she would totter again before the cycle repeated itself.

Maya, dressed in a simple white eyelet dress with strappy, heeled sandals, beamed with love and pride as she watched the child running to hug Aunt Ruby, who sat in the front pew of the sanctuary. She was everyone's favorite little girl. Whenever Maya had reason to take her to Alistair Bay High, where she now taught English and Spanish, Joy would be passed from one person to another as everyone took turns hugging her. She was a sweet-tempered child, and bestowed upon everyone a smile that made them feel they were the only person she had ever smiled at. She was truly a joy to behold.

But there could be no doubt that Joy reserved her sweetest smiles for the man both she and her mother adored. Just hearing Daniel's voice would set off a series of giggles from the child, and, ignoring everyone and everything else, off she would head in his direction. She would embrace his legs, and he would lift her high into the air before hugging her tightly to him, never failing to give a tickle or two that would elicit even more giggles and more than a few hiccups. This would continue until someone intervened. Her mother was such a spoilsport, as far as the two were concerned.

Perhaps it was a good thing that Daniel lived so far away, or Joy's mother would never get a moment alone with her. Ever since Joy had weaned herself at six months, Maya had been relegated to the

254

position of second-best. There was just something about Joy and Daniel that only the two of them understood. It would be useless for anyone else to try and come between them. Maya couldn't imagine anyone ever wanting to.

She had bloomed into a strong woman of God since she had recovered her memory. Like her best friend and neighbor, she was beginning to understand that because she had submitted her will to God, He was always working everything out for her benefit. She may have been violated, and her rapist may have escaped justice, but she would never have had Joy if things had happened differently. She was learning to forgive her attacker and was trying to embody kindness, patience, peace and faithfulness, along with the other fruit of the Spirit in her everyday life. As a high school teacher, she certainly had plenty of practice!

As if that weren't enough, there was Daniel.

Daniel was still the most infuriating man she had ever come across. She supposed it would have been almost impossible for two strong-willed individuals to come together in perfect harmony all the time, but the love they shared allowed them to forgive and move forward. Even when they were at odds over silly things like what type of cereal she should buy for Joy or where they should go for dinner, given enough time, they would eventually find themselves laughing at the disagreement before forgetting all about it.

ᴄ𝕤

Daniel, for his part, had never been happier. He was closer to God than he had ever been, and he was learning to focus on those things that were good, pure and true. He was still at the university; his book had been a reasonable success in the academic world, and he basked in the genuine love and appreciation of a good woman and a precious little girl. He had spent more time being annoyed with Maya than he had with any other human being—after all, she was just as stubborn, opinionated and outspoken as he was—but he was grateful that he always knew what she was thinking, and he couldn't imagine her keeping any secrets that would change his opinion of her.

Even before they both got individual counseling to deal with the issues from their past—Maya from a therapist who was experienced with rape victims, and Daniel from Robert Marsden—it was a foregone conclusion that he and Maya would eventually marry. From the very start of their relationship, he had known it, she had known it, and everyone around them had known it. One would have to be blind not to see the love they shared.

He had already begun the process of adopting Joy so that the three of them could one day be a family in every sense of the word and eventually share the same last name. The only thing that separated them from the divine destiny that awaited them was a marriage license.

But today was not about Daniel and Maya, nor was it about their precious girl. It was about a little boy named Martin who had made his appearance only three short months before. He slept peacefully in his mother's arms as she smiled down at him. Beside her in the front pew, Ryan beamed with pride. He and Jasmine finally had their long-awaited love child.

Unfortunately, they had gone through another loss with their second pregnancy when Jasmine had a spontaneous miscarriage during the seventh week. It had been different from the loss of Little Praise, but losing the baby they called 'Little Bit' had been no less difficult. It was a challenging state of affairs that was made harder because they had both expected that things would progress smoothly, if only to compensate for the loss they'd experienced before. But it wasn't meant to be.

Ryan had confided in Daniel that during that pregnancy, they had offered Little Bit to God soon after learning they were expecting, and once again they had to trust that His will and purpose would prevail. It had been a rough time for them, but as they had done before, they had found strength in each other and in God, and they had overcome.

Now, Daniel and everyone else could see that the two were beyond grateful to finally have their own little living, breathing bundle of joy. The pregnancy had been just as difficult as Jasmine's first, but this time they had been rewarded with a smooth and relatively short labor and the event-free delivery of a healthy boy who had his father's chin and his mother's eyes.

Today was the day of his christening, and everyone was thrilled to be worshipping with the family as they dedicated Martin James Phillips to the Lord. Jasmine's parents were visiting from Jamaica; Isaiah was back from another tour overseas, and an array of other relatives and well-wishers had descended upon Alistair Bay. It was a day of triumph, thanksgiving and celebration.

Martin's godmother, Aunt Ruby, was more than content to cuddle him while his mother led the praise and worship session. Jasmine had never seemed closer to God than she did that morning as she gave Him thanks for their little miracle, and the entire church was filled with the presence of the Lord.

As everyone clapped and danced to yet another inspired song choice, Daniel, holding a clapping Joy in his arms, looked at the woman he loved as she rocked beside him, caught up in the worship experience. The moment had come.

"I love you, Maya."

She grinned at him, "I know. You tell me at least once a week," she turned her attention back to the stage.

"And...?" he prompted her.

"I love you, too, Daniel."

"Well, a couple of months ago, you told me that when the right time came, I should ask, so I'm asking."

She smiled. Daniel was sure she knew exactly where this was going. "What exactly are you asking?"

"Will you?" He beat around the bush with a bright smile on his face and his eyebrows raised, their daughter in his arms oblivious to the magnitude of the moment.

She grinned as she continued to rock to the music, "Will I do what?" She teased.

"Will you marry me?"

"I thought you'd never ask."

"You practically told me to." It was his turn to grin, "So, will you?"

"Yes, Daniel, I will marry you."

And right in front of the first pew of the church, with Aunt Ruby close to them, Joy in their arms, and the Holy Spirit in attendance, Daniel and Maya sealed their promise with a kiss. In their arms, Joy began to squirm a little, so they took turns tickling her until she erupted into contagious giggles.

It was only then that Daniel looked up and had to make a supreme effort not to burst out laughing. It was the first time he was taking note of the framed painting featuring Jeremiah 29:11 that had been hanging on the wall of the church for years:

"For I know the plans I have for you," declares the LORD, "plans to prosper you and not to harm you, plans to give you hope and a future."

Daniel breathed a sigh of relief. He had finally found *his last hope*.

THE END

FREE BONUS CHAPTER

DDM

You're invited

DANIEL & MAYA

December XOXO

5:00 p.m.

New Covenant Community Church

Alistair Bay, FL

Sign up for the author's mailing list and get an <u>electronic</u> copy of "His Last Hope: The Wedding"

HIS LAST HOPE GROUP DISCUSSION GUIDE

1. In the prologue, Victoria chooses to run away from her immediate problems rather than face them. Is there ever a time when it's okay to put off solving problems for another time?

2. At the end of chapter two, Aunt Ruby tells the patient with amnesia that God always listens to her. Is there someone you often ask to pray for you when you're facing difficulty? Do you believe that person has 'a direct line' to God? Why or why not?

3. Aunt Ruby suggests that the pregnant woman take the name 'Hope.' Can you think of any other suitable names she could have suggested, based on their meaning?

4. Daniel set up hidden cameras in his office specifically so he could catch Hope snooping around. Is there ever a time that it's okay to record someone without their knowledge? Was there anything else Daniel could have done to determine Hope's honesty?

5. Jasmine loses her baby six months into the pregnancy. Do you know someone who has suffered pregnancy loss? How do you feel about God allowing someone to become pregnant if they are only going to end up losing the baby? What part of Jasmine's story could you use to encourage someone who has experienced profound loss?

6. Flashbacks reveal that Daniel also suffered a tremendous loss in his life. In what way(s) did his response then differ from

Ryan's response to losing James Lucas? What inspired the differences in their responses?

7. God used Jasmine and Ryan's heartbreaking experience for His glory. Can you think of a time in your life (or that of someone you know) that God turned a bad situation around for good?

8. The stranger who eventually comes to claim Hope turns out to be her brother. How would things have been different if he had been her husband, fiancé or boyfriend, instead?

9. Maya/Hope tells Daniel that she was raped and that the police did nothing about it. Should she have pursued the issue? How would the outcome of the novel have been different if she had?

10. Maya/Hope reveals that she considered aborting her child when she found out she was pregnant. Is there ever a time when abortion is an acceptable option? Can a woman who has aborted a child ever find complete healing and restoration?

11. Daniel and Maya/Hope agree that amnesia was probably the Lord's way of protecting Maya's unborn child. Can you think of any other situation in which the Lord has used or might use difficult circumstances to protect His people?

ACKNOWLEDGEMENTS

Words fail me, so only my spirit can express the full extent of my gratitude to the One who created me for a purpose, and who equipped me to fulfil it. You were my 'Holy Ghostwriter.' It was Your hand that wrote this, for I could not have done it in my own strength. I know, because I tried.

I am also grateful to:
- Radford—for your insight into Psalm 23:4 all those years ago.
- Kareem—for being the most fascinating person I've ever met.
- My parents, Churnley and Beryl Gray—for being here, there and everywhere I needed them to be. *Always*.
- My siblings and extended family—for not telling me I was crazy for pursuing this, even when I thought I was.
- All my nieces and nephews, but especially Rhian—for being so much like me that it makes me want to be a better me. Seeing me in the next generation is what got me saved.
- Lyndon—for your constant flow of encouragement. It has had a tremendous impact on this project and on my life.
- Barbara, Sylvanna and Ike—for enabling my decaf habit and for being remarkable human beings with the kindest of spirits.
- Robin and Andrea—for the listening ears, the shared tears and the endless prayers (I rhymed!); for brownies and muffins; for hugs.
- Reverend R. Oliver Ramsay—for everything, but mostly for the laughs.
- Marguerite, Nichole, Tracia, Cameisha and Olivea—for being my beta readers; for being kind and urging me to follow through.
- My personal cheerleader, Racquel—for thinking I'm awesome and telling me so.
- My work colleagues and Facebook friends—for the support.
- My client-turned-consultant-turned-mentor, Terri Whitmire—for everything you've been and everything you've done. You met me as a nitpicking copy editor, and your guidance has helped me become a published author. Thank you for being the channel God has used in so many ways during this process. Thank you for sharing your talent and your gifts. Thank you for helping me to appreciate and acknowledge my own talent and gifts. I thank God for bringing us together.

ABOUT THE AUTHOR

M. A. Malcolm, a native of Jamaica, is a wife, mother, stepmother, daughter, sister and aunt. She is a freelance copy editor, administrative service provider and self-publishing consultant who also works part-time as an educator. With a passion for enhancing the work of Christian writers, she is certified in copyediting and is the founder of Nitpicking with a Purpose (NitpickingwithaPurpose.com). Over the years, she has worked with a host of local and international authors.

While mostly fictional, *His Last Hope* was loosely based on Mrs. Malcolm's own painful experiences with pregnancy loss. She wrote the book to share a message of hope with those who have struggled to overcome their own personal tragedies. She was therefore shocked when *His Last Hope* was named the Christian Small Publisher Romance Book of the Year (2016).

A year after releasing *His Last Hope*, she became a children's author with the publication of her children's book, *So very… Max!* – a modern-day response to Hans Christian Andersen's *The Ugly Duckling*. She expects to release *His Last Resort*, the prequel to *His Last Hope*, in March of 2017.

Mrs. Malcolm has been a part of Faith in Christ Ministries in Westmoreland, Jamaica, for more than ten years. She spends her leisure time with her family, cuddled up with a cozy book, or catching up on much-needed sleep. She attributes her ability to produce fiction to her faith in God and her willingness to obey His command to write.

She loves hearing from readers, and can be reached via her website authormamalcolm.com. You may also sign up there for her mailing list if you would like to receive occasional emails and special offers, including free gifts. Book clubs may invite her to appear in person or via the Internet for live discussions surrounding *His Last Hope* and its uplifting message.

Made in the USA
Middletown, DE
01 May 2019